FIREFLY

FIREFLY

WARRIOR WOMAN OF THE SAMURAI
BOOK ONE

INDIA MILLAR

RED EMPRESS
PUBLISHING

Red Empress Publishing
www.RedEmpressPublishing.com

Copyright © India Millar 2019
www.IndiaMillar.co.uk

Cover Design by Cherith Vaughan
www.CoversbyCherith.com

ALSO BY INDIA MILLAR

Secrets from the Hidden House

The Geisha with the Green Eyes

The Geisha Who Could Feel No Pain

The Dragon Geisha

The Geisha Who Ran Away

The Song of the Wild Geese

The Red Thread of Fate

This World is Ours

Warrior Woman of the Samurai

Firefly

Mantis

Chameleon

Spider

Dragonfly

Scorpion

Cricket

Moth

Haiku Collections

Dreams from the Hidden House

Song of the Samurai

This book is humbly dedicated to Baizenten, the Japanese Goddess of writers and geisha. May both you and she enjoy the words written herein!

Though the sex to which I belong is considered weak you will nevertheless find me a rock that bends to no wind.
Queen Elizabeth I of England, 1558—1603

PROLOGUE

I no longer had any perception of the passing of time. My mind had ceased to function as it used to. All I was aware of was the need to hold on. I had forgotten the reason I was here in the first place. Vaguely, I knew that it had seemed important, once upon a time.

"Keep your eyes facing the rock, little sister. Look neither up nor down."

My brother's voice was very close, and he startled me. He also diverted my attention from the imperative of keeping my fingertips clenched tightly in the shallow cleft where I had wedged them. And of course, having been told not to look around, that was precisely what I did.

Worse still, I looked down.

And then I screamed. Not loudly, for I had little breath to spare for such noise. But it was sufficient. The movement of air in my lungs was enough to force me a tiny fraction from the slippery, icy rockface. And that, in turn, was enough to make the burden I had placed on my fingertips just too much. I scrabbled, desperate to renew my hold on the rock, but it was hopeless. My exposed belly rasped painfully against the jagged stone. My fingers were too numb with cold to feel anything. I cursed their inability to bear the slight weight of my body even as I felt myself begin to scrape back down the mountain. I suddenly remembered how long, how very long, it had taken me to get so far, and how much pain I had suffered along the way. All fear left me as I was suffused with mindless, instinctive fury.

How dare my own body betray me in this way! I bared my teeth. Even though I knew perfectly well that it was futile, I tried to bite at the moss that lay beneath my cheek, frantic to grasp something to stop me from falling. Unbidden, a wise proverb from *The Way of the Samurai* came into my mind.

"The way of the samurai is found in death. When it comes to either or, there is only the quick choice of death. It is not particularly difficult. Be determined and advance."

I closed my eyes. I could taste the earthy flavor of the moss in my mouth. Feel the bitter bite of the wind. Even the pain in my body made me aware that I was alive and that each second was precious to me. I wept silently. I had failed already, then. I would never achieve the state of mind necessary to become a samurai warrior. To do that, I would have to be indifferent to death. And I did not want to die.

Not now. Not ever.

ONE

You cannot hope to
Understand me until you
First wear all my clothes

*H*ad my elder sister not been so beautiful, my life might have been very different. Perhaps if she had been less certain of that beauty, less certain that the world would bend to her will, I would be in a different place now.

But then, what is the use of saying "if only?" As the saying has it, "Even the stone you trip on is part of your destiny." What has happened is gone; I cannot change it. And if I could, would I really want to? I must, I think, be honest and say that in spite of the sometimes extraordinarily cruel parts of my life, the answer is no.

My father had three children. The eldest was my brother, Isamu. The name means brave. A most suitable name for the eldest child of a samurai. Father doted on him, as was only natural. Isamu was born to Father's favorite concubine, a beautiful, talented woman who thought the gods' trod in Father's shadow. Even at a very young age, I found this puzzling. His mother outlived all of Father's other concubines. My sister, Emiko, insisted that the others had died of a combination of boredom and neglect. But of course, she never said that in front of Isamu.

My elder sister was the first child born to Father's wife and was very close to our mother. She was fond of telling me she was named Emiko because she was beautiful from the moment of her birth. The name refers to a child that is both prosperous and beautiful, so it was also a subtle compliment to Father's vast wealth. I could understand all of that. Emiko was truly beautiful, and of course, Father was both rich and of very high status. Our family was samurai, and—unlike other samurai who had fallen on hard times down the centuries—we had no need at all of the traditional allowance of rice we were given by the shogun each year.

I was the second child of Father's wife. And the last. It was a great sadness to me that my birth killed my mother. Emiko told me often that I was very fortunate that Father was such a noble man and that he adhered so strictly to the code of the samurai, the way of life called bushido. The code imposes seven virtues on the true samurai: loyalty, courage, truthfulness, honor, righteousness, politeness, and benevolence. In addition, a true warrior should appreciate and respect all life, as it is this quality that adds vital balance to the warlike character of the samurai. Emiko always pointed out that it was this last quality that had enabled me to live. Father had been quite fond of our mother, Emiko told me. Not so fond of her that he had hesitated to take concubines, of course, but that was perfectly normal. Had he been a merchant, or even belonged to the highest class of noble—the daimyo—he would probably have had me exposed as a just punishment for killing my mother. After all, I was only a girl child. A girl child who had been born prematurely and, in consequence, arrived into this world thin and whining and discontent. Perhaps it was a punishment from the gods for my sins, but I was also ugly. Altogether unlike my lovely elder sister.

I should be grateful for my good fortune, Emiko told me often. And behave suitably. By which she meant I should be quiet and respectful and always do as she ordered me without question. Even my name reflected my good fortune. I was called Keiko, which means lucky. There was no hidden meaning or irony in my birth name. It was meant to echo my circumstances, to make me understand that every time I heard it, I was fortunate to be alive.

Even though I understood that, I found it challenging to be as grateful as Emiko thought I should be. I was in awe of my lovely elder sister, to be sure. From a very young age, I understood that the gods had favored her with every blessing. She was not only lovely to look at, but she also had a naturally beautiful singing voice, and to see her dance was to wonder if her feet even touched the ground, so graceful was she. When she loosed her hair for me to comb out, it fell thick and straight almost to her knees. I thought it was wonderful hair, but Emiko complained about it, as she did most things.

"I want it to be longer," she said pettishly. "It should reach my heels. Look, like that."

She jabbed her finger at a very old print that adorned the wall in the main room of her apartment. She had many scrolls and prints in her rooms, but for some reason, that particular one saddened me. It had faded over the years, but the image was still clear. A beautiful woman stood straight and proud. Her head was tilted back slightly so that her cheek almost touched the man at her side. His head was on her shoulder, his lips a fraction away from her face. And as Emiko never tired of pointing out, the woman's hair—which was loose and pulled over one shoulder—fell straight and true down to her ankles.

I could never understand why Emiko saw only the length of the woman's hair. To me, that was irrelevant. Every time I looked at the print, I held my breath. The woman was smiling slightly, and I knew her smile was for the man who leaned against her. I suppose it was silly, but I always hoped that one day the print would be different when I looked at it. That her companion would have moved forward the tiny space that would have allowed his lips to brush against her skin. The print was very old. How many years had the couple waited to come together? Nonsense, I knew, but I always hoped that someday the miracle would happen and they would find the touch both so obviously craved.

I never mentioned it to Emiko. I shuddered at the mere thought of the withering contempt that would greet my words.

"Do you think if I had it trimmed a little, it would help it to grow?"

My thoughts had stayed with the print, and for a moment, I had no idea what my sister was talking about. She waited a heartbeat and then cuffed me with the back of her hand.

"Perhaps it would," I said quickly. "Shall I comb it for you a little while longer?"

"No, you're hopeless. You get the comb stuck and tug. I'll get the maid to do it for me in the future."

I knew she was lying. She always said that, even when I had combed her hair for so long my arms ached. I knew also that she thought she was punishing me by saying it. In a way, I suppose she was; although I knew perfectly well that she would never release me from the task of grooming her hair, each time did hope rise that perhaps, this time, she meant it. I looked suitably humble and hid a smile. I thought that Emiko would be bewildered if she could read my thoughts. She would never be subtle enough to look beyond the obvious. Why should she? As beautiful as she was, what need did she have to be perceptive?

"Will I ever be as beautiful as you, elder sister?" I blurted.

Emiko looked me over coolly. "No," she said simply. "You're too gangly. And skinny. Your skin's good enough, I suppose. And your hair's thick. But that nose! It sticks out like a tree branch. And your face is all angles. If a lover tried to stroke your face, he would cut himself on your cheekbones. Father said once that his grandmother looked like you. Just as well she did, or I doubt he would believe you were his daughter."

I stared at the floor miserably. I cursed my great-grandmother silently but bitterly. I avoided looking at myself in a mirror because of my face. I hated my own reflection so much that on the odd occasions when I caught a glimpse of myself, I instinctively looked away.

"I can't do anything about it," I said miserably. "Perhaps it doesn't matter that much. After all, great-grandmother found a husband, in spite of her looks."

"She did, but you have to remember that Father's grandmother was from a daimyo family. She married well beneath her station when great-grandfather took a fancy to her. And of course, she came with a splendid dowry as bait. I don't suppose Father would be willing to spend that much, not even to get rid of you. That's always assuming there was a suitable man out there who would even want you."

"Perhaps Father could find a match for me from outside our class?" Even as I said it, I knew I was talking nonsense. And if I hadn't known, Emiko's incredulous expression would have told me so.

"What? You mean a merchant or some other riverbed beggar? Such nonsense!" Emiko stared at me as if I had cursed her in the ripest possible language. "You would bring dishonor on the family. Father would never even think of it. I know great-grandmother married out of her class, but at least we're samurai. Our family has a name and a heritage that go back for centuries. No, for you to marry into the merchant class is unthinkable."

She stared at me with her lovely head to one side. "We could try plastering you with makeup, I suppose. You know, like geisha wear. No, that's not going to work either. You do have lovely skin, but if we covered it up, everybody would think you had been badly marked from smallpox and were trying to hide it." We were both silent, thinking about it for a moment. Emiko shook her head. "No, it's no good. You'll just have to live with the looks the gods gave you."

"There must be something I can do," I begged.

Emiko pouted, her full lower lip looking like the petal of a pale pink flower. Finally, she shrugged. "It would probably help if you kept your gaze downcast, like any well-bred lady should," she said reprovingly. "You have a terrible habit of staring straight at people. It's awfully rude. Anybody would think you were a peasant who didn't know any better."

"I'll try," I promised. Even as I said it, I knew I would not. I could do nothing about my face; it was my curse, I knew. But from the time I first understood that I looked different, it had seemed important that I should show my face without fear to people. I could not even try and explain it to Emiko, but I felt instinctively that a person's reaction to my flaws was an indication of their soul. Sometimes, I was certain that I saw a flicker of distaste pass over the face of whoever was looking at me. To show one's feelings in that way was grossly impolite. Often, such people were fulsomely kind to me to make up for their initial rudeness. It didn't fool me at all. I knew they saw me as pitiably ugly.

Others kept a stone face, but I sensed they were reluctant to get close to me, no doubt fearing that my ill-looks would bring bad luck down on them.

A few simply stared at me. That I could stand. It was rude, of course, but far better than concealing their distaste.

And a very few simply treated me as if I was another human being. Those few did I love with all my heart.

My brother, Isamu, was one of them. He had never bothered about my appearance. To him, I was simply his sister. Emiko said what she thought, and that was that. She was my elder sister, and it was my duty to love her. On the odd occasions when I was in the company of Father, he simply looked straight through me, as if I didn't exist. I understood that. I was not only a useless girl child—a dreadfully plain girl child, at that—but I had killed my mother to come into this world. In spite of all that, he fed and clothed me and gave me a home; I was grateful for his charity to me. I wished I could have been born a boy so I could have found a way to support my family in return.

Outside of my family, there was only one person in my whole world who was kind to me and saw the worthwhile person behind my looks. And because of it, I adored him with all the passion of a soul denied love. I dreamed of his touch and often awoke clutching my kakebuton—the thick quilt laid on top of my futon—as tenderly as if it had been him lying next to me. I blushed when he spoke to me and found it no effort at all to keep my face downcast when I was in his presence. When our fingers brushed accidentally as I passed him a cup of sake or poured tea into his bowl, I trembled.

After he had visited us—which was often—I lay awake far into the night, cursing the contrary fate that had taken delight in making him the only man who ever looked beyond my ugliness and into my heart.

Why, I wondered bitterly, did he have to be the man who was to marry my sister?

TWO

The sound of rain on
Hard ground is my heart beating
As I wait for you

"*I*t's all right for you, and Emiko as well," I said enviously. I was watching Isamu practice in the courtyard with his katana, the traditional samurai curved sword. Even though it was an inferior weapon—used only to hack at a wooden figure balanced on a swivel that moved at a touch and helped to improve the warrior's aim and sense of balance—the katana's blade was still wickedly sharp. I could feel my body twitching as it followed his movements. I memorized every curve of his arm, every turn of his body. Isamu finished his graceful movement before he spoke, standing back and sliding the katana carefully back into its scabbard before he turned his attention to me.

"What's all right for me and Emiko?" he asked. In spite of the vigorous exercise routine he had just finished, he was barely out of breath. He walked to the edge of the dojo area and took a dipper of water from a barrel. He offered me the dipper courteously. I took a drink even though I was not thirsty, grateful for his kindness. He slaked his own thirst and then poured water over his head, shaking the drops away like a dog.

"Everything is," I said simply. "You're the man of the family. Father loves you. As far as he's concerned, you can do no wrong. Emiko is beautiful and graceful and enchants everybody she meets. And she's going to be married to Soji, so her future is bright."

"Feeling sorry for yourself today?" Isamu said brutally.

I felt tears come to my eyes. Did even my adored brother not understand that I had less than nothing? That in our house I had as little status as a lowly maidservant? I would most likely never marry. I was doomed to live at home as a burden on my family until death gave me release from my useless life. I ripped at my fingernail with my teeth, disappointed that he had not understood my feelings instinctively. That he had made me feel even more depressed.

"I'm useless," I said finally. "Father's never going to be able to find anybody to marry me. Nobody is going to want me when I look like this. I'm going to die an old maid, unwanted and uncared for. It would be better if I died young, with at least the hope of some sort of honorable end." I raised my head and stared at him defiantly. I drew a sharp, indignant breath when I saw he was grinning widely.

"Great-grandmother looked like you, and she found a husband," Isamu pointed out cheerfully. "She must have, or we wouldn't be here. I'm sure Father will find you a suitable husband. Do you want me to talk to him about it? Would that make you feel better?"

His good-natured dismissal of my problem made me feel even worse. I frowned at him and shrugged my shoulders sulkily. If Emiko knew great-grandmother's story, then surely Isamu also knew. And if he knew, then he must know perfectly well that it was out of the question for me to marry down as she had done. And if I could not do that, then what was there left for me? Emiko had been betrothed to Soji when she was no more than a child. I was deeply envious of her good fortune. He not only came from an excellent family and was rich, he even appeared to be very fond of her. I was only two years younger than she was, and Father had never mentioned trying to find me a suitable husband. I thought about Isamu's words. Was that really what I wanted? What alternative did I have? Of course I wanted to marry and have many male children. It was the summit of any well-born woman's ambition. Knowing that, why did my tongue stumble and refuse to find words as I watched his smiling face?

"What else could I do?" I asked, even though I knew the answer. Nothing. It was have a suitable husband found for me or live out my life as an old maid, treated as no more than a servant by everyone in our household. I felt a cold emptiness in the pit of my stomach as I realized that neither alternative appealed to me in the least. If Soji had been available, now that would have been another matter. But he was not. And I could not believe that I would ever feel about another man as I felt for Soji.

"You can stop feeling sorry for yourself, for a start," Isamu said briskly. I glowered at him. "You don't have to get married, you know. Or end up as an old maid. There is another alternative. Have you never heard of the onna-bugeisha?"

I looked at his smiling face and threw my head back and laughed out loud at the absurdity of his question. I laughed so long and hard that tears came to my eyes. I wiped them away and apologized quickly. It was unutterably rude of me.

Had I been talking to anybody of a noble class apart from my dear brother, I would have been struck for my dreadful insolence. As it was, Isamu simply shook his head in mock severity.

"Are you surprised Father hasn't bothered to find a husband for you when you dare to laugh at somebody who is trying to help you? Have some respect for your elders and betters, sister!"

"I am sorry, brother." Even though Isamu had spoken lightly, I hurried to apologize. "I assumed you were making fun of me. Of course I have heard tales of the onna-bugeisha. But that is all they are, stories. Noble warrior women who fought alongside their men could never really exist. All samurai warriors are men, and that's all there is to it."

"You think so? Wait a moment until I put my robe on." He glanced at his costly robe, strewn casually on the wall of the well, and I hurried to fetch it for him. He slid his arms into the sleeves with casual grace and knotted the sash elegantly without bothering to glance down at it. Finally satisfied, he nodded at me. "Come along with me, little sister. I have something to show you." He walked away from me without a backward glance.

Hobbled by the tight skirt of my kimono, I had to scurry to catch up with him. I noticed sadly that I had grown taller. Even allowing for the height of my wooden geta, I guessed that I was now barely shorter than my brother, and he was quite a tall man. Yet another flaw in my tragic design. Not for the first time, I longed to be tiny and feminine like Emiko.

Once inside the house, I immediately heard Emiko scolding her maid for some trifling error. I noticed that my sister always spoke to me in precisely the same tone.

"Never mind about Emiko. Nothing ever really pleases her. Whatever you did for her would be wrong," Isamu said shrewdly. "If she has any sense, she'll be married before long and out of our way. She hasn't any sense, of course. More's the pity."

His words seemed odd to me, but I could not quite decide why. I followed him into his apartment and sat on my heels on the tatami, watching him delve into a cedarwood chest. After a moment, he came and sat beside me. He had a bulky package in his hands shrouded in a bag of very fine white silk. He undid the ties and pulled the mouth of the bag open very carefully, sliding his fingers inside and drawing out a large, leather-bound book, which he held out to me. I looked at it warily, the sight of it immediately bringing the memory of a long-forgotten event back to me.

I had deliberately pushed all thoughts of the incident away and done my best to forget all about it. That made the sudden recollection of it now all the more horrifying. Isamu obviously did not notice anything was wrong; his attention was all on the book in his hands. He stroked the leather binding delicately. My brother was not greatly given to daintiness, so I knew that this book must be very special to him.

I stared at it in revulsion. I was sure I had seen the book before, in different hands. I wanted Isamu to put it away. To slide it back in its cover and hide it back in the cedar chest where it belonged. I did not want to look at it. Isamu turned his head and looked at me curiously. I managed a smile. I had to be mistaken. It could not be the same book. Still, I closed my eyes in instinctive horror as Isamu very carefully lifted the front cover back.

THREE

On sand, our footsteps
Vanish with the tide. Memories
Linger forever

*S*everal years before, a friend of my brother named Choki had stayed with us. I did not like this young man at all. Perhaps he recognized my dislike and decided to punish me for it. Or perhaps he had taken a fancy to me. In any event, he invited me to his room—and politeness dictated that I had to go. He sat next to me, far too close for comfort, and showed me a book of which the cover looked to me exactly like the one Isamu had in his hand now. Very smooth, fine-grained leather. Light grey, so pale it gleamed in the light that filtered through the shoji screen.

"Keiko-chan," he said breathily, "I wonder if you have ever seen anything like this before?"

I shook my head. The book was beautifully bound. I ran my finger over the binding appreciatively. He seemed to take my gesture as approval and flipped the book open quickly. My mouth fell open in astonishment and I jerked back. Unfortunately, Choki was so close to me that my head hit his chin. I apologized wildly, desperate to cover my seething embarrassment. To be so close to any man I did not know very well would have been deeply uncomfortable. But in Choki's case, it was even worse. His odor was so rank I tried to hold my breath in an effort not to smell him.

"Do not worry about it. It is nothing. A blow from your delightful head could never be painful to me." His courtesy was so false it raised the hackles on the back of my neck. I knew he was mocking me, and I hated him for it. "Now, Keiko. Do look. Is my shunga not the most beautiful thing you have ever seen? Just look at the craftsmanship that has gone into executing the illustrations."

He was breathing heavily, and I knew he wasn't in the least interested in the skill of the illustrator. Before I could respond, he flipped a page over. I moaned out loud in mortification, trying to look anywhere but at the book. But Choki was having none of it. He put his fingers on my chin and forced my head around and down until I was looking squarely at the pages of the book. I could have clamped my eyes shut, I suppose, but what was the point? He would not let me leave until I had taken a good look.

I knew what it was. I had heard of such things. Shunga was the word for erotic art. But to call this book shunga was extremely generous. It was no more than a pillow book, a collection of sensual prints that lovers would use to arouse themselves. But we were not lovers. I was just a young girl, and Choki was my brother's friend. And although I longed to stand up and march out of the room, because Choki was both my brother's friend and a guest in our house, politeness dictated that I stay and tolerate his behavior. If I did not, I had no doubt that he would complain to my brother that I had been rude to him. Courtesy would dictate that Isamu believe the guest he had invited into our house.

To make matters even worse, I loved my brother dearly and would never wish to cause him shame. So, I sat, rigid with embarrassment, looking but trying not to see Choki's pillow book.

"It is beautifully done," I said tonelessly.

"Isn't it?" Choki had moved closer to me. I could feel his stinking breath on my cheek. "Have you ever seen anything like this before, Keiko-chan?"

"No," I muttered. Even as I spoke, I felt my gaze drawn to the illustration. As my initial embarrassment began to lessen, I almost laughed in disbelief.

The picture depicted a young woman, squatting down with her kimono raised so she could pass water into a stream. Hardly anything erotic about that! Then my gaze slid to the left and I saw a man, hidden behind a fence and watching the woman intently through a gap. His enormous tree of flesh was grasped firmly in his hand, and even in my innocence, I understood that he was excited by watching the woman pee and was pleasuring himself vigorously. I blushed deeply, my thoughts whirling in confusion. How could anybody be aroused by the sight of a woman carrying out her natural functions? Would I find it stimulating to watch a man urinating? Hardly!

"This one is by the master Utamaro," Choki said throatily. "Do you like it?"

I shook my head violently, feeling sick. "I don't want to see anymore," I managed to croak.

Choki laughed. "Oh, come now. No need to be shy."

I shook my head, mute with sick disbelief. Choki shuffled over and put his head on my shoulder. The book fell from his hands and for a brief moment I was deeply relieved. Then I felt him shuffling his robe about and realized he was touching his tree. I stared straight ahead, as much to avoid his breath as to hide my fear and humiliation.

"Come, dear. Just you put your fingers around that. I know it can't match up to the shunga, but then again, this is flesh and blood and not just a drawing."

I tried to pull away, but he held me fast, trapping one of my arms against his body. He grabbed my free hand and pushed it hard against his tree. I had no idea at all what he wanted and simply left it still and rigid against him. He sighed deeply and put his own hand over my fingers, forcing them to wrap around his tree, at the same time moving my hand up and down. His flesh was hot and faintly moist. I felt sick.

"That's right. Now, isn't that lovely? Would you like me to put my tree in you? I would give you very great pleasure, I assure you." His mouth was against my ear.

"I think I should go now," I managed to whisper.

"Go? When we are just getting to know one another better? Don't be silly." He licked my ear, shoving his tongue deep inside. It felt sticky and altogether unpleasant. With dawning amazement, I realized this was supposed to arouse me. "Have you ever been with a man before, dear?"

"No." I swallowed and choked at the same time. My heart was beating so fiercely, I was sure he could hear it and would think I was excited. "Please, I would like to go now. I'm sure I heard Isamu shouting for me just now."

"Oh, I don't think so. He told me he was going hawking with your father. I would have gone with them, but I have no real taste for takagari. Apart from anything else, the dust from the birds' feathers always makes me sneeze. And I rather thought it would be nice for us to have a little time to ourselves. And don't worry about your sister, she's gone shopping and took her maid with her. There's just the two of us left in the house, I promise you."

I clenched my hand fiercely in frustration, but Choki moaned with pleasure. Innocent as I was, I mistook his groans for pain and gripped his tree still harder, hoping that I would hurt him so much that he would push me away.

"Yes," he whispered. "Just like that. You obviously have hidden talents."

I tried to take my hand away from his tree, but Choki was far too quick for me. He immediately put his fingers very firmly around my hand, forcing me to rub his tree up and down. I froze in shock as he used his other hand to force its way inside my kimono, thrusting aside my robes and underthings as though they were barely there. I shrieked in fear, and he cackled.

"All you women are the same. The more you want it, the coyer you pretend to be, which wouldn't be a problem if we had more time. But as it is, I suggest we get down to things. Lie back. Give my tree a nice long suck and I'll seek the seed with you. That'll get your juices running good and proper before I match the bird to the nest."

I closed my eyes tightly. This couldn't be happening. Choki's fingers fumbled inside my robe and I knew that he was going to rape me. Here, in my own home. And there was nothing I could do about it. I was alone with him, and he was far stronger than I was. And if he did succeed in taking me, what then?

If I found the courage to tell Isamu his friend had taken me against my will, would he believe me? No doubt Choki would say it was all my fault. That I had enticed him and he had been unable to resist. Even Isamu would no doubt think it was perfectly understandable that his plain, neglected sister had been driven to desperate measures to satisfy her lusts. He would probably apologize to Choki for my behavior and never speak to me again. I could never complain to Father. He would never believe I was without fault. He would be so ashamed that he would immediately sell me to a brothel somewhere far enough away for me not to be known. Emiko, I knew, would accuse me of trying to make myself important and be furious with me.

Perhaps Soji might believe me? The thought gave me a small measure of courage. He would stand by me. I took a deep breath and winced as Choki's hand fumbled around. I summoned the image of dear Soji's face to my mind and my fear lessened slightly. If I had somebody who believed me, then I could find the courage to resist. I would *not* simply allow this to happen to me. I took a deep breath and tried to relax.

Choki raised his head and grinned at me approvingly. "Ah, I can see you're enjoying that." His mouth was ajar, and a thread of saliva connected his teeth. He flicked it away with his tongue. I tried not to flinch away from his breath. "I saw how excited you were with my pillow book. I knew all along you were not as innocent as you pretended. Tell me, how do you like it best? Do you want me to put my tree into your manko and match the bird to the nest or would you prefer me to split the melon with you?"

I had no idea what he meant, but as he seemed pleased, I smiled as enticingly as I could.

"Whichever you like," I whispered. The lies caught in my throat and I had to cough before I could continue. "But first, I would like to take your tree in my mouth."

I barely managed not to shudder at the thought. Choki wagged his tree at me happily, pulling the hood down and back and running it between his fingers. I stared at it in appalled fascination. I had never seen an erect tree before and could not believe that any woman could find it attractive. Choki's tree seemed to be threaded with numerous veins, protruding like so many worms that might begin to wriggle at any moment. The exposed head of his tree was bright red and streaked with what looked like beaten egg white. I felt nauseous at the very thought of putting it between my lips. But anything was better than having him put it inside me.

"I would enjoy that greatly," Choki murmured happily. He took one hand away from his tree and stroked my face with his fingers. I clenched my teeth to stop myself from biting him. "You don't look at all like your sister," he said with casual cruelty. "But if one doesn't compare you to her, you're not unattractive. And I do like a girl with an athletic figure. You know, if you prove your worth today, I might even be persuaded to put in an offer to your father for you."

I gasped in disbelief at his words. Choki smiled widely, obviously mistaking my incredulity as an indication of pleasure. My fear suddenly turned to anger. How dare this nasty, stinking man take advantage of his status as a guest in our house to attempt to seduce me?

"You are too kind, Choki-san." I could not believe he didn't hear the sarcasm in my voice. But it was obvious he had not. He preened, sticking the tip of his tongue between his teeth like a cat enjoying being stroked.

"We will see." He glanced at my stone face and must have seen optimism there as he went on quickly. "Not quite marriage, of course. My own bride was chosen for me years ago by our families. A girl from an excellent family with a good dowry. A placid, dutiful girl, and rather dull, but it doesn't matter. She will only be my wife, after all. But I may consider taking you as my concubine, my number two wife. There would be a ceremony, naturally," he added grandly.

I was dumb with fury. Had there been any sort of weapon at hand, I would have killed him at that moment and then committed suicide. I glanced around wildly, hoping to be able to find something deadly, but there was nothing other than the dreadful pillow book and the cushions we were kneeling on.

"Come. Enough of the pleasantries. My tree is longing for your attention."

I stared at it, bobbing at me from the pressure of his fingers. I would take his tree in my mouth, as he wanted. And once it was well between my lips, I would bite it so hard he would never be able to bring himself to show it to a woman again.

He would, of course, be incandescent with rage. He would complain to Isamu. No doubt tell him that it was I who had led him on and then assaulted him viciously when he had given in to me. Tradition and courtesy would dictate that it was the honored guest who was believed. If Isamu were angry enough with me, he would cut my head off with his sword and my name would be wiped from the family records. It was a matter of honor, I understood that. I also knew that whatever course I followed would end in disaster for me. At least this way, I would have the satisfaction of knowing that I had been true to myself. I rejoiced in the knowledge.

I bent down to Choki's tree. The very tip of my tongue touched his flesh, and I heard him exhale with the anticipation of pleasures yet to come. I couldn't do it.

"What? What is it? Why have you stopped?" He sounded pettish. Was it possible that he could have no idea how badly he stank?

"I am sorry, Choki-san. I...I cannot." I took a deep breath to calm myself and instantly wished I had not. I guessed Choki was becoming angry and that the strong emotion was somehow intensifying his bodily odors. Suddenly, I knew that he was perfectly well aware of his own stink. His face was twitching with fury. He hissed wordlessly, flecks of saliva spitting into my face.

"You nasty little bitch! I offer you the honor of enjoying my body and this is how you repay me? Well, if you won't give yourself to me freely, then I'll take you, simple as that. And don't think you can go running to your brother and telling him about it. He won't believe you."

I closed my lips tightly and shook my head. The wrong thing to do. Choki roared with anger and lunged at me, grabbing my hair and forcing my head down to his groin. His tree mashed hard against my mouth. The fish stink made my eyes water. I was determined not to open my lips. I would die first, and if possible, I would make sure that Choki died with me. Perhaps then Isamu would understand that my death had been greater than my life. That even though my body was nothing more than a weak and useless girl's, my spirit was truly that of a samurai.

Choki shoved his tree so hard against my lips that it hurt. Finding I would still not open my mouth, he struck me around my head, and then again. The more I struggled, the more Choki seemed to like it. His hands were on each side of my head, holding me tight. No matter how I tried, I could not get away from him. I gagged, my eyes watering as I tried to breathe without inhaling his stink.

Choki froze. My eyes were streaming with tears. I could see nothing. I was sure that Isamu—or even worse, my father—had come into the room unexpectedly. I blinked fiercely, trying to regain my vision. I flushed with shame as I understood how this would look to either man.

"Does he know you? Will he obey you?" Choki whispered. I looked at him in bewilderment and then followed his horrified gaze.

It was no man who stood in the doorway. For a second, I was bewildered, and then I understood what I was looking at and relief made me limp. Isamu's favorite hunting dog, an akita he had named Matsuo, filled the entrance to the room. Akita are used for hunting deer and are big, powerful dogs. Even for an akita, Matsuo was huge. His name meant shining hero. Isamu had named him that when his horse had thrown him once during a hunt and he had landed almost on top of a snake, a full-grown mamushi whose bite could have been fatal and would certainly have been horribly painful for a long time. Snakes nearly always slide away from men, but this one did not. Isamu said it looked as if it was about to shed its skin, the point at which snakes are most dangerous. Instead of fleeing, it reared up at Isamu and was about to strike when Matsuo rushed at it from behind and grabbed it by the neck. By the time Isamu had climbed to his feet, the snake was bitten in two.

From that moment on, Matsuo was Isamu's favorite dog. He adored my brother and would take orders from nobody but him. But Choki didn't know that.

"He will obey me," I said quickly. "But he doesn't like strangers. Matsuo, sit." Thankfully, the dog obeyed me, although it seemed reluctant. He sat silently, his lips peeled back from his white fangs.

"Tell him to go away. I don't like dogs. Especially not big ones like that. Good dog. Just you go away and leave us alone," Choki ordered. Matsuo growled even louder at his tone. Choki glanced at me and swallowed. "No, no. I see he's not going to take orders from a stranger. The dog obviously wants to protect you. I can see that." Choki's face had gone green with fear. "He's not going to leave, is he?"

"Not unless I tell him to," I said confidently. "He is very protective." And so he was, but not usually of me. Matsuo growled again, deep in his throat, his eyes never leaving Choki. Suddenly, I understood. Isamu was hunting with hawks today. Matsuo would have gotten in the way, so he had been left at home. Until Isamu came back, he would protect me instead.

Choki was fastening his robe, very slowly. I noticed that his rearing tree had shrunk so much it was almost hidden in his black moss. That pleased me greatly. I hoped that it would be a very long time before he dared display it to any woman again.

"Please. I really do not like dogs. They seem to know I'm afraid of them. Protect me from him and I promise I will never speak to Isamu about what happened between us."

A moment ago, Choki had been intent on violating me. Now he was trying to turn the tables so that the encounter would appear, if not my fault, at least with my agreement. I longed to order Matsuo to bite him. To maul him so severely that he would never want to show his face in public again.

Matsuo turned his gaze to me as if asking, "What do you want me to do with him?" and I relented. If the poor dog so much as nipped my brother's guest, then custom dictated that Isamu would have to kill him. I could not live with that on my conscience.

"Matsuo." I spoke firmly. The akita promptly left the door and came to stand at my side. I patted him gently. Choki groaned, a small sound that barely left his throat. "Smell him, Matsuo," I ordered.

Matsuo glanced at me enquiringly. When I nodded, he padded right up to Choki and sniffed him cautiously. It was clear the dog hated his smell; his lips curled and his ears went flat. When he got to the stage of shoving his muzzle right in Choki's robe and nosing at his tree, I clicked my fingers. It wasn't that I really wanted him to stop—Choki was groaning loudly and shaking, and the knowledge that he was terrified delighted me—rather, I knew if I allowed Matsuo to sniff for a moment longer I would burst out laughing. Matsuo backed away at my signal, and I was sure he looked relieved to be away from Choki's stench.

"Matsuo is an akita," I said gravely. "You may have heard of the skill of such dogs. Once they have the scent of a deer, they will track it for miles from the smell alone. And when they do find their prey, they tear it to pieces. That is their instinct. And Matsuo is very special. My brother has trained him particularly well. Once he gets a scent, he never forgets it. Just as he will never forget *you*. I suggest you leave this house immediately, before my brother returns. If you do, I will show you mercy. But if you linger, or if you ever come back here, all I have to do is click my fingers and Matsuo will tear you apart. It would be unfortunate for Matsuo, of course, as Isamu would be forced to take his head off to punish him. But I don't suppose that would be much comfort to you, would it, Choki-san?"

"No, no. No need for anything like that. I will leave now. This minute. I will leave Isamu a note to tell him that I have been called away on urgent business. I promise you, I will never return here."

I almost believed him. But I was still suspicious. I stroked Matsuo's dense fur and nodded politely.

"Perhaps you would like to leave your note with me? I'll make sure Isamu gets it as soon as he comes home. He will be most disappointed that you had to leave suddenly, I'm sure."

"You have a tight hold on the dog?" I nodded, and Choki scrambled to his feet. Matsuo delighted me by growling at him and lunging for his ankle as Choki passed him. He gave a high-pitched squeal and ran from the room with his robe flapping.

I gave Isamu his note, but only after I had read it myself. Choki's calligraphy was dreadful, although I suppose the unevenness of his kanji and the splutters from the brush could have been due to his encounter with Matsuo. He had done as I had asked and simply said that he presented his apologies but had been called away on urgent family business. I was surprised when Isamu seemed pleased he had gone.

"One has to be polite, of course. His bride is a distant cousin of our family, and as I knew him somewhat, Father felt we had to invite him as our guest. But, between the two of us, he was a terrible bore. Didn't want to hunt. Couldn't even compose a decent haiku." He paused and I waited for him to comment on Choki's dreadful smell. He didn't, as that would have been outside the bounds of politeness. When he did speak, I was astonished. "He dropped a couple of hints about you. I rather thought he'd taken a fancy to you. He didn't say anything to you, I suppose?"

I shook my head. "Not a thing," I lied cheerfully.

FOUR

Snow bends the boughs to
Its will. But once the thaw comes,
Their time will return

*T*he memory of horrible Choki was so vivid that it took me a moment to focus on what Isamu was actually showing me. Even if Isamu possessed anything as vulgar as a shunga pillow book, he would never dream of showing it to me. Besides, he was handling this book with such reverence, I knew at once that it was very special and that I was mistaken.

"This book is very precious, little sister. Grandfather gave it to me when I was a young child."

Isamu was opening the cover as he spoke, and I looked at it with interest.

The leaves inside were curious. They did not turn like normal pages, but folded out like the pleats of a huge fan. I knew at once that the book was very old indeed. The paper was called washi and was made from the fibers of mulberry bushes. Because of its construction, the paper could remain intact for centuries if it was well cared for. This book had obviously been kept very carefully for a very long time. The washi was still intact and the grain very fine, but it was beginning to yellow at the edges, and I noticed that Isamu took great care as he unfolded the pages and spread them out before us. They crackled faintly as they were laid flat.

"Don't touch!" he said sharply. I snatched my hand away as though he had burned it with fire. Isamu was rarely impatient. If I had not understood before, I now knew how important this old book was to him.

"I'm sorry." I tucked my hands beneath my knees to show how careful I would be from that moment on. "I will be very careful not to hurt your book. Is it very old?"

"Centuries. Not even grandfather was quite sure how old. I think it may have been made in the time of the Genpei War." I tried to look intelligent, but I had never heard of it. Isamu obviously understood my confusion. "That means nothing to you, does it?"

"No," I said simply. "Will you tell me about it?"

I was fascinated without knowing why. Perhaps Isamu felt my interest. He balanced the book on his knees carefully, his expression alight with enthusiasm.

"The Genpei War took place over six hundred years ago. Two clans went to war for supremacy—the Tairo and Minamoto."

"I remember hearing Father saying once that our family descended from the Minamoto clan," I interrupted. "Is that true?"

"It is." Isamu nodded seriously. "You should be very proud of our heritage, Keiko."

"Oh, I am," I assured him. As the mere youngest girl child, I had never been instructed in our family history. Now, I understood how well connected we were and why

Emiko had sneered at the idea of me marrying anybody who was not a full-blooded samurai.

Isamu prodded me to ensure he had my attention. I sat straight and tried to look intelligent. "It was illustrated to commemorate the courage and daring of the Minamoto samurai. And not just the men of the clan. The women as well. Look."

He held the fanned pages out carefully, and I followed his finger where it was pointing at the first illustration. It showed what was unmistakably a woman mounted on a horse. I held my breath in astonishment as I saw that she was wearing full armor, and the traditional two swords of the samurai were thrust into her sash, ready to be drawn at any moment. A long, curved naginata—a wickedly sharp curved blade mounted on a long handle—was draped almost casually over her shoulder. She was utterly feminine in the beauty of her face and hair, and at the same time undeniably masculine in her clothes and bearing.

"Who is she?" I breathed. "Why is she dressed as a samurai warrior?"

"She is one of our ancestors," Isamu said quietly. "Her name was Tomoe Gozen, and she was onna-bugeisha. She is dressed as a samurai warrior because that is what she was —a warrior woman of the samurai. One of the women you dismissed as no more than a children's tale."

"Really?" In spite of the evidence before my eyes, I could hardly believe it. I wanted to know everything that Isamu could tell me about this lovely warrior. "Who was she? Did she really fight like a man?"

"I told you, she's one of our ancestors." Isamu tried to look bored, but a smile broke through as he recognized my enthusiasm. "She fought in the battle of Awazu alongside her man. It is said that she was a greater warrior than any man who fought that day." His voice became suddenly formal, and I understood that he was reciting something he had learned by heart. "Tomoe Gozen was especially beautiful. She had white skin, long hair, and charming features. She was a remarkably strong archer, and as a swordswoman, she was a warrior worth a thousand men, ready to confront demon or god, mounted or on foot. She handled unbroken horses with superb skill. Whenever a battle was imminent, her husband sent her out as his first captain, equipped with strong armor, an oversized sword, and a mighty bow. She performed more deeds of valor than any of his other warriors."

Isamu's voice trailed off and he stared over my head as if I wasn't there. I was disappointed. I wanted so much more. Where had this extraordinary woman learned to fight? What had she done to persuade the gods to give her such courage? And above all, what had happened to her? It was this last question that I asked Isamu. He blinked at me in surprise as my voice called him back to the present. He seemed to find my question irrelevant as he shrugged impatiently.

"Oh, there are various theories. Some say she was killed during the fighting. Others say that when her husband understood he was finally defeated, he told her to run away because he wanted to die alongside his brother. He would have been ashamed for it to be known that he died alongside a woman. Does it matter?"

I stared at Tomoe Gozen's picture and wanted to say that it mattered very much to me. But the more I looked, the more certain I became that I knew the truth anyway. Her husband had probably told her to flee, but it was not because he was afraid to die alongside his woman. Unlike every other man I knew, he had loved his wife. And he had known that the only way he could ever persuade her to leave him to die in battle was to make it a matter of pride. Every samurai—male or female—would understand that. She would have wanted to die at his side, but she would have listened to what her husband was telling her. *I love you. Go. Save yourself for my sake. This way, I will die with honor and you will live with pride in me. If you stay, we will both die needlessly.* Yes, that made perfect sense to me.

"No, of course it doesn't matter," I lied cheerfully. "Are all the rest of the illustrations of her?"

"Yes. Look." Isamu pointed his finger at the next illustration. Tomoe Gozen's horse reared in the heat of battle. She had drawn her long naginata—intrigued as I was, I still wondered how she had managed it without unseating herself—and with it had skewered a man with a raised sword in his hand. Most of the rest of the illustrations were similar, except for one that was particularly gory. In that one, she had decapitated a samurai and was holding his head aloft, his blood spattering her armor.

"Isn't she wonderful?" Isamu's tone was so reverential that I glanced at him in surprise. He might have been speaking of a woman he knew and admired rather than one who had lived and died centuries ago. "I tell you, little sister, there is no woman walking the earth today who could ever match Tomoe Gozen. If I ever found one who could, I would marry her tomorrow."

He was speaking more to himself than me, and I allowed my thoughts to wander. Isamu was nearly twenty. He had been betrothed to a perfectly nice girl—the daughter of a friend of our father's—for years. By now, they should have been married and his wife installed in our house. The rooms should have echoed with the sound of children playing. Male children, of course. I often wished that he would marry and bring his bride to our home, as it would have given Emiko somebody other than me to sharpen her tongue on. Could it be possible that he was really languishing in passion for this long-dead warrior woman? Greatly daring, I spoke carefully.

"But even if she were alive today, it would be impossible. Himari-chan is waiting eagerly for you to name the day you are to be married. It's all arranged. You know that."

Isamu made an impatient gesture with his hand. "Oh, Himari-chan must wait. You sound just like Father, nattering at me to marry. Of course I will. The family name depends on me. I'll get around to her eventually and sire enough children to keep everybody happy."

He sounded angry and I stayed very still. Himari was a nice girl. Not too pretty—but then, who wants a pretty wife? That is what a man has mistresses for. I had never gotten the impression that she was particularly bright, but she clearly adored Isamu, and I was sure she would be as dutiful a wife as any man could expect or want.

"I see," I said seriously, even though I didn't. And then, even more cautiously, "The story of Tomoe Gozen is very interesting, brother. And I can quite see why you would admire her. But what has it got to do with me? There is no place for onna-bugeisha in this modern world of ours, sadly."

Isamu began to gather the fan of washi pages together. He pressed them carefully into place before smoothing the leather cover back into place firmly. He did not speak again until he had slid the silken cover back over the book and drawn together the threads that held it close.

"What would please you most in life, little sister? A husband? Is that really what you want?"

I stared down at the floor miserably. I knew I should say

yes and pretend to be enthusiastic. But why bother lying to my brother? He would see through my pretense at once in that irritating way that elder brothers had.

"No," I said instead. A surge of bitterness made me speak far more plainly than I had intended. "What use is a husband to a woman? All you men are the same. You just look on us as an unfortunate necessity. None of you love your wives. None of you even enjoy being intimate with them. All you want a wife for is to bear your children and make sure the servants keep the house clean and tidy."

I was panting with my vehement outburst. I thought Isamu would be furious with me, but to my surprise, he laughed long and loud.

"Dear little sister, if only you had been born a man! What fun we would have had together. But that's the way of the world. You are not a man. You are my little sister who only thinks and speaks like a man. I think it would be a very brave man who took you as his wife! Alas, I have no idea where we could find that special man for you. So, if you will not marry, what will you do?"

"Live out my miserable existence as an old maid," I said bitterly. "When you finally marry poor Himari, I suppose I will get the chance to bully someone who has even lower status than I do. At least until she has a son and becomes important. And then I will go back to living on Father's charity and being at everyone's beck and call."

I was so filled with resentment I didn't even bother looking at Isamu. Why bother? He would only be laughing at me again.

"And what if you had the chance to do something else?" Isamu's voice was so soft that I had to look up and watch his lips to catch what he was saying. "What if you had the chance to make Father proud of you? To make him forget that he only kept you about the place because of his obligations as a samurai? What if you could make him take notice of you at last?"

His words bit home, sharply as a snake. I had never spoken to anybody about the one thing that would make me happy above all else. I had never even considered making Father proud of me. It would always have been enough if I had managed to make him even acknowledge my existence. Somehow, Isamu knew what lay tightly enclosed in my heart. I stared at him in silent astonishment.

"How did you know?" I managed to say at last. My mouth was so dry, my voice was a croak.

"Because I know you, little sister," he said gently. "I've seen the envy on your face every time he tells Emiko how beautiful she is. I've even seen your jealousy when he spares a kind word for one of the dogs." He was right; the knowledge that Father cared more for his hounds than he did me was salt in my mouth. "I saw your expression a few days ago when he called you Kiku instead of Keiko. That hurt, didn't it?"

I kept my eyes wide and did not blink. I would not cry. I thought nobody had noticed Father's—uncorrected—mistake except for me.

"Yes, it did hurt me. But what else can I expect? Nobody is going to marry me whether I want to be married or not. Father's stuck with me until I die. I'm useless to him. A burden. I'm grateful that he allows me to live here as part of our honorable family."

"No, you're not," Isamu said smugly. "You hate every moment of your existence. Every time you look at Emiko, you resent her beauty. And above all, you hate Father for not loving you. Don't bother to lie, Keiko. I've watched you grow. Watched your resentment swell with every day that passes."

"So?" I shrugged, desperate to appear uncaring. "Nothing I can do about it, is there?"

"Nothing *you* can do about it, little sister. But perhaps there is something *I* can do for you. Would you be happy if I made Father look at you with respect? If I made Emiko look like the shallow creature she is next to you? If I gazed at you with admiration, would you be happy then?"

I thought that Isamu must have been smoking too much opium. He took a pipe now and then. Most men did when they were tired of sake. I managed a laugh.

"I think you are making fun of me, brother," I said politely.

"Then you are wrong."

He rose and put his book away in the cedar chest. He smiled down at me. Politeness dictated that I should also rise. As I did so, I grimaced in pain. I had been sitting on my heels for a long time and my calves were cramped. To my astonishment, Isamu gave my shoulder a brisk slap. The blow was hard enough to hurt.

"Do you trust me, little sister?" I nodded. I was close to him now, and there was no opium fragrance in his clothes. Nor could I smell sake on his breath. Excitement shivered in my belly as I began to hope that he was not playing games with me. "Good. Then we shall begin. Take that as your very first lesson. Pain is nothing. It is not worthy of the attention of an onna-bugeisha."

He fell silent. I waited hopefully, but eventually realized there was no more to come, so I bowed politely and walked out, my back very straight in an effort to hide my pleasure.

FIVE

You will not make me
A slave unless I will it.
Am I then a slave?

*I*samu took it for granted that I would not question his decision about my future. Would I have defied him if I'd had doubts? Probably not. I could not refuse my elder brother anything. But it didn't matter. I was going to be onna-bugeisha, and I wanted that with all my heart and mind.

But I had to summon all of my patience. Several weeks passed before Isamu spoke to me again about the onna-bugeisha way of life. I had begun to think that he had either been teasing me or had simply found something else to catch his attention and had forgotten our conversation. Isamu was like that. His mind was a butterfly, flitting from interest to interest and rarely returning to any one thing. It seemed to me that the only two things that were constant in his life were the bushido code—the way of the samurai—and his love of hunting, either with hawks or, for bigger prey, with Matsuo as his companion. I wasn't shocked that he had forgotten our conversation, but I was disappointed.

At least I was until the day he roused me out of bed early and waited as I found a warm robe and dressed. His glance flicked around my bare room as if he had never seen it before.

"Ready?" he demanded impatiently.

"What for?" I asked as I slid my feet into wooden geta.

"To begin your training, of course." He spoke in such a matter-of-fact tone that it might only have been yesterday that we had looked at his book of images of Tomoe Gozen.

"I thought you had forgotten all about that," I blurted.

Isamu stared at me as though I had insulted him. "Then you are far more stupid than I thought you were," he snapped. I flinched, but Isamu had not yet finished with me. "If I am to teach you anything, you must never question what I say or do. I always have a purpose, understand?"

"I suppose so." I was hurt and wanted to let him know.

"Little sister." His tone had softened slightly. I raised my eyes and looked at him woefully. "You are to learn the code of bushido, the traditional code of all samurai. It is said that the tiny tongue can fell a man two yards high. That may well be true, but I promise you that a sword would hurt you a great deal more. To become onna-bugeisha, you must have great strength of both mind and body. Insults must not trouble you at all. Nor must you ever give way to pain. Now, we will try again. Do you understand?"

I thought about his words carefully. "No, not at all. But I will if you teach me."

"That's a start." He pursed his lips and I thought he was angry with me. "You are very like Emiko, you know. Both of you say what is on your mind without thinking about it. Neither of you is at all submissive as a good woman should be." I saw his eyes were alight with amusement behind the pout and I smiled. Apart from anything else, I was delighted to think that I resembled my beautiful elder sister in at least one way. Isamu obviously realized my attention had wandered as he poked me in the shoulder. "You're not listening. Do you remember when I was much younger, Father sent me on the first and last day of each month to take food and sake to Aya-san?"

I was puzzled by the apparent change of subject, but I nodded. I remembered Aya very well. He was an old retainer of Father's who had been given a house to live in when he became too old to perform his duties as estate manager. I did not like Aya at all. I tried to avoid him when I was a small child and he was still about the house, but it rarely worked. Although he was old then, his hearing was obviously still good as he would often waylay me. He always pinched my cheeks and rubbed his face against me. Often, he would slide his arms around my waist and pick me up, pretending he was making me fly like a bird. Even then, I knew his intentions were improper. I could see it in the way his face flushed and his tongue snaked out to lick his lips. I was delighted when he was pensioned off.

"I remember him," I said shortly.

"You didn't like him," Isamu said calmly. I was surprised; I had never spoken of Aya's actions to anybody. I would have been far too embarrassed. "I imagine he touched you in the same way as he touched me. He was always patting my face and slobbering over me. When he moved out of our house and I took his food to him, he dared to go much further. Often, he would tell me to take my robe off so he could see how much I had grown. After a while, he got even bolder. He often pulled his own tree out of his robe and played with it in front of me."

"No!" I gasped in disbelief.

Isamu smiled and nodded calmly. "Oh, but he did. And it got even worse. Eventually, he told me to come close to him. Then he took my hand and put it on his tree. I was so horrified, I didn't know what to do. I just stood there like an idiot, wishing I could find some excuse to leave and never come back."

"Why didn't you?" I asked curiously. "If you told Father, he would have had Aya punished for doing that to you. He might even have taken his head off his shoulders himself."

"You're wrong." Isamu shook his head. "I think Father knew exactly what Aya was like. I'm sure he must have realized he had a taste for young children."

"Why did Father make you go to see him, then?" I asked. I was bewildered; if Father knew what Aya was doing to Isamu, I would have expected him to have put the old man to death instantly.

"To teach me that the code of bushido, the way of the samurai, is not just words. By doing as Father told me and visiting Aya even though I hated it, I was learning obedience. And not just obedience, but duty and self-sacrifice. Those principles are not the whole of bushido, but everything else in the code stems from them. Do you now understand why I couldn't tell the filthy old man to keep his hands to himself? Father had sent me. I had to obey."

I grimaced in sympathy.

"I had to. I told you, I was fairly sure Father knew what he would get up to. It was a test to see if I had the strength of will not to let it disturb me. He must have known because a short while later, Father asked me if I got on well with the old man. I lied, of course. I said it was a great honor to be of service to a man who had dedicated his own life to our family. Father smiled at me when I said that and told me that he thought it was time that one of the women servants took his food and drink to him."

I stared at my brother in awe. Had I been a man, could I have shown such fortitude, I wondered? I was always obedient, of course. But that was different. I was a girl. It was expected of me. A man had a choice in the matter. That was what made Isamu's submission so exceptional.

"You were very courageous," I murmured.

Isamu smiled. "Not at all. I have always known I would follow the code of bushido. If I did not, I was not worthy of following in Father's footsteps. There were other things almost as bad as Aya, but in different ways. Father would send me to walk to the nearest village and back in midwinter with no shoes. Even though my feet were bleeding and so frozen that I couldn't feel them when I got back, when he asked if I had enjoyed the exercise, I always said that I had. He taught me the art of swordsmanship himself, and he had no mercy. Even though we used blunt training swords, he still cut me frequently or walloped me with the flat of the blade. But I understood why he did it. The more hurts I received in the first few months, the quicker I learned how to avoid it. The day I parried Father's thrust and got my own blade to touch his ribs was the proudest of my life."

I thought that I would have been sorely tempted to slide the blade between Father's ribs, but I stayed silent.

"Will you be gentler with me when you teach me to use a sword?" I asked.

"And did I say I would teach you, Keiko?" He grunted.

"No. But Tomoe Gozen was a superb swordswoman, so surely you would expect me to be at least her equal?" I said slyly. I had spoken lightly and was surprised to see Isamu was thinking about my words.

"You're right, of course. Well, there's a chance, I suppose. She was your ancestor. We can try. Stay here for a moment. There's something I must attend to before we get down to business."

Hope and excitement fluttered in my belly like moths. Had I known what was in store for me, I wonder if I would have changed my mind then and there.

SIX

The bee that stings me
Also brings life to the fields.
Mine is such small pain

*M*y new life began with a pair of shoes. A pair of rather well-worn zori, to be exact.

Isamu had been gone for so long, I grew tired of waiting for him. Eventually, I decided that he must have been distracted by something more important, or perhaps Father had called for him. I got to my feet and glanced out my bedroom door and there they were, two black lacquered zori right in the middle of the corridor. They were not at all neat. In fact, they looked exactly as if somebody had just kicked them off and left them abandoned on the floor. They puzzled me. Father was a stickler for many things. Punctuality, politeness, respect, and—above all else—tidiness. If he happened to come this way and see the zori—and he could hardly fail to notice them—whichever servant had neglected to put them away would have been dismissed at once.

They were not my zori, nor Emiko's, they were far too big. I tried to remember if Isamu had been wearing zori when he visited me earlier. He had not. I recalled he had been casually dressed in an informal cotton yukata robe and equally informal wooden geta. They had made a clacking noise when he left me, so these zori were not his. I decided that I would pick them up and put them in my room. I would ask one of the servants to return them to their owner later, after a mild scolding about leaving them there in the first place.

I was bending to pick up the shoes when I heard a whisper of movement. Before I could straighten up, a cloth was over my eyes and I was lifted into the air and thrown over somebody's shoulder. I opened my mouth to scream, but thought won out over instinct. I wanted to kick and struggle, but I guessed at once that it would be useless. I was bent double, my head hanging down and my legs captured behind my knees in a powerful grip. I was also being moved. My thoughts swerved like starlings dancing at twilight; I had no time for fear. I forced my taut body to relax so that I hung like a sack of rice. It was the right thing to do. My captor's rhythm slowed marginally and I sensed hesitation in his step. It had to be a man. No woman would have been strong enough to pick me up as if I was nothing. I took advantage of his surprise. My arms were dangling free. Although I was blind, I could still feel. I stretched quickly and managed—by sheer luck—to find the baggy web of robe between his legs. A second later, I had grabbed the cloth and yanked it as tightly as I could up and toward me. The effect was immediate and gratifying. I heard a high-pitched groan and the man's grip slackened. I slid to the floor, pulling my blindfold away and running at the same moment.

"Keiko, stop!"

I almost lost my balance, I was so shocked. I turned and stared at Isamu. He was leaning against the wall, bent almost double.

"Brother! I am so sorry. I had no idea it was you. Did I hurt you?"

I stumbled to him, far more worried about the hurt I had inflicted on him than my own ordeal. I reached out to pat his chest and Isamu straightened immediately, folding me in his arms and squeezing me so tightly that I yelped.

"You did well, little sister. You almost had me fooled."

Almost? I was certain he had been totally confused by me playing dead. Luckily, he was gripping me so tightly I could not speak.

"But this is your first lesson. Even if you think your opponent is dead, never approach so close that you can be taken. Stick a sword in his heart first, then look." He released me and I slumped, panting for breath. "At least you have the virtue of patience. I thought you were going to stay in your room all day. Come on, we have work to do."

I walked briskly behind Isamu, my stride almost matching his. It must have irritated him, as he began to walk faster. I was having none of it. If it meant I ended up winded, I would not allow him to outpace me. We were both panting and trying to hide it when we arrived at the beaten earth arena where Isamu and Father practiced their swordsmanship and challenged each other at kenjutsu. I was immediately excited. This was more like it! I had never watched Isamu and Father fight together. It had never been explicitly forbidden, but there was no need for it to be. I would never have dared to intrude on them. But whenever I sensed he was in a good mood, I watched Isamu practice alone with his katana. His effortless grace always astounded me. It seemed more like a dance than something that could inflict pain.

Today, having already managed to outwit my elder brother, I felt cocky.

"Is there any point in teaching me to use a sword, brother?" I said slyly. "I have often heard you say that arquebuses are the weapon of the future. Should you not be showing me how to fire one of those instead?"

Isamu tensed. Still, I did not worry. They were only words. Father had two arquebuses in his study. He used one of them occasionally to scare birds into flight so he could fire at them with arrows. But I doubted he had ever fired one in anger.

"And what do you know about warfare, little sister?" His tone was soft. I began to understand that I had made a mistake.

"Nothing, except what you have told me."

"Then stay silent and do not show your ignorance. An arquebus takes no skill to use. Even a peasant can inflict death with it after a few moments' instruction. It has no place in the code of bushido. Here, take this."

He selected a practice katana from the rack at the side of the dojo area and threw it to me. I caught it, but clumsily. It was old and well used. The hilt felt greasy in my hand and the blade was speckled with rust. I was surprised by its weight. The weapon that looked so fluid and graceful in Isamu's skilled hand was nothing but a lump of old metal in my grip. Isamu had stripped his yukata off while I was getting the feel of the sword and now faced me wearing nothing but loose harama trousers. I realized that he had planned all this. I was hampered by my tight kimono while he had nothing to restrain him.

Isamu didn't bother to ask if I was ready. He chose his

own weapon and pivoted on the balls of his feet, immediately slapping me across the stomach with the flat of his sword. I grunted in pain and slashed my own sword in the air in front of me.

An hour later, I felt as if every bone in my body was broken. Isamu had been careful to draw no blood, but time after time after time, he had inflicted hurt on me with the flat of his blade. From knee to neck, I screamed with pain.

"Enough?" he asked finally, holding his own sword at arms' length in signal that the contest was over. I wanted nothing quite so much as to drop my own sword. My arms felt like lead. The sword was so heavy, I had been forced to change my hand grip frequently. It did no good at all. I was equally useless no matter where I put either hand. I hurt and was tired and thirsty and so deeply dispirited I could have howled out loud. I would never become onna-bugeisha. My dreams were dust even before I had finished my first lesson.

Isamu was grinning smugly.

I forgot my aches and pains and my tiredness. I raised my sword and screamed at the top of my voice and lunged for him. My sword point made contact with his shoulder and slashed a long cut into Isamu's flesh. It began to bleed freely. I was so astonished, I dropped my sword and backed away. I knew perfectly well that I should fall to my knees and kowtow to my elder brother in apology. If I did that, he might not beat me for my dreadful disrespect. But I did not. I had come so far, I would not back down now.

Instead, I stood my ground and raised my head and looked him straight in the eyes. Or at least it appeared that I did. I had learned many years ago that the easiest way to appear to meet the gaze of strangers and at the same time avoid seeing the distaste in their faces was to stare at the bridge of their nose, right between their eyebrows. I did that now.

"I apologize for cutting you, brother. Had you not been so merciful to me, I would never have been able to do it. It was sly and underhanded of me." It was nothing but the truth, of course. Why, then, did I feel a flush of triumph as I watched the blood oozing from his shoulder?

"That's true." Under the circumstances, Isamu sounded quite calm. "But it is also true that you have learned your lesson well. Didn't I tell you this morning never to approach a fallen enemy until you were sure he was dead? I should have listened to my own words! Come, little sister. We will go to the bath."

He threw his arm around my shoulder in a warrior's hard embrace and I almost screamed with pain. But I was so flattered by his gesture, I managed to turn my grimace into a smile.

SEVEN

Paper. Scissors. Rock.
Which is the greatest when each
May win in their turn?

That inauspicious beginning was how I came to be clinging to a mountainside in the depths of winter, wishing with all my heart that I had given in and embraced my bitter future as an old maid.

It was utter madness. We had been doomed to failure from the start. The thing was undoable, and I should have told him so. But when Isamu had suggested it, it had seemed so very right. A bright and shining thing. The thing that would make Father proud of me at last.

We had been sitting at the side of the dojo when Isamu told me he had arranged for a monk to come instruct me from the monastery that Father sponsored. The monk turned out to be wiry and small and so very old that only politeness kept me from laughing at the thought that he was going to teach me anything at all.

Isamu had introduced him with great courtesy. "Riku-san, I am honored that you have agreed to come to our home. Please, allow me to introduce my worthless sister to you. This is Keiko. She wants to learn the way of the onna-bugeisha."

The old man bowed gravely to me. He was dressed in the traditional robes of a Buddhist monk with a white under-robe and a saffron robe over that, but there was something very odd about him. As I bowed back, I watched him carefully and suddenly understood what was unusual about him. All the Buddhist monks I had ever met held an air of subservience. They carried begging bowls but never asked for food, merely inclining their heads in thanks if somebody put something in their bowl. This monk stood erect. His old eyes gleamed, and I guessed they would miss nothing of importance. I met his gaze and saw a spark of humor there that startled me.

Remembering my manners, I murmured, "I am honored to meet you, Riku-san." Still, I was bewildered. What could an old monk teach me about the way of the samurai? Humility, perhaps?

Without speaking, Riku moved to the middle of the dojo. Isamu gestured at me to go to him. I approached as close as politeness allowed and waited. A moment later, I was flat on my back on the hard beaten earth of the dojo.

"You have not been trained well, Keiko." The old monk's voice was as whispery as paper turning. "You do not know me. There is always danger in the unknown."

He leaned down and offered me his hand. I took it warily and he pulled me to my feet as if I were as light as a leaf. Before I could detach my hand from his grip, he had thrown me down again.

I could not understand it. I was at least a head taller than the old man, and certainly heavier than he was. Above all, he must have been far older than my father. How could this be? Still, now I was wary. I circled around him, never taking my eyes from his face. He cackled and spoke over his shoulder to Isamu.

"I was wrong, Isamu, she learns quickly. I remember when I first taught you the art of kobudo, it took you many lessons to learn to look for my next move in my eyes rather than my arms."

I preened under the old monk's praise and even managed to avoid his next throw. But that was the best I could do. Finally, he took pity on me and bowed.

"I look forward to meeting with you again, Keiko," he said politely. I noticed with astonishment that he wasn't even breathing heavily, whereas I was gasping for breath. With supreme effort, I managed to bow. He grinned, showing gaped yellow fangs, and walked away without another word.

"I do believe you've managed to impress Riku," Isamu said.

I glared at him, suspecting sarcasm. But he looked surprised, and I relaxed.

"Who on earth is he?"

"He taught both Father and me the art of kobudo. Today, you had a taste of jujutsu, bodily fighting without weapons. Riku is also a master of swordsmanship and fighting with a staff. Also, the use of the naginata, Tomoe Gozen's weapon of choice. They all form part of the samurai tradition. You will learn them all in time, from both Riku and me."

"But he's a monk!" I protested. "How did he come to be a master of kobudo?"

"Your education is sadly lacking, sister." Isamu smiled. "Centuries ago, there were warrior monks who rose to be as

Firefly 53

important as samurai. They served their lords in battle, just as we serve the shogun now. They fell out of favor long ago, but down the years there have always been monks who have passed the tradition on to their own sons. Riku is probably the very last of them. He never married, nor has he ever taken a concubine. When he dies, there will be no one to follow in his footsteps."

"I am sorry for that," I said sincerely. "Such a man should have a son to follow him." We sat in silence until I got my breath back.

"Are you ready for your next lesson, little sister?" Isamu asked eventually.

I shifted carefully. I was stiff and wanted nothing more to soak in the bath and then crawl into bed. "Most certainly, brother," I said cheerfully.

"You're sure?"

I nodded, offended. Here I was, doing my best to pretend I felt no pain and was ready for anything, and Isamu was doubting me.

"Certain," I said firmly.

"Excellent." Isamu's next words threw me completely. "What do you think would please Father more than anything?"

I thought carefully before I replied. Father was rich. I could think of nothing he could not buy if he wanted it, apart from status. Although our family was samurai, we still ranked below the daimyo, the nobles who were only surpassed in status by the shogun himself. And the emperor, of course, but the *shogun* spoke for him, and we all knew where the real power resided. Tradition dictated that a samurai could never rise to be a daimyo. But Father was a regional governor, and a proud man. Could it be possible that he aspired to surmount the social barriers and become a daimyo somehow? As soon as the thought came to me, I dismissed it. That could only happen if Isamu married into a daimyo family, and Harami's family was samurai. Then I recalled that Father often complained that he had not enough time on his own estate; his duties as governor often kept him away for long periods.

"More time?" I said doubtfully. I was surprised when Isamu nodded.

"You're not too far off. Think, what does Father like to do above all else when he is home and has time to himself?"

"Hunt," I said immediately. Father loved the thrill of the hunt. In the correct season, he hunted deer. But above all, he loved the sport of takagari. He had men who did nothing but breed his goshawks for him and look after their every need. They did not train the birds; Father insisted he do that himself. I often thought that he loved his goshawks almost as much as he loved Emiko. Certainly far more than he cared for me.

"You are very perceptive, Keiko—for a woman. Father has often spoken to me of his dream to have a golden eagle for hunting. If we could give him that, then we would give him his heart's desire. Nothing could raise us higher in his eyes, I promise you."

I was silent for a moment. Isamu stared at me, tapping an impatient rhythm with his fingers. I frowned.

"Are there any golden eagles near here? And if there are, how do we get one? They nest high, don't they? To avoid people?"

"Oh, I have that all figured out," Isamu said smugly. "The falconers say there is a nesting pair about half a day's ride from here, in the foothills of the mountains. I can climb well enough. I will take care of you on the mountain, have no fear. What do you say, sister? Will you come with me?"

Isamu laughed. I had no need to speak, my beaming face spoke for me. My trust in my elder brother had been so great I had not even considered being frightened.

Now that the moment for action was before me, I shivered with doubt. The mountain seemed impossibly high and impossibly smooth. Isamu shrugged off his robe and told me to do the same until we were both wearing only our small clothes.

"Robes would get in our way," he instructed. "They would catch on the rocks and could make the difference between success and failure. At the very least, they would slow us up."

With as much dignity as if he was fully clothed, he led the way to the base of the peak and began to climb briskly. He also took care of me, in a brusque, brotherly way. He pointed out fingerholds to me, waiting impatiently as I fumbled. But the higher we climbed, the dizzier my senses spun and the slower I climbed and the further away Isamu drew from me.

Now, he was so far above me, he was no more than a gray blur and I knew I was doomed to die this day. The moss encrusted on the rock might have taken the whole of my life to grow into a velvet-smooth platform, but it tore beneath my fingers as easily as paper. A particularly vicious blast of icy wind shot past me, and it was the final assault. My body was forced another fraction away from the viciously jagged rock beneath me and my world stood still for a final moment.

I was going to fall. It had taken me hours to climb this high up the mountain face, feeling carefully for each crevice to wedge my poor, bleeding fingers into. My toes were still poised on a narrow shelf of rock, but they could not hope to hold me in place. I was mute with terror.

"Do not fear death, little sister. It is not the samurai way." Isamu's voice was close again, and a moment later, his cold hand was clamped into the small of my back as he pushed me firmly back against the mountain face. My nose scraped the bare rock where I had dislodged the moss. My belly shrieked with pain as it rubbed against a jagged edge. I didn't care. I was alive! My time for death had not come yet!

Elation gave me the boost I needed and my fingers found a shallow depression in the rock. Relief made me brave. I turned my head and laughed at Isamu, jerking my chin upward.

"Race you!" I called. He laughed with me and began to move at once, his movements so smooth it was like watching a dancer. I would have none of that. I swung myself up alongside him and then, finding a fairly deep fault, I gripped tightly with my aching fingers and hauled myself past him. I was first to a shallow overhang, Isamu beside me a moment later. We sat together panting, both too exhausted to speak. Isamu put his hand on my shoulder and gripped it tightly. I recognized the gesture as one of mutual respect and my entire body filled with joy.

"Relish the moment, Keiko," he said finally. "It will never come again. This is your first mountain. The second and the third and all the rest will be easy after this."

I understood he was speaking symbolically. There was no need for me to climb any more mountains after this one. But there would be a need for me to conquer my fears in other ways. For me to prove myself time and time again. But each time, I would know that I had climbed my mountain. That I had nothing more to fear.

I smiled at him happily. "How much further?"

"Not far." Isamu leaned so far out that I was afraid he would lose his balance. "See up there?"

I followed his pointing hand with my gaze. A long way up, I could see what looked like a haphazard collection of twigs, perhaps thrown together by the spiteful wind that whistled around me constantly. Even though Isamu was clad only in a loincloth, he appeared not to be affected by the cold at all. I wondered in amazement how he did it. In my own loincloth and another cloth around my breasts, I was freezing.

"That's it?" I had expected something much grander.

"Yes. Can you hear anything?"

I listened carefully. There was nothing but the sound of the wind, biting at us with icy teeth. "Nothing." I was reluctant to admit it; if Isamu was asking me to listen, then surely there should be something for me to hear?

"Neither can I. That's excellent. I saw the mother bird fly off to hunt just before we started to climb. If she finds prey, she will be back soon. That will be dangerous for us. She'll do anything to protect her chicks."

Isamu sounded delighted. I had visions of him tearing the mother golden eagle apart with his bare hands and shuddered. I put my arms around myself, hoping he would think it was the cold that was making me shiver. The afternoon was becoming old, and I was growing nervous. I did not want darkness to catch us. I glanced upward, and Isamu nodded.

"Time to move. From now on, you must be very quiet. Do not speak. Try not to breathe heavily. Make sure wherever you grip, there are no stones that might fall. Understand?"

I nodded. Since Isamu had stopped me from falling, I had not been the least bit nervous. Now, I was apprehensive again. He swung away from me easily, and I followed in his tracks. Only this time, I did not look down.

The going was easier here, and we reached the nest quite quickly. Isamu put his finger to his lips as we reached the ledge with the untidy pile of twigs. He leaned forward and began to part the sharp branches carefully. I craned around him, anxious to see our prize at last.

We were both so engrossed, neither of us heard the mother eagle returning. She was on us like a vengeful demon, throwing her head back and shrieking her anger. I had a spare moment where I saw the dreadful beak gawping wide, and then she was attacking Isamu, lacerating him with her talons and pecking fiercely with her beak. I screamed in panic, and I was sure for a heartbeat that Isamu, too, was terrified. Then he was shouting instructions at me.

"Grab one of the chicks! It doesn't matter which. Shove it as far into your loincloth as you can, then go. I'll follow."

I reacted impulsively. Perhaps it was because I was a woman and understood in the depths of my own body what the mother eagle was feeling. Would I have let a strange monster steal one of my babies? I would not. Instinctively, I felt sorry for the poor bird and knew she was as frightened as I was. But I also knew with terrible certainty that if I left my brother to the mercy of this particular mother, I would never see him again. She would die before she let the male intruder who was trying to steal her babies leave this mountain alive. Already, she had cut him in many places. He was streaming with blood. In the space of a heartbeat, her talons ripped at his face and I saw blood stream down his cheek. If he could see at all, it would only be out of the uninjured eye. I was certain it would be impossible for him to climb down the mountain alone. She would harry him all the way down until he could no longer resist trying to beat her off and his other hand lost its grip, leaving his body free to follow the call of the earth as he plunged helplessly to his death.

My elder brother was helpless. He had no room to draw the short dagger thrust into his own loincloth. Even if he somehow managed to do it, the effort would unbalance him and he would fall to his death. As I watched, he put his hand out to fend the golden eagle off, and she immediately fastened her beak into the back of it, tearing the skin. As she panted, I saw her tongue was reddened with Isamu's blood.

The great onna-bugeisha Tomoe Gozen had listened to her man when he ordered her away from him in his last moments on earth. I would not. I knew what I had to do with an icy clarity that had nothing at all to do with thought. I was governed by sheer instinct. I would not let my brother die here in these desolate mountains. Nor did I want to hurt this beautiful bird that was doing no more than defending her own babies.

I pulled my own dagger out of my loincloth and set it down on the icy ground. It was useless in this situation and would only get in the way. I was so cold that the blade cut me quite deeply when I pulled the weapon out, but at that moment, I didn't notice. I straightened, glancing around to get the lay of the land—or rather the ledge—where we were trapped. I may be tall, but I am also very slim. I guessed I had just enough room and moved quickly before terror could tell me otherwise.

Isamu had his back to the rock face. He must have seen me moving in his peripheral vision. He screamed at me, "No! Keiko, no. Get down. Get away from here. Grab a chick while she's distracted by me. Save yourself. Go!"

I ignored him and moved quietly and slowly to the

eagle. There were eight paces between us; I counted each one in my mind. She turned her incredible head to face me as I got within touching distance and I saw the anguish in her yellow eyes. I apologized to her silently for the further terror I was about to put her through.

When I thought I was close enough, I paused. Not to get my balance, but to ensure that she was watching me. As soon as I was sure that she was facing me, as quickly as I could, I thrust my arms out, my fingers hooked into claws that mimicked her own talons. I threw my head back and screamed. The sound echoed around the mountains, coming back at us time and time again, finally diminishing into the sigh of the wind. The golden eagle flicked her head from side to side but continued to claw at Isamu. I screamed again, thrusting my head as close to her as I dared. I felt her pain in my own throat as something gave within me in response to the impossible noise I had made.

Finally, she gave way. With a great scream of her own, she backed away and took flight, circling above us. Isamu grabbed my arm and dragged me to the lip of the shelf. I tore myself away from him for as long as it took to push my hand in the nest and grope around until my fingers found feathers. I scooped the protesting chick out and thrust it blindly into the folds of my loincloth, fumbling it around to my side.

"Quickly," he mumbled. His voice sounded as if he was speaking through a mouthful of food. I glanced at him and shuddered as I saw that his lips were so torn, they looked like strips of raw meat. "I'll go first. Follow me."

There was no finesse in our descent. The battle with the eagle had taken longer than I had realized. Dusk was falling and the cold air was beginning to take on a crystalline quality that forecast frost. My elation was ebbing rapidly and I began to shake. My hands were so cold I couldn't feel the rock surface; twice I would have fallen if Isamu hadn't grabbed me. The second time, he hung onto me by my hair.

Darkness fell around us quickly. The true dark of a night without stars or moon. No matter how hard I peered around, I could see nothing at all, not even the rock face almost in front of my eyes. I had no idea we had reached the bottom until my searching foot hit the ground. Even then, I was so numb with cold and so exhausted that I kept searching for the drop with my toes, sure that we had simply come to another ledge.

"We've done it, Keiko. We're safe."

It took a moment or two for his words to penetrate. Suddenly, I was laughing out loud. I was alive! Not only that, but I had achieved the impossible. Isamu laughed with me until suddenly his amusement faded abruptly.

"The chick. Is it alive?"

EIGHT

The winter wind makes
Me shiver. In summer, I
Enjoy a cool breeze

I was horrified. I had been so intent on getting down the mountain I had not given a thought to our precious prize. I slid my hand into my loincloth and was immediately rewarded with a vicious peck. I held my bleeding finger up to show Isamu, forgetting he could not see in the intense darkness.

"Well? Is it alive?" he demanded.

"Alive and well, I think. It just bit me."

"Excellent. Come on, we need to get it home."

I grabbed the back of his robe and followed him blindly. Until the horses moved, I couldn't see them. We wasted no time, just threw our robes over our loincloths and knotted our obi clumsily with fingers that could barely feel. Isamu helped me mount. I was deeply touched until I realized his concern was for the chick's safety rather than mine.

As we set out, a thin, cold moon peered through the

clouds. I rarely rode, and the brisk pace he set worried me. How ironic would it be after all the danger we had already faced if we fell from our horses and perished on even ground?

But it didn't happen. Isamu was a superb horseman. He seemed to guide his mount by instinct, avoiding the worst of the ground expertly. I clung on for life itself and simply allowed my docile mare to follow his lead.

Occasionally, he called back to me, asking if the chick was all right. As it spent most of the journey either scratching or pecking me, I reassured him that it was. It was only when we got home that I began to worry.

Isamu stood in my room, beaming down at the eagle chick. I had gathered together a makeshift nest of old clothes, and it sat in the middle, making annoyed peeping noises. But I could see that the bird was not right. It was listing to one side and barely moving.

"What's the matter with it? Is it hurt?" Isamu demanded anxiously. "Don't say it's going to die on us!"

I was angry with myself. Just like Isamu, I had not given a thought to anything beyond catching our eagle. Now, I felt guilty. I had snatched this poor chick from its mother without giving a thought to its welfare. It peeped again, sadly this time, I thought, and I snatched it up and cuddled it against my breasts. It did not fight, but simply snuggled against me, stealing my warmth.

"It needs food. Go to the kitchen and get some meat for me. Thin strips. Rabbit would be best, but if there isn't any, chicken will do."

"No. Give me the bird. You go."

Of course, the kitchen was women's territory. No samurai would ever go there. I didn't have time to argue, the eagle needed food quickly. I handed it to him, and immediately it became agitated, struggling and peeping loudly. Isamu held it at arms-length, bewildered.

"Oh, give it to me." I took the bird from his willing hands and snuggled it against me. Immediately, it was quiet again. "Please, brother. There will be nobody in the kitchen at this time of night. Nobody will see you. Bring me a plate of meat for him as quickly as you can. His mother must have been on her way back to feed the brood when we took him. He's starving to death."

Isamu sucked a fresh cut the chick had inflicted on his hand. I heard him grumbling to himself all the way down the corridor.

He brought me rabbit. I dangled it in front of the chick. He ignored it. In the short time Isamu had been gone, the bird had grown weaker. He felt cold and no longer struggled even when I held him away from my body.

"Is it going to die?" Isamu whispered.

I shook my head. Had we risked our lives to lose our prize now? "Not if I can help it!" I said firmly.

I wiggled the meat. Smeared it against the chick's beak. Still, he turned his head away. Finally, in desperation, I put the raw flesh in my own mouth so that it dangled on each side of my lips. I leaned across to the chick and pushed my face close to it. It hesitated, so I did it again. My hair fell on each side of my face with the movement. Perhaps, to the bewildered chick, it resembled its mother's feathers as it suddenly pecked at the meat, tearing off a morsel and swallowing it hungrily. I kept the rabbit in my mouth until the chick's beak was almost tearing at my lips and watched with delight as the bird swallowed what was left. As soon as it was gone, he raised his head, his beak gawping wide, peeping for more. This time, he took the food from my fingers. He ate until his belly was bulging and then fell over, asleep before he hit his nest.

"How did you know to do that?" Isamu sounded awed. I stared at him in surprise. He was looking at me with a curious mixture of emotions evident in his face. I saw astonishment, and not a little respect. And, perhaps, fear? I burst out laughing.

"All I did was to try and mimic how his mother would have fed him," I explained.

Immediately, Isamu's face relaxed into amusement. "Oh, is that all? I see."

It was on the tip of my tongue to retort that he would never have thought of it, but I bit the words back. On the mountain, we had been almost equal. Here, he was my elder brother and was to be respected.

"It's a good thing Father enjoys meat," I said instead. Father would never simply leave a deer or a rabbit he had killed in the hunt. He insisted that everything that existed had a life, whether it was vegetable or flesh, and hence we could not discriminate between the two. Besides, once they were dead, the animals he hunted were food, and the gods would never approve of food going to waste. So, he insisted we eat flesh. It made sense to me. And anyway Father was Father and automatically correct.

"Will it be all right, do you think?" My brother, asking my opinion? Now that was surely a first!

"I believe so. I'll feed him again in the night if he wakes up. When do you want to give him to Father?"

Soon, I hoped. Today, if he was at home. I longed to see the delight on his face when we presented our gift. But I was disappointed.

"Not yet." Isamu stared at the chick and frowned. "It's too small at the moment. It barely has any feathers. It could be anything. You need to care for it until it begins to look like a golden eagle."

I took a deep breath and looked at my chick through his eyes. He was right. The bird was very young indeed. It was amazing it had survived the trauma of us stealing it and the subsequent journey. I smiled at it, proud that it had clung on to life. I would not let it die, of that I was certain.

"I'll need a box for it," I told him. "And a chicken would be good."

"You've already got enough rabbit to feed a family. What do you want chicken for?" Isamu looked scornful.

"Not for it to eat. A live chicken, a placid, fat hen. It can nest beneath her to keep warm."

Isamu scratched the back of his neck. He shrugged and yawned widely. "I'll leave all that to you. I'm going to have a bath to wash away all the blood and muck. Do you want to come with me?"

The invitation was flung at me casually, but I was only too aware of the honor he was doing me. I glanced at my chick, and it stirred in its sleep, peeping softly. What would it feel like if it awoke and found I was gone? I shook my head.

"Thank you, but I think I had better stay with the chick. I'll take my bath in the morning after I've got him settled under his hen."

"Suit yourself." Isamu turned on his heel and left without a backward glance at either me or my new pet.

I slept with the eagle snuggled at my side in his nest.

The next day, I sent an astonished servant to bring me a nesting box with the biggest, broodiest hen he could find. The man obviously thought I had run mad, but he did as he was told all the same. I put my chick in the nesting box and held my breath as I lowered the hen on top of it. The eagle was already nearly half the size of the hen, but neither seemed to worry greatly. There was a moment's silence as the hen settled, and then the chick's head popped out from beneath her and regarded me gravely. The hen clucked and fanned her wing over him, and I closed my eyes with relief.

Almost, I was persuaded that Isamu had forgotten our trophy. I saw nothing of him for days. When I went to look for him, his apartments were empty. I mentioned his absence casually to Emiko, and she shrugged.

"Oh, he's gone off to enjoy himself in Edo. Says he's tired of the sticks and wants to see some life in the Floating World. He'll be back as soon as he finds a courtesan skilled enough to wear him out."

I wasn't as disappointed as I had expected at the news. My eagle chick—who I had named Soru—sky—was thriving. He was now nearly as big as his foster mother, and his infant down had begun to give way to real feathers. He was very tame and liked nothing better than to perch on my shoulder and peck at my hair. I loved him, and I would be sorry to see him go to be trained to hunt at Father's command. He would, of course, have hunted for his own food in the wild. But to be told to kill for sport, that was different.

And yet, when Isamu finally lounged in my doorway and demanded to know how our bird was doing, I was delighted to show him off. I held out my arm to Soru, and he immediately hop-skipped up my arm to his favorite perch on my shoulder. Isamu's eyes were wide in astonishment.

"You've done well with him. He's beginning to look like an eagle."

"And how do you know he's male, brother?" I smiled. "I've looked and looked and I can't tell."

"Of course he is," Isamu said smugly. "How could he be anything else? Come with me. Father's home and I want to present his gift to him."

Even though Isamu kept a stone face, I could see he was simmering with excitement. Soru clung to my shoulder as we walked the corridors, uttering little cries of interest as he ducked his head up and down, watching everything.

I became increasingly nervous as we approached Father's apartments. I had never been inside before. Even Emiko was rarely summoned here. Other women entered more often. Father occasionally had a courtesan brought in for him to enjoy. When he entertained, geisha came here to sing and dance and entrance his guests with their wit. I had seen the geisha often, as I peered at them from my window, and sighed at their lovely grace. When I was a little girl, I had thought I would like to be a geisha. I had confided my desires to Emiko, and she had howled with laughter.

"You? You're far too tall and gawky. And sullen. Geisha are supposed to be beautiful and graceful and so witty they can make any man feel as if he is the equal of the *shogun* himself. And anyway, what nonsense! Whoever heard of a samurai lady wanting to be a riverbed beggar, which is all geisha are for all their airs and graces."

And that was that. Next time a quartet of geisha came to entertain Father's friends, I turned my face away from them and told myself they were only riverbed beggars.

"Give me the eagle." Lost in my thoughts, I had not realized we had reached the door to Father's apartment. Isamu tapped politely on the screen frame and waited. When Father did not answer, he called out. "Father, it is Isamu. I have something that will interest you greatly. A present."

Still, Father did not reply. Soru remained perched on my shoulder. Becoming impatient quickly, Isamu clicked his fingers, and I reached up and took hold of Soru carefully, handing him to Isamu as our father's voice finally instructed us—him—to enter.

"Gently, Soru," I whispered. "I am here. Do not worry."

Isamu glared at me scornfully. He was holding Soru all wrong. Instead of allowing him to perch on his wrist, which the eagle might have tolerated, he had wrapped his fingers around the bird's legs. Soru opened his beak in a wide gape and then sank it into Isamu's hand. I kept my head dutifully bowed as we walked forward, but even then, I could see the blood dripping from the deep gash in Isamu's hand.

"My son. It is good to see you." Isamu had stopped, so I drew to a halt behind him. Even though Father sounded in a good mood, I kept my eyes carefully downcast, fastened on the *tatami*, as I made a deep bow. I stayed crouched, waiting for Father to tell me to stand, but he did not. I felt both stupid and humble, bent as I was, and wondered suddenly if Father was leaving me like that on purpose to humiliate me. The idea gave me courage and I straightened, ignoring the consequences.

I glanced at Father from lowered eyes and understood at once that I had been wrong. Father had eyes for nothing at all except Isamu and Soru. I was invisible to him.

"Isamu, what do you have there?"

Poor Soru was struggling and fighting for his freedom. I could see he had dug his talons deeply into Isamu's palm, and he was biting constantly at the back of his hand with his sharp beak. I felt my pet's distress; I was not worried about Isamu, he could look after himself.

"A golden eagle chick, Father." Isamu held himself erect, refusing to acknowledge the pain Soru was inflicting on him. "He will make the finest hunting bird in Japan. He is my present to you."

Isamu bowed and made to hand Soru to Father. Seeing his chance, Soru stopped tearing at his hand and in the pause between Isamu loosening his grip and Father taking him, he was in the air instantly, flying around the room, trying to alight on the beams and—unable to get a purchase there—screeching in distress. I felt his pain. Forgetting I was in Father's presence, I stepped forward and held my arm out straight, making the *tkk-tkk-tkk* noises I used to alert Soru to my presence. My relief was beyond reckoning when the eagle chick immediately flew down and landed on my shoulder, rubbing his head affectionately against the side of my face.

I stayed very still, my attention focused on my eagle. Isamu spoke quickly.

"Keiko has had charge of the eagle since I fought his mother for him, high in the mountains."

I blinked. *Isamu* had fought the mother bird for her chick? Had we not been in Father's presence, I would have spoken. Even as it was, I almost did, but Isamu cut me off.

"She is very good with animals. They seem to like her. Even Matsuo chooses to spend time with her when he is not with me."

"Keiko, you may approach me." Father spoke my name as if he had to think about it first. I moved carefully, concentrating on achieving at least a semblance of grace. When I was close enough, Father put out his finger to Soru. My eagle bit him, hard. I was amazed when Father laughed.

"The bird is both courageous and willing to take instruction. He will make a wonderful hunter." Father offered his finger again, and to my surprise this time, Soru ignored it, walking a few steps away from him instead. "Only the *shogun* himself has a golden eagle for a hunting bird, and I have been told that his eagle isn't Japanese. He had one imported from the Kingdom of Chosun. This bird will be the talk of Edo province, if not the whole of Honshu Island. Isamu, my son, I thank you for this wonderful gift. Keiko." My world stopped as I waited for the words of praise I had longed to hear since the day I first understood my lowly position in our household. "Keiko, you should thank the gods for the affinity they have given you with animals."

That was it? After I had risked my life to get him his new pet? I should be grateful for the fact that animals recognized a kindred spirit in me? And Isamu? How dare he stand there beaming, relishing Father's praise? It was me! I was the one who defeated the mother eagle and stole her chick. Me! Not Isamu! Why did I stand with my eyes lowered modestly, smirking with pleasure at the fact that my father had deigned to notice me?

"Give me the bird. Come," he commanded. I held out my arm wordlessly, and Soru hopped down to my wrist and climbed on to his outstretched arm. I felt betrayed. As Father turned away, he threw a scrap of praise at me from over his shoulder. "You have done well, daughter." My heart raced; he had called me his daughter at last! "I am not ungrateful for your care of Isamu's trophy. Emiko will be married soon. Perhaps it is time we looked for a husband for you as well."

And that was it. Father sat down with Soru balanced on his wrist. We had obviously been dismissed. I wanted to cry, but did not. Nothing on earth or in the heavens would have made me show Isamu how devastated I was.

"I told you Father would be delighted." Isamu rubbed his hands together happily and grimaced as the blood from his wounds stained both palms.

"He was delighted with you, anyway," I said sourly.

Isamu stared at me with eyebrows arched in apparent

astonishment. "Surely you didn't expect me to tell him that you came with me to capture the bird? He wouldn't have believed me. And if he had, he would have rejected it immediately. He would probably have told me to take it straight back to the mother's nest."

"But she would kill it!" I exclaimed.

Isamu shrugged. "Probably. But Father could never have accepted it, knowing a mere girl had captured it. If he knew, it would have been less than nothing in his eyes. As it is, he will gain great face from possessing a native hunting eagle. And we will also bask in his pleasure, I promise you."

"He said he might find a husband for me," I said slowly.

"He did, and if he said that, he meant it. Don't worry." In his exuberance, Isamu buffeted my back with his knuckles. "It needn't get in the way of your training to become onna-bugeisha. I don't suppose Father will want to spend too much on your dowry, so the only husband he'll be able to find for you will probably be an elderly widower. As long as you please your husband on the futon and stay out of his way the rest of the time, he won't care what you do with yourself."

He almost skipped down the corridor in front of me. I walked slowly, dragging my feet.

An elderly widower? I was supposed to be pleased about that? I was barely sixteen and had never even traveled as far as Edo. And now I was going to be given to an old man as his bride?

And Isamu thought it needn't get in the way of my hopes of becoming truly onna-bugeisha? If the thought hadn't been so ironically amusing, I would have cried.

NINE

Your hand curls around
A seashell. Take care, it may
Not be quite empty

*E*ven the ordinarily self-centered Emiko noticed my gloomy mood.

"What are you so upset about?" she asked. Before I could speak, she answered her own question. "You should be content. Your belly is full. You have a roof over your head. You don't have to work hard for a living like peasants do. Isamu says Father has finally decided to find a husband for you. What else could you want? You should give thanks to the gods for your good fortune."

She picked up her hand mirror and lifted her chin, turning her head from side to side and smoothing her neck. "I've heard that the shogun's wives have mirrors made of glass that reflect their faces perfectly. I would like one of those. I will ask Soji to buy me one as a token of his fidelity." She tossed the copper mirror to one side as if it bored her.

"I'm sure he will if you ask him," I replied politely. I

meant it. Soji was the most generous of men. He never came to the house without a present for Emiko, and quite often a trinket for me. Oh, how I loved that man!

"You are very fortunate to have him for your betrothed, Emiko. Isamu thinks Father will find an old man to be my husband. Probably a widower who has outlived a couple of wives already."

My sister looked at me as if I had bitten her. Her beautifully arched eyebrows rose in surprise.

"So? A husband is a husband, isn't he? He'll be from a good family and rich. You can be sure Father will see to that. If you're lucky, he'll die in no time and then you'll be a free woman of good birth and good fortune. Some people have all the luck."

I stared at her in disbelief, but she was in full flow and didn't even notice.

"But what about me? You really think I'm fortunate to have Soji? Don't you mean it the other way around? It's Soji who is lucky to have me as his bride." She frowned and her forehead creased into lines. I thought it was fortunate that she no longer had the mirror in her hand or she would have been furious with her own image. "If our marriage hadn't been arranged when we were both children, I would have persuaded Father to find me a different husband."

"But Soji is such a nice man!" I protested. "He's generous and kind. And he obviously worships you. And he's handsome as well. And rich. What else could you want in a husband?"

"Almost everything," Emiko said simply.

I goggled at her in disbelief. She sighed deeply and drew her legs up to her breasts, putting her arms around her knees. She rested her head on them and suddenly, she was no longer my terrifying elder sister, but a mere young girl.

"I know he's rich. Even richer than Father. He'll buy me anything I want. But he can't buy my heart, Keiko! I want a *man,* that's what I want. Not a weakling like Soji. I need a husband who will tell me what to do. A husband who rules his own house. One who will make me work to keep him at my side and away from courtesans. Once we're married, I just know that Soji will do what I tell him."

She was silent for a moment and I saw she was blushing. I was so shocked I was speechless.

"I don't desire him. When he walks into the room, I shudder at the idea of sharing his futon for the rest of my life. And he's a young man. He could live longer than me out of spite! I know he's going to be a faithful husband. I don't think he's even got enough go in him to take a concubine, so I'll be stuck with him at my side night after night. And of course, I'll have to let him make love to me or there'll be no children." She brightened suddenly. "Perhaps that's the answer. If I refuse to let him have me, I can't have children and he'll put me aside."

I was beyond astonished. Emiko must genuinely be desperate to talk to me so frankly! I could hardly believe what she was saying. Soji was perfect. How could she not be happy to marry him? I took a deep breath and forced myself to concentrate.

"But if he did put you aside, what would happen to you?" I asked cautiously. "Father wouldn't have you back here. Soji would say that you were barren. He could never admit that you wouldn't let him have you; the loss of face would be too much for him. He'd be a laughing stock if it came out. You would have no money, nowhere to go. You would never get another husband, you know that."

"I don't care." Emiko's lower lip jutted petulantly. "I hate him. I can't stand it when he touches me. When he looks at me with those loving puppy dog eyes, I want to hit him just to see him look shocked."

"Perhaps if you told Father how you feel, he might talk to Soji? End the betrothal and find you a husband you liked better?" I blushed. I wasn't thinking of Emiko's welfare at all —just my own. Might it be possible that if she refused Soji, he would turn to me instead? The thought of it made my toes curl. My beloved Soji for a husband instead of an old man I didn't even know? Ah, but that would surely be heaven!

"I have." Emiko sounded suddenly weary. "I tried to explain to Father how I felt, and he just looked at me as if I was raving. He told me I would marry Soji or I would no longer be his daughter."

I had no doubt that Emiko was making a perfect tragedy out of nothing. "You know perfectly well that Father didn't really mean it. You're his favorite. You could always wind him in your obi." I spoke without bitterness; it was the simple truth. Father doted on his lovely daughter, and she was his pet. Anything she wanted, she got.

"You think so?" Emiko's voice was so shaky, I stared at her in surprise. Tears were running down her cheeks. They must have stung, as she screwed her eyes up and her lovely face was suddenly plain. Overcome with surprise—and not a little guilt at my own hopes—I rushed to her side and put my arms around her shoulders.

"Emiko! No! Don't cry, please. I'm sure Father will think about what you said and agree to find you another husband. Once he gets over his temper, everything will be fine."

Emiko buried her head in my shoulder and spoke

without looking at me. I had to listen carefully to make out her muffled words.

"You're wrong, Keiko. I thought the same thing. I left it for a while and then asked him again. I'd thought about it very carefully. I rehearsed what I was going to say over and over again. I needn't have bothered. I barely got past the first few words." She paused and I could wait no longer.

"Go on. What happened?"

"Father didn't even seem angry. That was almost the worst thing. He just put his hand up to stop me talking and turned a stone face to me. He had that damned eagle Isamu got for him on his shoulder and he didn't stop stroking it all the time he was talking to me.

"'The first time you spoke to me of this, I was gentle with you,' he said. 'I thought it was just some passing nonsense you had gotten into your head. I thought I had made it clear then that you would marry the husband that I had selected for you. I see now that I was far too lenient with you. You will not speak of this again, Emiko. You will marry Soji. You will marry him willingly, with a smile on your lips. You will be a good, dutiful wife to him for however long the gods spare you on this earth. You will accept his desires and bear him many male children. My grandsons.'"

Emiko raised her head from my shoulder and looked at me as if she could hardly believe her own words. She spoke softly, in barely more than a whisper.

"I was about to speak, to explain why I could not follow his will, but Father didn't wait for me. He stood and put his hands on my shoulders and shook me, Keiko. Father has never laid as much as a finger on me in my whole life. I was so surprised, I shrieked out loud. That seemed to make him even more furious and he hit me. He slapped me on the side of my face, hard. When I tried to get away from him, he hit me again, even harder. I had a black eye and a bruise all over the side of my face that didn't fade for many days. And all the time, that bird stayed on his shoulder as if it had been fastened there. It kept opening and closing its beak. I'm sure it was laughing at me."

I recalled that not long ago, around the time of the New Year celebrations, Emiko had taken to her room and refused to come out for the festivities. I thought it odd at the time, but had not dared ask her if anything was wrong. Now, I understood.

"Did he really hurt you?" I asked softly.

"Oh, yes. I didn't have the sense to give in, not even when he hit me again. I shouted at him, told him I wasn't going to marry Soji, no matter what he did to me."

I stared at Emiko in awe. Such courage! I would never have believed that she would dare.

"He must have believed me finally. He stopped hitting me and took his hands off my shoulders and just stood back, looking at me, he and the eagle both. Do you know, I think the way Father looked at me was even worse than when he hit me. He looked at me not so much as if he hated me, I could have understood that. Hate is a strong emotion, and I suppose I had invited it, the way I spoke to him. But it was more as if it wasn't me who was there anymore. As if I were just a maidservant who had annoyed him."

"If I had dared to defy him like that, he would have beaten me to a pulp," I said simply. Emiko shrugged, accepting the truth of my words. "What did he do?"

"He didn't do anything," she said. "He just stood there and looked at me. He looked at me as if I was a stranger to him. As if I was...worthless. That frightened me. I knew I had gone too far. I kneeled down and kowtowed to him. I grabbed his ankles and bent my head to kiss his feet. What else could I do?" She sounded indignant, as if I had dared to say she should have stood her ground and continued to defy Father.

"Nothing at all," I said quickly. "I think you were amazingly brave to go that far. What happened? Did he come around in the end and agree to dissolve your betrothal to Soji?" I couldn't believe it would be otherwise; Emiko had always gotten what she wanted. Or in this case, what she didn't want. Father had vented his anger on her. No doubt he would go away and decide she had been punished enough.

On this day of surprises, the greatest surprise was yet to come. I was wrong. Completely wrong.

"No," she said flatly. I stared at Emiko in disbelief. "He let me grovel until I had run out of breath to plead with him. Then he stood on my fingers until I screamed, it was so painful. He stepped back from me and just looked at me for the longest time. When he spoke, his voice sounded as if he was making polite conversation with somebody he didn't greatly care for."

"'From this day on, I have only one daughter,' he said. 'You are dead to me. Do not ask me for anything. Do not even speak to me. If you come into a room and I am already there, then you will leave. If you pass me in the corridor, turn your face to the wall until I have gone. You will marry Soji. I will speak to his father soon and see if it is possible to bring the wedding day forward. You will marry him, and you will be a dutiful wife to him.'"

"Did he really mean it?" I asked. I could barely control the tremor in my voice. Father had said he had only one daughter—me! The daughter who had not existed for him at all until recently. I felt a bitter sense of satisfaction—now

Emiko knew what I felt like to be an outcast. To dwell in the same house as the rest of the family, yet be apart from it. The family where I was now a member while she was not.

"I still couldn't believe that he meant what he said." Emiko's face was screwed up to keep the tears back. "I had to stay in my room until my face healed, so I had plenty of time to think it over. After a while, I decided I had gone about things in the wrong way. I should have been the dutiful daughter. Begged and pleaded with him rather than just telling him."

A chill ran down my spine. I stared at my sister in disbelief. Father had told her she was no longer his daughter. He would never have said that if he didn't mean it.

"You tried again?" I asked, the amazement clear in my voice. Emiko nodded miserably.

"I had to. The more I thought about marrying Soji, the more I thought I would rather be dead. I might have better fortune in the next life, who knows? And I had kept out of Father's way for a long time. I was sure he must have forgiven me. I waited until Isamu had gone hunting. I sent you on an errand for me? Remember?"

I nodded. Ironically enough, she had sent me to Soji's house to tell him she was not feeling well and wanted to be excused from some event she was to attend. Soji had smiled at me and asked me to sit down and take tea with him. I had been thrilled, even though he had spoken of nothing but Emiko. A curious train of thought occurred to me. Did she really hate Soji so very much? Or was she contrary because the decision that they were to marry had been made for her? Or—and I held my breath at the thought—did Emiko fancy herself in love with somebody else? Could even she be that silly?

"As soon as you were well away, I went to see Father,"

she continued. "I didn't bother speaking, I just prostrated myself in front of him and begged for forgiveness."

"What happened?" I asked more out of politeness than anything. Clearly Father had forgiven his dear daughter. She was still here, wasn't she? Still alive and well, without so much as a bruise left to cloud her lovely skin.

"He walked away from me without a word." Even now, it was clear Emiko could hardly believe it. Her voice rang with amazement. "When he got to the door, he stopped and called to me over his shoulder.

"'I do not know you. I have only one daughter.'" Emiko was sniffling with self-pity.

"Was that it?" I kept my voice even. After all, it was no more than I had suffered every day for as long as I could remember.

"No!" Emiko howled. I jumped at the fear in her voice. "It wasn't." Her voice sank to a whisper. "He said that if I didn't agree to marry Soji, he would not have me in his home for a day longer. And if I dared to say one more word to him before my wedding day, then he would take me to Edo himself and sell me to the meanest brothel he could find for whatever they were willing to pay him."

I almost laughed out loud at the drama of it. It was beginning to sound more and more like the plot of a kabuki play to me, not real life at all.

"Emiko! No! Did you believe him? You were always his favorite. He would never do that to you. He was just trying to punish you, that's all. If you're good and do as you're told for a while, he'll forget all about it. I think you must marry Soji, though," I added. "If you carry on refusing, he might go so far as to put you in a monastery for a year or so to punish you. And even then, I'm sure Soji would be waiting for you the moment you came out."

"They would shave my hair off!" Emiko wailed.

I shook my head in disbelief. Father had threatened to sell her to a brothel, yet she was more worried about losing her hair.

"Anyway, I don't care what Father says or does. I'm *not* going to marry Soji, and that's all there is to it. I'll kill myself first, and then he'll be sorry."

"Emiko, have you met somebody else? Is there another man?" I asked hesitantly. Emiko promptly held her lovely head up, every fraction the wronged heroine. I stared at her in disbelief. "Emiko, no. Who is it?"

She stared around as if making sure that Father had not entered the room without us noticing and then leaned forward and lowered her voice to a whisper.

"You remember late last year when Father had guests?" I remembered, but I did not know them. I had kept out of the way, as I always did when we had visitors. "One of Father's friends brought his son with him. Reo."

She was glowing. I felt terribly mean when I had to shrug and say I had not seen the young man.

"What was he like?"

"Oh, he was beautiful!" Emiko said at once. "Tall and manly. Not only that, but he was so very iki."

I tried to stop my lips from twitching. Iki meant somebody who was immensely fashionable and urbane. A truly iki man would be welcome in all the best teahouses in Edo. Courtesans would fight amongst themselves for the joy of being his lover. It was an indefinable quality, but obviously Emiko had recognized it in Reo.

"Do you know, he spent one whole evening composing haiku to my beauty? I was in heaven!"

"I'm sure you were," I said drily. "And does he feel the same way about you?"

"Of course he does." Emiko was indignant. "He came to my room before he left." I gasped and she glared at me. Her nostrils were pinched, her head held high.

"Emiko, that was a dreadful thing to do. He should have known it was forbidden as he was a guest in our house." I thought of the dreadful Choki and shivered. That, of course, had been different. I had been nothing but the youngest girl child with no status at all. Emiko was—or at least had been—the favored daughter. "Did you lay with him?" I asked bluntly.

"I did. Why shouldn't I?" she asked defiantly. "He told me how much he loved me, Keiko. He promised he would talk to his father and ask him to speak to our father about marrying me."

I stared at my lovely sister wonderingly. I had seen nothing of the world, yet even I knew that Emiko was deceiving herself.

"And have you heard from him since?"

Emiko pursed her lips. She stared at the ceiling, at the floor, anywhere but at me. "No," she whispered finally. "Not a word. I was so desperate, I sent him a message with one of the maids who was going into Edo on an errand." She caught sight of my appalled face and went on quickly. "Oh, I made sure it was all very carefully worded, just in case it fell into the wrong hands. When she came back, I asked her straight away if she had put the message into Reo's own hands. She insisted she had. She said that he had read it and told her there was no reply."

We sat in silence for a long time.

"What am I to do, Keiko?" Emiko asked finally. "I didn't want to marry Soji before I met Reo. Now, I would be miserable every day I had to spend in his company. But Reo doesn't love me either. The only honorable way out for me is to commit suicide, but I don't want to die, Keiko! What can I do?"

My lovely, confident elder sister was asking me for advice? I pulled my scattered wits together and tried to think.

"Wait a while. Forget about Reo." Emiko closed her eyes and made a small, distressed noise. "I don't care how iki he was, he was a horrible, sneaking creature to make you fall in love with him and then use you like that." Something occurred to me, and I added curiously, "Was it good when he made love to you?"

"Not really," Emiko said sadly. "I had no idea what to expect, and it was all over very quickly. I suppose I should have known then that he didn't really love me. If he had, he would have tried to make it nice for me, wouldn't he?"

I didn't bother answering that since I knew nothing about it. I focused on her other problem instead.

"Wait a while," I advised finally. "I'm sure Father's temper will mend itself eventually. Keep out of his way if you can, and when you do chance to be in his company, make sure you're the most dutiful of daughters." A sudden thought struck me and I looked at Emiko in horror. "You're not pregnant, are you?"

"Thank the gods, no." She shuddered. "I've had three courses since Reo was here."

"At least you can be grateful for that. You're going to have to marry Soji," I said bluntly. Emiko shook her head, but I was having none of it. "You must. He's so mad for you, he'll take you even though you're not a virgin. And he's probably the only samurai in Japan who would accept a bride who had been deflowered already. If you refuse him, you'll end up an old maid, just like I was going to."

I thought she was still going to argue. I watched her

thoughts flicker across her face and slumped with relief when she finally smiled.

"I'll make an offering at the temple to Amaterasu-O-Kami, the god of love. He'll help me, I know he will. I suppose it might not be too bad being married to Soji. As you say, he's so besotted with me, I'm sure he'd turn a blind eye if I found myself a lover, so I could take some consolation elsewhere."

She tossed her lovely head and smiled, her tears already forgotten.

For once, I did not envy her.

TEN

Where has yesterday
Gone, you ask me. Why worry?
It will never change

I put Emiko's woes out of my mind. I had other, more pressing things to consider.

Father would keep his word. If he was determined to find a husband for me, then before I exchanged one prison for another, I was going to see at least a little of the life that had been denied me so far.

I would go to Isamu and tell him what I wanted him to do. Not ask—tell. I was excited by my decisiveness. What, I mused, had caused it? Was it because my arrogant elder sister had asked for my advice? Or because I had literally climbed a mountain? Or perhaps it was the fact that Father had finally acknowledged my existence? I smiled to myself; I knew that it was none of these things.

A few months ago, none of them would have happened. They had only happened now because of the change in myself. I was the catalyst for all the changes, nobody and nothing else. I was learning to fight like a man and to think like one. For a moment, I felt almost sorry for my future bride-groom, who was no doubt expecting a dutiful, obedient wife.

I caught Isamu practicing with his sword at the dojo. Impatient as I was, I forced myself to wait until he had finished.

"Well, little sister?" he called cheerfully. "Come for another beating, have you?"

"No." I said not another word until Isamu turned to look at me, waiting for me to carry on. "I want to go to Edo, Isamu. To the Floating World."

I had expected him to laugh, and he did. But I was sure I caught a flash of puzzlement in his eyes.

"Do you, now? And I'm going to take you, am I?"

"You are," I said calmly.

"And how am I going to explain what you, a girl, are doing there? Dress you up as a yujo? Pass you off as some-body I picked up for a bit of fun?"

He seemed to find the idea hilarious, as he started chuckling to himself again. Yujo were women of pleasure. They could be anything from a highly-paid courtesan to a prostitute so pitiable she could not even find a place in a brothel and had rented herself out in a back alley to anybody who had a few coins in his purse. I stared at my brother steadily.

"How perceptive of you, Isamu!" I said sweetly. "Obvi-ously, such an iki man as you could never be expected to take his younger sister to the Floating World."

Even as I spoke, I realized with a mild shock that my brother was probably just as iki as Emiko's lover. He was handsome and very confident. He was rich enough to dress superbly, and he had that indefinable something that marked him as a man of the world.

"I don't think you quite know what you're asking." Isamu had stopped laughing and was frowning. "You'd never pass as a yujo, not even if we plastered you in makeup and loaded you with cheap jewelry. And if you're thinking of pretending to be a geisha, forget it. The geisha in the Floating World are the most beautiful and elegant anywhere in Japan. You're far too tall and skinny. Everybody would think you were a man trying to pass as a woman. Not that anybody in the Floating World would find that particularly odd."

His amusement bit hard. I had always envied the beautiful, flower-like geisha who had come to entertain Father. When I was younger, in the privacy of my own room, I had spent hours tiptoeing about, trying to mimic their pattering walk. When I was sure nobody could overhear me, I had even tried to speak as they did, my voice high-pitched and deferential. Until Emiko's stinging contempt had made me feel profoundly foolish. I smiled at Isamu sweetly, determined he would not see my hurt.

"I have no wish to pretend to be something I'm not, brother. You know the Floating World, so I'll leave the practicalities of it to you. I know you'll think of something," I said cheerfully.

Isamu's mouth was opening and closing like a fish, all the laughter gone from his face. I watched him patiently, waiting for him to find words.

"You're serious, aren't you?" he said finally. "You really thought I would agree to take you to the Floating World? Show you a few of the best teahouses. Drop into a performance at the kabuki. Even take you to a brothel or two. And what makes you think, little sister, that I'm going to risk making a laughingstock of myself by doing that? Have you run mad? Or is it perhaps the wrong time of the month for you and it's addled your wits?"

If it hadn't been for Isamu's final comment, I might not have been quite so angry. As it was, I was furious. And all the more determined.

"I'm not mad, brother. Nor am I on the rag." It was a disgustingly common thing to say, but it gave me great satisfaction to see Isamu flinch. "I want to go to Edo. To the Floating World. I can't go alone, so I've decided you're going to take me. You owe me the favor. If it hadn't been for me, you would never have gotten Father's eagle for him."

Isamu's face darkened. His mouth pinched into a thin line. He glared at me. I stared back calmly, elated at the knowledge that he no longer held any fear for me.

"You think so?" he snarled. I smiled sweetly. "I could have taken the bird without your help. All you did was care for it. I owe you nothing. And I will not take you to the Floating World."

"We took Soru together," I said calmly. "And you will take me to the Floating World."

Isamu stared at me incredulously. His expression suddenly became sly. "I suppose you'll keep on making my life a misery with your nagging until I agree, won't you?" he said.

"I certainly will."

"Very well. I'll take you to the Floating World with me. On one condition."

I was delighted; I had never expected it to be this easy. I was about to agree immediately, and then caution laid hold on my tongue. Isamu was grinning widely, so I knew he was hiding something.

"And what is your condition, brother?"

"I'll take you if you fight me and win. Here and now."

I thought about it, but not for long. "With swords or jujutsu?" I asked casually. Isamu blinked, and I knew I had surprised him. Good, the first point to me!

"Better make it jujutsu," he said. "I could beat you with a sword using only one hand. I don't want you whining that it wasn't a fair fight."

"Fine." I turned away from him and unfastened my obi. The knot was stiff, and I fumbled at it angrily, hoping that Isamu didn't take my slowness for fear. I discarded my kimono quickly, standing in only my undergarments—a han-juban undershirt and sasoyoke loose underskirt. They were fluid enough to move with me. I kicked off my zori so I wouldn't topple on them.

It was a chilly day. Gooseflesh pimpled my exposed skin, but I didn't worry about it. I would be warm soon enough.

Isamu glanced at me curiously and bowed his head without speaking. We faced each other across the dojo and —even though we were brother and sister—bowed politely to each other. Had this contest been between sumo wrestlers, the man-mountains who entertained crowds with their skills throughout Japan, there would have been a strict protocol. No action would have taken place until the referee gave the word. But we had no referee, only ourselves, and once the traditional bow had been given, there were no more rules.

We circled each other like a pair of crabs preparing to fight over a choice morsel. I watched Isamu's body, not his eyes. He would keep a stone face and give nothing away. Isamu had not thought it necessary to discard any clothing. I saw his kimono tighten over his chest and a scant moment later he rushed at me. Isamu was quick, but I was quicker.

Before he could try again, I grabbed his kimono front and attempted to throw him.

Jujutsu is all about using the strength of one's opponent and turning it against them. But Isamu was far more skilled and practiced at the art than I was, and of course he knew that. I had no advantages except speed and surprise. I grunted in annoyance as he slipped from my grip at once.

"Riku has taught you well," Isamu said. I didn't answer. I needed all my breath for fighting. "But is it enough?"

He was smiling, tilting his head to one side, inviting me to look at his face. I did not; I concentrated on his mid-section. Riku had told me to do that, over and over again.

"You are a weak woman. Your opponent is always going to be bigger and heavier and stronger than you. If you are fighting a samurai, he will also be far more experienced than you." He threw me almost casually as he spoke. He finished his lecture standing over me. "You must use the talents you have that your opponent does not. You are very perceptive, so depend on that. Watch his body. He can control his face, but not his muscles. He will tense before he moves. Wait for that before you decide to attack or defend. If it is a matter of defeat or victory, do not hesitate to fight outside the rules. If you are down and have nothing left, knee him in the kintama."

In spite of my aching back, I laughed out loud. "That is hardly honorable, Riku-san!" I protested.

"No, but it's better than being taken prisoner or—in your case—being violated by some man who thinks he has won the right."

I remembered Riku's wise words now. Sadly, I decided I could not disable Isamu by kicking his kintama. If I did, once he got his breath back, he would no doubt accuse me of cheating and say our bet was void. I would fight fair, and if I lost, I would have only myself to blame.

Isamu lunged at me again. I feinted to the right, but he was not deceived. He followed me immediately and in a moment, his arms were clamped around my waist. He lifted me off the ground, and I thought the fight was over.

I was wrong. Instead of throwing me to the ground and keeping me there, Isamu hesitated. His grip faltered. I took my chance at once, wriggling away. My evasive maneuver was too good. I found myself on the hard ground with the wind knocked out of me.

Isamu circled me warily. I didn't stop to think, I just acted on instinct and took my chance. I snaked across the ground, stuck my foot out, and tripped him neatly.

He hit the floor so hard I was sure the air must have been knocked out of his lungs. To make sure, I sat on his back, my legs straddled on either side of his ribs.

"My game, brother!" I crowed.

He was silent and still and for a brief moment, I wondered if I had killed him. Then I realized I could feel his lungs heaving between my legs and I relaxed.

"You cheated," he panted.

"I did not," I said firmly. I slid away from him and stood up, still concerned that I had really hurt him. He rolled on his back immediately.

"I won," I repeated firmly. I was about to say, *Now will you take me to Edo with you?* But I changed my mind. "You will take me to Edo. To the Floating World." It was a statement, not a question.

"I suppose so," Isamu said sulkily. I saw a crafty gleam come into his eye and waited suspiciously. "I will, but only if you cut your hair first."

"No!" I spoke automatically. Emiko had told me often

enough that I would never be pretty, but I was very proud of my hair. It was as thick and glossy as a freshly-washed cherry. Unlike Emiko's hair, which was inclined to be straggly, my hair fell to well below my knees in a straight curtain, as thick at the bottom as it was at my shoulders. I knew that if I wanted it to be longer, I could grow it so that it trailed on the floor behind me, just like the lady in Emiko's print. And now Isamu was telling me to cut it!

"Why? Why should I cut it?"

"So you can come to the Floating World with me," Isamu said. His gaze ran down the front of my body assessingly. He grinned and raised his eyes to my face. "It needs to be no longer than this." He reached out to me—the movement awkward as I was now standing so far away from him —and cut his hand through the air just below my shoulder blades.

"Why?" I asked again, suspicious that this was some trick to make me change my mind.

Isamu laughed. He bent and scooped up my kimono and threw it to me casually. "Because I cannot take a lady into the Floating World with me. A woman—unless she is a geisha or a yujo—has no place there. I will take you if you're sure that's what you want, but I will not take my little sister. I will take a boy. Cut your hair, Keiko, and we will see."

ELEVEN

I wonder if my
Reflection looks back at me
And sees what I see

I clenched my teeth so hard to stop my lips from trembling that they ached. I wanted to cry. It was only the knowledge that a true onna-bugeisha would never shed a tear over something as trivial as having her hair shorn that stopped me from bawling. That and the knowledge that Isamu would be overjoyed if he thought he had upset me.

"Can't I just wear a wig?" I asked hopefully.

"No," Isamu said. "It wouldn't work. You have far too much hair to tuck up. Anyone would be able to tell you were wearing a wig at once. If you want to go to the Floating World, then you must become a boy and your hair has to go. It needs to be the same length as mine so I can show you how to put it up in a topknot."

He was enjoying himself. Isamu never did anything half-heartedly, and now that he had committed himself to my demand, he was going to do things properly or not at all. I looked at his hair and ruefully agreed with him. His hair was smoothed back loosely from his face and tied on the top of his head in a loop. All samurai wore their hair like that, but Isamu was fortunate to have very thick, glossy hair, much the same as mine. On him, the style looked fashionable rather than martial.

"There, little sister. Done," he announced. He waved the scissors in front of my face to emphasize his words.

I turned my head, trying to see over my shoulder, turned my head to see if I felt any different. Instead of flowing around me as it always had when it was loose, my hair flopped over my face. I pushed it back and shook myself. I had expected to feel bereft, as though some vital part of my body had been lost. Instead, I felt liberated, as though a weight had been taken from my shoulders.

I stood and turned my head from side to side. Ignoring Isamu, I picked up a hand-mirror and moved it up and down until I had seen myself as far as my waist. Isamu was grinning widely at me. I returned his smile.

"I don't look like me," I said slowly. It wasn't quite what I meant, but I couldn't put my real feelings into words.

"No, you don't," Isamu agreed. "It's not just your hair that's different. It's the way you're standing. The way you're holding yourself. You're nearly ready to go to the Floating World, Keiko. There's just one more thing."

I stared at him suspiciously.

"I need to pluck your eyebrows. They're the wrong shape."

After losing my hair, this was nothing. I sat patiently and let him nip at my eyebrows for what seemed forever. When Isamu handed me the mirror finally, my mouth fell open in shock.

The face that stared back at me was no longer mine. I raised my brow, and the effect was immediately even stranger. My face looked foreign, even to my own eyes. I wiggled my brow again and bit my lip. The face that stared back at me was neither—or did I mean either?—male or female. I could have been a young woman or a boy just growing into manhood.

"See?" Isamu said triumphantly. "Before, your eyebrows were shaped so that your face looked womanly. Now, if you could stop smiling and frown a bit, you would look more like a young man." I turned my mouth down and saw that he was right.

While I peered at my reflection, Isamu gathered up my shorn hair. He had tied it with a ribbon and bowed as he handed it to me.

"You will probably want this made into a wig. That way when you return, you can wear it and nobody need know that you have cut your hair so short."

I took the hank of hair from him and stroked it almost nervously. Already, it felt distant from me, as if it had never been part of my body. I put it down quickly. I would have it made into a wig. Oddly, I thought I would be happy to wear it that way. A wig was impersonal, something that could be put on or taken off at will like a kimono, not something that had ever been a part of me.

Matsuo chose that moment to wander in. He went straight to his master and waited patiently to be petted. As soon as Isamu stroked him, he came and sat in front of me. I felt as if he was inspecting me, and I was pleased when he made a small huffing noise and thrust his wet nose into my hand.

"See? Even Matsuo approves." Isamu grinned. He clicked

his fingers at the dog. I was amazed when Matsuo hesitated and glanced at me before obeying his master's command. "Well, sister? Are you ready for a taste of life in the city? If you are, we shall go to Edo tomorrow. Father will be away for a few days. I doubt Emiko will notice we are gone. And if she does, I'll tell her I took you to visit a prospective suitor."

I looked at him reproachfully, thinking his words were a joke in bad taste. I was horrified when he smiled and added, "It's not far from the truth. Father told me that he had several husbands in mind for you. One of them lives in the suburbs of Edo, not too far from the shogun's palace. We might even see him in the Floating World."

"Do be sure to introduce me to him if we do," I said drily. "Dressed as a boy and with my hair in a topknot, with a little good fortune he'll be terrified of me."

"Oh, I don't know. Speaking for myself, I rather like the idea of you looking like a boy. In fact, I think I shall introduce you to everybody in the Floating World as my kagema."

I stared at him stonily. A kagema was a male prostitute, not a role I relished at all. Seeing my expression, Isamu went on.

"You don't care for that idea? Very well, what about a wakashudo relationship? Now that is perfectly honorable. Everybody knows about the samurai tradition of an older samurai taking a much younger male lover. Most samurai do it."

"Father never did," I pointed out.

"Yes, he did." I gawped at my brother in sheer disbelief. "It was before you were born, though. I was too young to realize it at the time, but after I had my genpuku coming-of-age ceremony when I was thirteen, Father took me to one side and told me all about it. You know his lover, he's been to the house many times. Eiji-san."

My mouth hung open in disbelief. I had seen Eiji often when I was a child. He had been kind to me in a pleasant, distant fashion. As the years passed, he came to visit us less and less often and had finally stopped altogether some time back. I had thought nothing of it until now.

"Really? Why happened between them? I haven't seen Eiji in years."

"He got older," Isamu said simply. "Wakashudo only works where the much older man takes pleasure in teaching the younger one. Eiji reached an age where he was no longer a boy. Perhaps he began to look for a boy of his own, I don't know. In any event, Father never bothered to replace him."

"And you, older brother? Do you follow the tradition of wakashudo?"

"If I find a younger lover who appealed to me enough, I might." Isamu shrugged. "But then again, I like women."

I pulled on the divided-leg hakama and tied a robe on top of them, finishing with a plain obi. I took a couple of steps and found I was walking with a swagger. Isamu regarded me with the tip of his tongue poked between his lips.

"I'm beginning to think that taking you to the Floating World might be quite fun," he said.

TWELVE

Clothes are the shape of
My body, but only when
I am wearing them

"Jun, stop dawdling. Come along."

I turned in my saddle to see who Isamu was talking to. I had been lost in my thoughts as we trotted along the well-worn track leading to Yoshiwara, Edo's great pleasure center better known as the Floating World.

Such was the glamor of the tales of the great city of Edo, I had always imagined it must be many days' journey away from our home. I was shocked to discover it was only slightly more than half a day's brisk ride. Still, I was delighted to find it so close. Unused to traveling on horseback, I was already saddle-sore and my back ached. My mare was the same mount Isamu had given me for our adventure to secure Father's eagle. She was a sweet-natured, docile creature who responded to my tentative kicks and tugs immediately and gently.

"Jun, for the gods' sakes, pay attention when I speak to you. And try not to gawp so. You look the perfect country bumpkin with your mouth hanging open like that. It really will not do my reputation any good at all if people in the Floating World think I've taken a rustic for my lover."

I still didn't understand. "Who's Jun?" I asked.

"You are, you idiot." Isamu tutted at my stupidity. "You are dressed as a young samurai. While we are in the Floating World, you are a boy, not my stupid little sister. I can hardly call you Keiko, can I? Jun is an excellent name for you in your new incarnation. Remember it and make sure you respond promptly when I speak to you."

"Yes, Isamu," I said humbly. Even though he was pretending to be annoyed, I caught the sound of humor in his voice and guessed the source of it at once. Jun is a name that can be given to either a boy or girl and is often given to dogs as it means obedient. No doubt Isamu's idea of a good joke.

"And another thing." Isamu reined his horse to a slow walk. The track was wide enough to ride side by side and I drew my mare forward. "This is important, so listen carefully. You look like a boy. But you do not sound like one. Once we are through the gates of the Floating World, if there is anybody close by, you must be silent. No matter what you see or hear, you will not say a word if there is a chance of you being overheard, understand?"

"Won't people think that's a bit odd? Are you going to tell them I'm mute?"

"By all the gods, no." Isamu looked greatly offended. "Do you really think I would take a lover I couldn't hold a conversation with? Certainly not. Think, sister. But if anybody hears you speaking, the game will be up immediately. The easiest thing is for me to tell everybody that you have taken a temporary vow of silence to appease the gods. Nobody will think anything of it."

"What have I done that's so bad that I need to appease the gods?" I asked doubtfully. "I haven't had a chance to do anything at all yet, still less anything bad enough to make the gods angry with me."

"Shut up and stop arguing. I've told you time and time again, the Floating World is different from anything you've ever experienced. The only important things are that you have plenty of money, which you're willing to spend, and are sophisticated enough to be welcomed in the best places. It will probably make you more intriguing that you've done something so dreadful at an early age that you must make such a vow."

"Yes, Isamu," I said meekly. Still, I couldn't resist staring around me.

"Ignore him," Isamu said without looking at me, and I wondered if he had suddenly grown eyes in the back of his head. How else could he know what I was looking at? A man—a wealthy merchant, judging by his dress—his expression tired and deeply sad, was standing in the shade of a large old willow tree planted just outside the gates to the Floating World. His hand rested on its trunk and his face was turned back to the gate. As I dragged my reluctant gaze from him, I saw him squaring his shoulders and moving away from the gate, pausing to give a final, lingering glance into the maze of streets behind him.

"Almost everybody does that when they leave the Floating World behind them," Isamu said casually. The inference was obvious; everybody else might do so, but Isamu would not. "That willow is famous. On the way in, it gives shade so the expectant visitor can stop and compose himself for a moment, anticipating the pleasures to come.

On the way out, it is the last thing the lovelorn pleasure-seeker sees. The tree has stood there since the Floating World came to life many centuries ago. I remember grandfather telling me that when he first visited the Floating World as a very young man, he too stood in its shadow as he left."

"Will this tree still be here when your sons visit, I wonder?" The sense of tradition made me sentimental, and I was surprised when Isamu glanced at me angrily.

"Perhaps. If Himari is sensible enough to bear me sons." Then he added with sudden vehemence, "Which she *will*. I'm the last of our family line. I always thought that Father would adopt another son to ensure that the line would continue. I even suggested it to him, but he says he's too old to go through all the fuss. So it's down to me, I suppose." He frowned, and I decided not to pursue the subject.

We dismounted before we approached the gates. Isamu patted his white stallion's muzzle and handed the reins casually to a boy who seemed to have appeared out of nowhere.

"Guard him well," Isamu warned, "and my friend's horse also." The boy bowed to us both and tugged our mounts away carefully. "From here, we walk, Jun. There is no room for horses in the Floating World. Are you tired? We can hire a palanquin if you want, but the best way to enjoy the place is on foot, that way you miss nothing."

I was about to speak but remembered I was to be silent and nodded instead. Isamu looked at me approvingly. I noticed that the guard outside the great gate stood to attention and bowed deeply when Isamu threw him a small coin. He also ignored Isamu's weapons. We walked through as if we—or at least Isamu—owned the place.

My brother was suddenly almost a stranger to me. I

observed him carefully, trying to copy his lazy slouch, the bored expression on his face. This, I thought, was truly iki! Alas, I could not do it. As soon as I relaxed my body, every ache and pain inflicted by the journey multiplied ten-fold. Everything was so interesting, I had to constantly tell myself not to stare around in rustic fascination.

The noise threatened to overwhelm me as soon as we crossed the bridge across the deep, waterless moat and stepped through the gate into the Floating World. Living in the country as we did, my hearing was excellent. I could pick out the song of different species of birds, hear the change in the wind that heralded much-needed rain. And of course, as a girl, I had always spoken very quietly, as had Emiko. In the perfect quiet of our home, neither Father nor Isamu had ever needed to raise their voice.

The row here almost hurt my ears. I turned my head from side to side. The street that ran straight in front of us was crowded and fluid with movement. Trees were planted on each side. Although they were not in blossom this time of year, I recognized them as sakura trees. Immediately, I decided I would try and persuade Isamu to bring me back in the spring so I could see the trees in bloom. Distracted, I had allowed Isamu to get ahead of me and I almost ran after him, certain that if I lost sight of him, this strange, busy world would swallow me up.

"This way." He flung the words carelessly over his shoulder, without looking to see if I was there or not. "I sent word to my favorite teahouse to say I would be coming today. They will be expecting us."

The crowd parted grudgingly before us. I watched Isamu anxiously. It seemed to me that people were not at all respectful of his status as a samurai. I expected him to draw his sword and cut a swathe through them to teach them a lesson. He did not, and I understood at once that the normal rules of life were different here.

Isamu was taller than most of the throng, and I was grateful as it made him easier to follow. At first, I almost had to run to keep up with him as I was automatically walking as if I was still hobbled by a kimono. Concentrating hard, I forced my legs to imitate his long, swaggering strides. After a bit of practice, I found it not just easy, but delightfully liberating. He turned abruptly onto a side street that was almost as wide as the thoroughfare we had left and stopped in front of a single-story building, discreetly shielded by opaque shoji. It had a small garden in front of it, which I supposed, given the apparent lack of space in the Floating World, must signify great splendor. There was no sign at the door to say what it was nor a bell to ring.

Isamu pushed open the screen door and stepped inside, kicking off his shoes. I followed. As we entered, a young woman was standing in front of us, bowing deeply.

"It is an honor and a pleasure to welcome you to the Green Teahouse once again, Isamu-san."

Her voice was high-pitched and breathy. She smiled as she spoke, her eyes never leaving Isamu for a moment. I inspected her critically, hiding my disappointment. She was far less magnificent than the geisha who had visited Father. She was pretty enough, and her kimono obviously expensive, but she lacked the fluid elegance I had expected. Nor was she as confident of her own beauty as they had been.

"Thank you." Isamu bowed, but not very low. I copied him at once. "I believe I saw you last time I was here. Your name is Megu, isn't it?"

I thought the girl was going to go into a fit, she was so delighted that my brother had remembered her name. She bowed repeatedly, giggling and covering her face with her hand.

"So kind, honorable samurai, to remember a humble maiko's name! So very kind! Please, will you and your companion come through? Hana-san is expecting you."

She stood aside and we passed her by without a second glance. I was quite pleased, both because she didn't look at me oddly and because I understood now that she was not a geisha. Not yet, anyway. Maiko were geisha in training. She was still learning her trade, and I thought—rather unkindly —that she had a long way to go before she could hope to entrance a man with her wit and beauty.

Then we were in the main room of the teahouse and I sighed with pleasure. This was more like it! The room was large and airy. The fragrance of incense mingled delightfully with blossoms. I stared around as casually as I could manage. The walls were hung with brightly colored prints. A few vases, each with a single ikebana arrangement of flowers, were carefully placed on low pillars. As a girl from a good family, I had been instructed in the art of ikebana, and I saw at once that these sparse displays had been beautifully arranged by expert hands. The room was almost severe in its disciplined elegance. Everything was of the very best, but nothing was overstated.

"Isamu-san! I welcome you to my humble teahouse. It is so very good to see you again. And your companion, of course." The woman who spoke had entered so silently I had not noticed her. Her voice, although not loud, made me jump. "Please, will you both sit in front of the tokonoma?"

She led the way to a recessed area, simply decorated with a single scroll on the wall. I watched Isamu fold himself elegantly to the tatami matting and did my best to imitate his graceful movement.

"Hana, it is excellent to see you again. May I present my friend, Jun?"

I bowed my head politely. Was it my imagination or had Isamu put a certain emphasis on the word "friend?" I guessed I was right when I saw Hana's lips quirk into the smallest of smiles.

"I'm afraid Jun must remain quiet. He has taken a vow of silence. Only temporarily, fortunately."

"Indeed? A silent samurai? Now that is a novelty! One hopes it does not last for so long that you are driven to talking to yourself, Isamu-san."

I was amazed when Isamu burst into loud laughter. Had either Emiko or I been so impudent, he would have beaten us for it.

"I doubt I shall want for conversation in your teahouse, Hana." Both Isamu and Hana smiled knowingly. I felt very gauche and lowered my head humbly.

The courtesies over, Hana clapped her hands briskly. A shoji slid back at once and three geisha entered with mincing steps. Immediately behind them, an older, very plain maid carried a tray laden with tea making equipment. Within seconds, the geisha were seated around us, cooing their delight at seeing Isamu once more. I was introduced and blushed ripely beneath their approving gaze. Isamu frowned at me, and I understood his displeasure. A real samurai would not be so easily flustered by the presence of mere women, even geisha.

Once the geisha had fawned over Isamu, two of them turned their attention to me. One passed me a brimming cup of green tea. Another came and sat beside me, chatting happily into my silence. Only the eldest of the geisha stayed beside Isamu, her head on one side and her expression rapturous as she listened to every word he said as though pearls of wisdom passed through his lips with each syllable. He seemed smugly pleased, but despite the attentions of my own geisha, I watched the interaction between them and wondered.

Isamu's companion leaned toward him, her gaze never leaving his face. Every line of her slender body expressed pleasure at being at his side. And yet, I was doubtful. Perhaps it was feminine instinct, but I guessed that she was bored. She glanced across at me at that moment and caught my gaze. She lifted her eyebrows in surprise and a frown pursed her reddened lips—there and gone in a flash. But I knew she had sensed that I had seen through her act and was flustered.

Once the tea was finished, Hana smiled at Isamu. "Would you like the girls to play and dance for you? I remember that you greatly enjoyed Miho's skill with the samisen the last time you honored us with your presence."

Isamu stretched. "You are kind, Hana. I thank you, but no. This is Jun's first visit to the Floating World. Naturally, I had to introduce him to the best and the most famous teahouse in Edo first, but there is a great deal else I would like to show him, so I think we must leave you now."

"His first visit!" Hana's brows rose in amused astonishment. "In that case, we must do our best to make it very special for him." She glanced at me, and then her attention was back on Isamu. I was annoyed. I might be pretending that I had taken a vow of silence, but I could still hear! She had no need to behave as if I was deaf, blind, and stupid.

"Did you have something in mind?" Isamu was sitting a little straighter. His attention was on Hana, not the geisha at his side, who was fanning him tenderly.

"I rather wondered if you—and Jun, of course—might like to pay a visit to the Hidden House? I have a new girl to tempt you with. A hunchback, very small. Also, spectacularly ugly."

I stared from Hana to my brother. What nonsense was this? Why would he be interested in a hunchback dwarf? Isamu was licking his lips, and I glanced at him in amazement.

"Really? If she is in the Hidden House, then no doubt she is truly a treasure. Perhaps next time, when I am on my own," Isamu said. "I don't want to shock my dear Jun too much on his first visit!"

"As you wish." Hana rose to her feet. All three geisha stood with her, bowing as Isamu and I stood up. Hana bowed as well, but I noticed it was just low enough for courtesy. I could barely wait until we were outside again to pester Isamu with my questions.

"Why did Hana think you would ever be interested in an ugly hunchback? What's the Hidden House?"

"Jun, you are supposed to be silent," he reproved me. I sighed, and he took pity on me. "Very well. If you have to speak to me in the street, try to do so very quietly. I will tell you, so you don't let everybody know how unworldly you are. The Hidden House is Hana's other place of business. It is behind the Green Teahouse, on the other side of the courtyard. It is open only to a select few. No man can go there unless he is introduced by an existing patron. Even then, Hana vets all prospective visitors very carefully. She rejects many more than she allows to pass through the Hidden House's doors. A man must be rich to be allowed in. But money alone is not enough. One must also be very well bred and well connected. The soul of discretion. And above all, Hana must like you. The shogun himself would not be allowed to enter if Hana took a dislike to him. Many people think the place does not exist, that it is only a legend. But that is not true."

"What is so special about the Hidden House?" I mumbled, trying not to move my lips. Isamu glanced around and then gripped my arm, drawing me into the mouth of an alley so narrow we blocked the way.

"We can talk safely here. If anybody wants to pass, we will see them coming. Talk of the Hidden House isn't for everybody's ears. It's simply unique. Even in the Floating World, there's nothing that can match it. Hana describes all of the girls there as flawed jewels. None of them are what you would call normal. She charges a fortune for a man to taste their pleasures, and there's never any lack of customers."

He looked at me with his eyebrows raised, as if to ask if I understood. Although I was reluctant to appear ignorant, I shook my head.

"Why would a man pay a lot of money for a girl who isn't beautiful and talented? There are plenty of lovely yujo available in the Floating World without paying a huge amount for somebody who is less than perfect."

"I didn't say the geisha in the Hidden House aren't talented." Isamu frowned, obviously irritated. "They are. They are all skilled musicians and dancers. And no woman in the Floating World could ever beat them for wit. And do not let Hana ever hear you compare them to yujo. All the girls in the Hidden House are true geisha, with all a geisha's talents. It's just that they are a little different."

Isamu tailed off into silence. I thought about what he had said and brightened.

"It's all a matter of being sophisticated, isn't it?" I said. My hopes were dashed when Isamu shook his head.

"No. That has nothing to do with it. The geisha in the

Hidden House are worth every coin a man spends on them, believe me. Last time I was there, I had a girl who was blind, deaf, and dumb."

I goggled at him in disbelief. Isamu, who was so fastidious about every aspect of his life, wanted to lie with a girl who was deformed? He was sweating lightly; his tongue snaked out and licked his upper lip.

"She was amazing. She was intensely beautiful and refused to kowtow to me at all. If I hadn't had Hana's word for it that she could neither hear nor see me, I would never have believed it. She seemed to sense what I wanted before I knew myself. I took her in every way possible, and she taught me things even I had never dreamed of before. And I just knew that she hated every second of it. If she had been able to stick a dagger between my ribs, she wouldn't have hesitated. She was wonderful."

I stared at him, wondering if the deformed geisha had perhaps put a potion in his sake to bewitch him. Isamu shook himself as if he was shaking off his memories.

"You would never understand. It's a man's fantasy, not a woman's. Even if I took you there, I doubt you would appreciate it. And by the way, Hana must have taken a great fancy to you, *Jun.*" He sounded amused as he spoke my name. "It's unheard of for her to invite a first-time visitor to the Green Teahouse to move on to the Hidden House. I know I'm a favorite of hers, but even for me, if she hadn't liked you, she would never have mentioned it."

"Oh, good," I muttered. I had liked the Green Teahouse well enough, but so far, the Floating World had left me disappointed. I had not expected to take tea with well-trained geisha; there was little excitement in that. Nor did I have any inclination to taste the exotic delights of the Hidden House.

Isamu smiled. "Time for us to move on, Jun." He saun-tered casually back out into the street and was immediately surrounded by people. I was about to thrust my own way into the seething crowd when something made the fine hairs on the back of my neck prickle. I closed my eyes, the better to allow instinct to take over from my senses. I was right. We were being watched. I felt it.

I stood on tiptoe, pretending I was trying to keep Isamu in view. There was no need for it; he—and I, for that matter —were far taller than most of the people who surrounded us. I mimed anxiety, turning my head as if I was worried I had somehow lost sight of him. The sensation of being watched intensified, but nobody appeared to be paying us any attention at all. I hesitated and then darted after Isamu, tugging at his robe to let him know I was there.

All the way down the street, I felt the weight of a gaze between my shoulder blades. It was so intense it made my back itch.

THIRTEEN

You say I am blind.
How then can you hope to know
What it is I see?

*A*fter that, I made sure I was not separated from Isamu again. I walked so closely to him, if the streets hadn't been so crowded that I couldn't see it, I would have stepped on his shadow.

By the time we reached the end of the long, straight main street, I felt excited by the Floating World. All my senses were reeling from the impact of the sights, the smells, and above all, the exuberant noise that surrounded us. When I was sure Isamu wasn't looking at me, I stared around like the rustic I was, increasingly breathless with excitement at the sheer strangeness of my surroundings.

I had never dreamed that anywhere could exist where everybody—regardless of their class or sex—could rub shoulders so comfortably. Many of the men who drifted past us were merchants. Most of them were well dressed, but there was a certain vulgarity to their robes and obi that gave them away. But there were also working men. They had no pretensions to appear better than they were, but wore their work clothes with a kind of defiant pride in the way they held themselves. I even saw a couple of samurai who were unknown to me but exchanged nods of recognition with Isamu. But not just men, the streets were thronged with women as well.

Many of the women were yujo, no doubt out looking for customers. They were easy to spot from their gaudy kimonos and the ostentatious, overelaborate ornaments bristling from their enormous wigs. A few of them gave Isamu languishing glances and then saw me walking close to him and sighed in disappointment. There were also geisha and maiko, as richly dressed as the yujo but with a quiet elegance that the women of pleasure lacked.

My stomach rumbled, distracting me. Isamu must have heard it as well as he stopped.

"I suppose you're hungry?" I nodded. "I'm taking you to the kabuki theater. If we buy something to eat as we walk, will that do?"

"Oh, yes." I was so excited I forgot again that I was temporarily dumb. Isamu sighed and raised his hand, waggling his fingers. In a moment, we were surrounded by food sellers.

"Take your pick." Isamu grinned.

I peered around the ring of men who surrounded us, all with trays strung from their necks. A man who was selling rice dumplings held out his tray to me temptingly calling, "Dango, dango!" He was elbowed aside by another man selling boiled red beans, who in his turn was pushed out of the way by a vendor of sliced tofu. Yet another tempted me with noodles. Isamu made my mind up for me. He beckoned to a man who was peddling sushi and made a rapid selection of seafood and rice delicacies. The man wrapped our purchases in paper, and in return, Isamu handed over what seemed to be ridiculously few coins. The other food sellers, disappointed, followed us for a few steps until Isamu turned and pretended to draw his sword to threaten them.

"Does everybody in the Floating World have something to sell?" I asked through a delicious mouthful of raw sea urchin and rice.

"One word out of you when we get to the kabuki and I take you home!" Isamu threatened. "What do you mean, anyway?"

"Well, look at them all." I waved my hand at the crowded street. The yujo, of course, were looking for customers, as were the food vendors. But at every step, there seemed to be somebody offering something. Fortune tellers squatted with their backs to buildings, calling out to everybody who passed that theirs was the only true forecast. Every now and then, somebody stood in a ring of spectators, hoping for coins in return for their rendition of bawdy comic songs. I felt my ears go red as I heard the lyrics of one of them. Flute players competed with them for attention, as did dancers. Beggars threaded amongst them, their hands outstretched as they whined their woes. An obviously blind woman, her hands planted on the shoulders of a small boy, ambled past us. I felt sorry for her, trying to make her way in this place of constant noise and movement.

"Can you not give the poor blind woman some money, Isamu?" I asked.

"Why? She already makes a good living." He sounded amused, and I looked at him reproachfully. "She's a masseuse. In the Floating World, masseuses are always female and blind. That way, they can't be distracted by their customers' bodies, and their sense of touch is intensified by their lack of sight. Look." He nodded toward the blind woman as a man tapped her on her shoulder. He spoke briefly, and then the oddly-assorted trio turned down a side alley. "Some say the best yujo of all are blind." Isamu finished his sushi and crumpled the paper wrapping up, throwing it to the ground. One of the beggars immediately picked it up, searching for scraps. "They make up for the lack of one sense by the use of others, if you get my meaning, Jun."

"And have you tried one for yourself, brother?" I asked cheekily.

Isamu pretended to cuff me around my head, but I ducked the blow easily. "Onward!" he said cheerfully.

I followed him, but my thoughts stayed with the blind masseuse. Isamu's words made perfect sense to me. He had soon become bored with watching Riku teach me the art of unarmed combat and stopped coming to see us practice. When we had been left alone for perhaps a month, Riku had amazed me.

"Today will be different, Keiko-chan," he said. I waited, anticipating some new move. Instead, he delved into his obi and produced a blindfold. "Turn around and I will tie this for you."

Riku tightened my blindfold securely and moved away from me silently.

"I cannot fight when I cannot see!" I protested. A hand touched my shoulder and I jumped, spinning around. A second later, the hand touched my face. Both touches were gentle, but I did not like this new game at all. Not because I thought Riku might hurt me. I had long ago come to understand that he tempered his punches when he fought with me. I might emerge from a training bout bruised, but never any worse. But a moment ago, I had had perfect vision. Now, I was blind.

"Where am I?" Riku said softly.

I put my hand out in the direction of his voice and felt his robe.

"And now?"

I had not heard him move, but still I turned in the direction of his voice. Again, my seeking hand found cloth.

"You see?" Riku said. "You think you are blind, but you are not. You have five worldly senses, and a sixth that is a gift from the gods, given only to a few. I know that you have been blessed, and that you possess that extra sense. Your vision is not only unnecessary when you fight, it is a hindrance to you. I have taught you to fight well as a woman. Now, you will learn all over again as a creature of instinct."

With that, he pulled my hair. I darted around, trying to catch the slightest noise from him. Useless. He was as silent as a moth. He touched me again, from another direction. I turned quickly, pushing my hand out to grab him. Nothing. Again, the quick touch. And again.

The next time, I stood still. I felt his touch, but did not move. I waited until I felt contact again, and that time grabbed his hand before he could withdraw it.

"Good. You are fast. But you will learn to be much better than that. Where am I now?"

I listened. There was no sound. I held my breath and—ridiculous as it was beneath the blindfold—closed my eyes. My ears told me nothing. Nor could I smell him. I stayed still. He remained silent. Suddenly, I felt his presence. I darted forward, my hand outstretched. He was not there, but I *felt* the displaced air where he had been only a moment before.

"Very good. You are learning." I listened and understood at once that I had made a mistake. Riku had hold of my robe before I could gather my thoughts and he threw me to the floor effortlessly. "I told you. Do not rely on your ears or your nose. Not even your sense of touch. If you do not learn, I will plug up your ears and nose so that you are senseless."

I shuddered at the thought. I felt defenseless blind-folded, how much more terrifying would it be if I couldn't hear either?

"I do not hear you, Riku-san," I said softly. "Nor I do I see you. But I know you are there." As I finished speaking, I lunged. My fingers slipped on his robes, and I heard him laugh.

"Did you smell me?" he asked.

I nodded and sighed. The blindfold had made my sense of hearing and smell a hundred times more efficient than they usually were. Riku had been so still, I could not hear him. He smelled of nothing more than clean flesh, but I had located him by that smell.

"Come here."

I shuffled forward, my arms outstretched to find him. He waited until my fingers found his robes, then he grabbed me. I panicked at once, forgetting everything I had ever learned and struggling in his grip. I felt his fingers poking at my ears, and the world was silent. I wanted to scream and drew on every reserve of willpower I possessed to stay still and quiet. Worse was to follow. As good as his word, he plugged my nostrils with soft wax pellets.

I stood completely still. My world had ceased to exist. There was nothing outside my own body. I had become senseless. I waited for Riku to touch me again. Waited until my legs ached from the lack of movement. Had he gone away? Left me like this as a test, to see how long it would be before I gave in and removed the blindfold? I felt as if I had been thrust into a deep, dark prison, so far removed from all that was human that I might as well have been dead. I wanted to shriek with fear. Instead, I thought of Tomoe Gozen. Isamu had told me that Riku was the last of a line of fighting monks whose lineage went back centuries. Was it possible that one of his forebears had taught *her* in this way?

If Tomoe Gozen had learned to fight in this way, then so must I. I relaxed, concentrating on the pattern of my breath, in and out. Panic drained out, leaving in its place the sweetest sensation of nothingness. I was no longer tied to the earth. I was elemental. My soul was free of bodily ties.

I caught Riku's hand before it touched me. Caught it and used his own strength against him to throw him to the ground. I felt the displacement of the air as he jumped silently to his feet and circled me. I did not move. When I sensed he was behind me, I waited, anticipating that he would try and rush me from there, as that would be my weakest point. I was right. I feinted to one side, but this time he was too quick for me and his arm snaked around my throat. No matter. I relaxed my body until it was as fluid as water and I felt, rather than heard, his grunt of surprise as I freed myself from his grip.

And so it went. That first time, Riku had the advantage over me perhaps half the time. But I got better. Soon, I was able to fight far more efficiently when I was deprived of my senses than when I could see and hear. I began to love the sensation of being one with the wind and the sun and the earth. My body was no more than a vehicle for my instincts.

Isamu continued to instruct me in the art of sword fighting and the use of the naginata. I knew that the pupil had exceeded the master in at least one area when he announced loftily that he would not work on my skills with the naginata any further. It was a woman's weapon, he sneered, and of no use to a man.

I exulted in the knowledge that I was now the superior warrior, even though Isamu would never admit it. At the same time, I was reluctant to share my new self-knowledge with my brother. Hesitatingly, I asked Riku's opinion on the matter.

"You can tell him." He shrugged. "He won't believe you. But at the same time, it will make him uneasy, and he will laugh at you because of that. Your brother is an excellent samurai, and a very great warrior. But he has no instinct. He knows only what he has been taught, not what he can really achieve."

I agreed with Riku and was grateful for his understanding. But when I was practicing with Isamu, I never relied on my sixth sense. It seemed unfair.

Isamu's voice recalled me to the present and I nodded quickly, pretending I had heard every word.

"Of course, it's alright for an old woman like her." He was talking about the masseuse again. I nodded. "She's old and ugly. Some of the younger women are quite pretty, and it's often the case that their customers think they're entitled to a happy ending after the massage is finished." He chuckled happily and I wondered how he knew that.

The kabuki performance was already well underway when we arrived. Isamu handed money to an attendant and we were led to a box near the stage, which stuck out into the audience like a tongue protruding from a giant mouth.

"What play are we to see?" he asked.

The attendant nodded at the stage. "You're in for a treat, my lord. At the moment it's the famous drama, *Shunkan*. It's barely started. May I send some sake for you?"

Isamu nodded, and very quickly, another attendant was at the side of our box with sake and cups. I drank cautiously, afraid I would get drunk and disgrace myself. Isamu tossed his first cup off as if it were water and held out his cup for a refill.

I watched the action on the stage avidly. The rest of the audience members were obviously regulars at the kabuki. They hissed and booed loudly at appropriate places, and I noticed the man in the next box to us weeping unashamedly at a particularly poignant moment. He shared his box with a geisha, who mopped his tears solicitously.

As the play finished, Isamu sat back with a sigh of content. "Nothing like the kabuki to drive away the worries of the world. There are several theaters in Edo, but this one is by far the best."

I had been so entranced by the kabuki, I almost felt that some of the worldly glamor of the Floating World had rubbed off on me. I raised my eyebrows and shrugged nonchalantly.

"Come, Jun." Isamu climbed to his feet. We had been sitting for hours, and I heard his knees crack as he stood. "It's getting dark. That will be the last performance today. Now the Floating World will come alive. I have something interesting I want to show you."

I followed him eagerly. The kabuki had thrown its dream dust at me and I was sorry the performance had finished. I wanted to see more. Much more. I would persuade Isamu to bring me back to the Floating World as soon as possible.

We moved out, carried along in the surge of the crowd. I had been so entranced by the drama that I had all but forgotten about the feeling that we were being watched. As the crowd thinned, I was sure somebody was looking at us intently again. I leaned close to Isamu, pretending that I was worried the press of bodies would separate us, and under the cover of his body, I stared around carefully.

There were so many people. It could be any one of them who was following us. In spite of that, my eyes were drawn to a single figure. He was neither tall nor short. Medium height, medium build. Not a youth, but neither was he middle-aged. He was even dressed in very simple robes. There was just a certain *something* that I could not quite identify that made me sure he was the man who had been following us.

I tugged on Isamu's sleeve. "I'm sure somebody has been staring at us ever since we came through the gates. Do you have enemies here in the Floating World, brother?"

"None that I know of. Possibly the odd jealous husband, I suppose. Can you point him out to me?"

I was grateful he was taking me seriously. I turned my head to nod at the stranger, but he was no longer there.

"He's gone!" I spoke louder than I had intended in my surprise.

"Well, if you see him again let me know."

We moved casually with the crowd. I glanced from left to right carefully, but there was no sign of the man. Why, then, did the hairs at the back of my neck prickle again as though my body was certain we were still being watched? We were beside the river now, and I was grateful for the cool breeze that came off the water

"Isamu-san! It is so very good to see you again. It has been far too long."

Isamu stopped abruptly. "Reo-chan. It's good to see you. Please, allow me to present my good friend, Jun. I am afraid you'll find him nothing of a conversationalist. The silly boy has taken a month-long vow of silence to try and appease the gods." I almost winced at Isamu's fond greeting.

"Indeed!" Emiko's despoiler ran his gaze down my face and along the length of my body.

She had described him as iki, but I couldn't see it. I thought his robes were a little too flamboyant for true good taste, and there was a distinct lack of good manners in the way he stared at me, as if he wanted to eat me up. I smiled, hoping he wouldn't notice the way the muscles around my mouth bunched with the effort.

"What a deliciously unusual face! I wonder, does it indicate anything else that is exotic about the dear boy? I am enchanted to meet you, Jun."

I bowed. At the same time, I thought curiously how very odd it was that in my incarnation as a boy, my features were not only acceptable, but Reo appeared to regard me as deeply attractive. When I was a girl, Emiko told me constantly that I was ugly beyond redemption. Truly, the ways of the world were weighted in favor of men! Isamu put his hand on my shoulder in an overt declaration of ownership.

"This is Jun's first visit to the Floating World. I was just about to show him a lattice brothel."

"Really? I would have thought that a little uncouth for you, Isamu!" Reo was smiling far too broadly for my liking.

Isamu shrugged. "Jun has to learn to distinguish gold from dross," he said easily. "But so far he's proved an excellent pupil. He's already made a remarkably good impression on Hana. She invited him to visit the Hidden House."

"Really?" Reo's jaw dropped. "By all the gods, he must have something special. I've been dropping hints in Hana's ear for months that I would be honored to be invited to taste the joys of the Hidden House and still haven't gotten there. I suppose you have?"

"Most certainly. Many times." Isamu's smile was inscrutable. "And I can tell you, you must intensify your efforts to gain admittance. There is nothing else like it anywhere."

I smiled with him. I had disliked Reo when Emiko told me about him. Now that I had met him, I would have taken great pleasure in pushing him into the serene waters of the river and seeing him drown before my eyes. I had to force myself not to jerk back when he leaned toward me and spoke with apparent sincerity.

> "There is no greater
> Joy in this life than watching
> Youth become a man."

Emiko had said that he had spent an entire evening composing haikus in celebration of her beauty. And now he was paying the same compliment to me, the rat.

"Come now, Reo. Would you try and steal my treasure? I really don't think I can allow that. Would it amuse you to come with us to take a look at a lattice brothel?"

"Normally, no. But in the company of Jun—and yourself, of course—how could I refuse?"

He walked far closer to me than was polite. His gaze never left me, to the extent that he tripped and would have fallen if Isamu hadn't caught him by the elbow. I willed Isamu to tell him to mind his manners, but my brother found the situation extremely funny. I could see the laughter in his eyes and the way he was fighting to stop his mouth from twitching with amusement. I longed to break my vow of silence and tell him how this monster had deflowered Emiko and then thrown her aside heartlessly. I stayed silent. It was impossible. Isamu would be furious with me if I so much as spoke in Reo's hearing and spoiled his joke. If I told him what Reo had done to Emiko, the shame of it would probably be enough to force my brother to commit seppuku—vulgarly known as belly slitting—the most painful and lingering suicide available to an honorable samurai. And I was fairly certain he would dispatch both Emiko and me before he took his own life. Emiko for the shame she had brought on our house and me for revealing it to him.

I bit back the words. I had survived the nightmare of the cliff-face. I had no intention of dying here on the streets of the Floating World. Instead, I smiled sweetly at Reo, even as I cursed him in my heart.

"Here we are." Isamu tugged my sleeve to attract my attention. I glanced at the building that ran alongside us and coughed to cover my startled grunt of horror.

"Anything that meets with your approval, Jun-chan?" Reo leered at me. He rested his head on my shoulder, his chin sharp in my flesh. I wondered with revulsion how the yujo we had seen could possibly accept this sort of arrogant behavior from their clients night after night. And for these poor girls behind the lattice, it was even worse. They didn't even have a yujo's freedom to choose their clients.

Reo was obviously out to impress me. He raised his head from my shoulder and almost danced the length of the building.

"What about this one?" he called. He poked a finger through the slats and tugged cheekily on one girl's hair. I would have bitten his finger off. She smiled and put her head on one side coquettishly.

"Or this one?" He went even further with the second

girl. She leaned forward against the wooden lattice, and Reo promptly fingered her breasts. I could hardly believe it, but she giggled.

"Oh, stop playing with the whores, Reo," Isamu called. He sounded bored, and I was glad of it. "I don't actually want to take Jun in there. I just wanted to show him one more of the delights of the Floating World."

"Oh, I don't know." Reo seemed to have found a girl who appealed to him. He was tickling her under the chin, his tongue stuck between his lips. "I quite fancy the look of this one. I don't recollect seeing you before. New, are you? What's your name?"

"Hayami, my lord," she whispered. "I only arrived here yesterday. This is the first time I have been offered to the honorable gentlemen."

"Did you hear that, Isamu? Her name means rare beauty. Bit of an exaggeration, but she's not bad. And fresh as well."

"Believe that if you will, Reo," Isamu said drily. "Still, if you want to dirty yourself here, that's up to you. I think Jun may have seen enough for a first visit. Are you tired, Jun?"

I was nearly asleep on my feet, but I was determined not to show it. I shook my head firmly. Isamu was having none of it.

"Come on, time we were on our way. It will be very late before I get Jun to his home. Reo, are you staying here?"

I glanced at Reo and swallowed hard. The girl he fancied had pulled her kimono apart so that her breasts were fully displayed. Reo had slipped one hand through the bars and was fondling her left breast happily. The girl sighed and put her head back, her eyes closed and her mouth ajar in apparent ecstasy. Just arrived today? Even I wasn't fooled! But apparently Reo was.

"Of course, if Jun is tired, you must take the poor boy home." His eyes remained fixed on the whore's breasts as he spoke. "I rather think I will venture inside and see what price they want for Hayami here. I hope I may have the pleasure of calling on you soon, Isamu."

"Of course. You are always welcome in my father's house, Reo. Goodnight. I hope your flower is well worth her price."

Reo took his eyes off his choice of whore long enough to dart over to us. He bowed courteously to Isamu. I had expected a quick bob of his head toward me, but instead, he slid his hands inside my sleeves in an oddly intimate gesture and squeezed my wrists.

"Do take care of this delicious creature, Isamu." He smiled into my face. "I am so looking forward to meeting him again!"

Hayami appeared worried that she was losing a customer. She leaned against the bars and made kissing noises. Immediately distracted from me, Reo turned and walked back to her, rubbing his hands together briskly.

Isamu was grinning widely. I guessed he was amused by Reo's choice of where he was to spend the remainder of the night. I kept a stone face. Surely my iki brother could see a fool when he was in front of one. Besides, look at the way Reo had treated Emiko. My anger lasted only a moment before it gave way to exasperation. How could Emiko ever have been fooled by that shallow idiot? Surely, even she could see that Soji was worth a thousand of Reo?

"Give any man the sniff of a bit of manko he really fancies and he's lost to the world." Isamu snickered.

I nodded absently. The lattice brothel had disturbed me greatly. I was filled with pity for the poor girls behind the lattice. Suddenly, Father's plans to give me in marriage to a man I didn't know seemed a great deal more tolerable. At least I would have only the one husband, whereas those poor girls had to accept strange men into their bodies every night. How could they live, I wondered, knowing that each day of their lives would be a repeat of the same humiliation. I think my thoughts must have been written on my face, as Isamu was suddenly quite serious.

"You feel sorry for those yujo, don't you?"

"Yes," I said seriously. "I can't imagine what it must be like, having to display yourself like that. And then to be made to give your body to any man who wants you. It must be hell on earth for the poor women."

"They enjoy it," he said brutally. I stared at him in astonishment. Could he really believe his own words? "It's an easy life for them, sister. All they have to do is open their legs for their customers and take pleasure in what is being done to them. In return, they are fed and clothed. They have somewhere to live. Unless they misbehave, they are not beaten. For most women, that would be more than enough."

"But they're not free," I said lamely.

"You can't eat freedom," he said cheerfully. "Look at it this way. Most of those women were sold by their parents when they were young girls. Their fathers would have been delighted to get rid of them. If they had stayed at home, they would have been one more useless mouth to feed. It's likely they would have been sold off as slaves sooner or later. As it is, they not only bettered themselves by becoming whores and earning decent money, but they also gained great respect by sacrificing themselves for the good of their families."

There was a flaw in that argument, but I could not find

the words to explain it to Isamu. "I would commit suicide before I allowed myself to be used like that," I said finally.

"Would you? That is the onna-bugeisha in you speaking. I have obviously trained you well, Jun."

"Will you bring me back to the Floating World, brother?" I dared to ask. When Isamu did not reply, I added, "Soon?"

"Perhaps. If I have the time." He shrugged. I hid a smile as he added, "It has been quite amusing."

We walked out of the great gate in companionable silence. Isamu would allow me to come back with him, I was sure of it. I was also certain that there was much more here that I had yet to experience. I looked forward to it!

I was so tired I worried I might drop into sleep on the way home and fall from my horse. Perhaps I did sleep and dream, for I was sure that there was somebody behind us all the way, the rhythm of their horse's hooves exactly matching ours. But whenever I glanced behind me, the road was empty.

FOURTEEN

I see. I hear. I
Feel. How much more good fortune
Could I ever need?

*P*erhaps I was simply too tired to sleep. I had often been like that as a young child. Emiko used to scold me constantly, telling me to stop talking and go to sleep. But if I'd had an exceptionally interesting day, sleep always refused to claim me.

I threw my—or rather, Isamu's—robe to the floor. I would see to that in the morning. But sleep eluded me still. I tossed and turned on my futon until the kakebuton—the top quilt—was a wrinkled mess. I was physically tired, but my brain refused to slow down. I replayed the events of the day over and over again in my mind.

Should I, I wondered, tell Emiko I had seen Reo? I quickly decided not to. She would immediately demand to know whether he had asked about her, and I am a terrible liar. Besides, how could I explain what I had been doing in the Floating World with Isamu? If she believed me—which was unlikely—she would shame me for it. What if she told Father? No, I would not tell her.

My mind finally at rest, I turned over, ready to find sleep at last.

I was wide awake again in a flash. I could hear a voice. Not a voice I knew, nor was it coming from inside the house. It was outside my shoji, very soft, repeating a single word over and over again. My name. Or, rather, the name I had taken for this evening's adventure.

"Jun." Pause. Then again, softly as the wind sighing through the grass. "Jun."

I sat up and shook my head. Surely I had fallen asleep after all and was dreaming. My palms had blistered from gripping the horse's reins. Very deliberately, I squeezed my fingernails into my own flesh and winced with the pain.

So, I was awake. I was not dreaming. I had been right when I thought we had been watched. And whoever the watcher was, he had the nerve to follow us home. Oddly, I realized I was almost jittery with energy rather than feeling frightened. Instead of shouting for a guard, I spoke softly.

"Who are you?" I asked quietly. I was sure I had spoken too softly and that he would never hear me, but I was wrong.

"Ah, sweet Jun. Shouldn't you ask me why I am here? What I am doing outside your window in the hours before dawn calling your name?"

"Would your answer mean anything to me if I did?"

"I don't know. That is something you must ask yourself." He was laughing at me. I could hear the amusement in his voice. I smiled to myself with him.

"Then why should I bother asking you?" I responded.

I used the time before he answered me to listen to my own body. I should have been terrified, I supposed. A stranger had followed me all the way from the Floating World. Not only that, but somehow he had slipped past the guard who patrolled the garden around our house at night. I was exhilarated and excited, but afraid? Not at all.

"How much did you bribe the watchman to let you through? I hope it was a lot. If Father finds out the man has taken a bribe, he will not live to enjoy it," I said conversationally. Under the cover of my words, I got to my feet and padded over to the window on silent feet.

"Watchman? Oh, you mean the man who was huddled over a brazier heating water for his tea. I assure you, he never saw me."

I was at the shoji. I jumped with surprise as I realized the voice was no longer coming from there, but was over by the screen that led into the garden. The path that ran outside the house was graveled, both for beauty and to make it impossible for an intruder to approach without being heard. How had he moved without me hearing him? And more to the point, how had he heard me approach the window? I had not even heard myself move. I spoke calmly, taking care to show no fear.

"Well, my mysterious visitor, tell me. Why are you here? Why were you watching us in the Floating World?"

He laughed, very low. A finger of pleasure tickled my spine.

"I wasn't watching your brother. I had eyes only for you, Jun."

"Then you will be disappointed." I moved very slowly, putting one foot carefully in front of the other, walking on my toes. "I was Jun only for tonight's amusement. For the rest of the time, I am Keiko."

"Of course you are. It is a lovely name, but not as lovely as the girl who bears it." That caught me unawares. I teetered, one foot in the air and the other so arched it could barely support me. "Take care, Keiko. I would not have you hurt yourself."

I put my foot to the floor quickly. There was a full moon, and a gentle wind caused the shadows of the shrubs to move languidly. But there was no shape of a man. How could he move so silently? How could he see me when I could not see him?

"I will not hurt myself. And neither will you. I'm not afraid of you," I called at once. I heard him laugh, quite softly. His voice was as warm and rich as honey dripping from a spoon. I could barely remember what he looked like from the brief glance I had had of him in the Floating World, but it hardly mattered. I was beyond excited that somebody could be so taken with me that they had followed me about all night and taken the trouble to pursue me to my own bedroom.

"Of course you're not afraid of me," he said. "Why should you be afraid of the man who is going to be your lover? Dearest Keiko, do open the door and let me in. I can hear your night watchman stirring. He may be deaf and blind, but even he can't fail to notice me crouching here."

I dithered for a moment. I should simply stay still and allow him to be found. I had told Isamu somebody was watching us, so this was not my fault. Instead, I darted forward and slid open the shoji. A shadow glided through soundlessly. A moment later, I heard the watchman clatter past. He was so clumsy, I wondered how he failed to wake me every time he passed.

I held my breath until the crunch of his feet on the gravel died away. I thought ruefully that even if I had been snoring loudly, he would never have heard it over the noise he was making himself.

"You are very beautiful, Keiko. I like you far more as a woman than I did as a man. And I have to say you entranced me even when you were a boy."

This was ridiculous. And undoubtedly dangerous. I should be screaming for the watchman to return and take this upstart who had dared to follow me and invite himself into my room. He stood in front of me, almost close enough to touch if I stretched my hand out to him. I did not call out. Instead, I whispered, "Who are you?"

"Do you mean, what is my name?" I nodded. It would do for a start. "I am called Yo."

I took a deep breath and spoke as evenly as if this was an everyday event for me.

"So, Yo-san. What are you doing here? Didn't anything tempt you sufficiently for you to stay in the Floating World? I find it difficult to believe that you were so entranced by me after a single glance that you decided to follow me all the way home and risk having your head taken off your shoulders if you were discovered. Or do you perhaps prefer men to women? If that is the case, then as you can see, you are already disappointed."

Yo did not speak, but instead held his hand out to me. I made my mind up quickly. I would not allow him to think I was afraid of him. I placed my fingers in his. His skin was cool and smooth. My mouth dropped open in shock as he raised my hand to his face and put his lips on the back of it.

The gesture was as delightful as it was strange. I shivered at the same time as I scolded myself inwardly. What was I thinking, allowing this unknown into my life, letting him touch me, kiss my hand?

"This cannot be. I'm not some green girl, sighing for romance. I'm onna-bugeisha. A warrior woman of the samurai." I had no idea I had spoken out loud until Yo answered me.

"You are. That is why I watched you. Not just tonight, but for many months. I saw your brother teach you how to use a sword. I saw the master teach you jujutsu. Did you never wonder why Riku no longer came to you?" I shook my head at the same time as I wondered how he knew Riku was my sensei. How he came to know his name, speak of him as if he knew him? "It was because the pupil came to excel the teacher. Did your brother never tell you that?"

"No, he didn't." I was bewildered by how much Yo seemed to know about me. Isamu had long ago ceased to watch me practice with Riku. I had assumed it was because he had become bored. My heart lifted as I understood that I had made him jealous. One more wonder on this strangest of nights! "How did you watch us and I not see you? How do you know Riku-san?"

Yo ignored my questions. "You use a staff as well as any man. I could perhaps beat you with a sword, but not with the onna-bugeisha's weapon of choice, the naginata. And I think we are certainly equal in the art of unarmed combat. You are truly onna-bugeisha. That is why I am here. You are unique. I have waited and waited for you to give me my chance, and now I am in your hands, Keiko. Tell me to go, and I will leave you. Shout for the watchman to come back, and I will allow myself to be taken and face my punishment. But I hope you do not."

"I still don't understand. If you have watched me for so long, why didn't I see you until tonight?" I wanted to know the answer, but even more did I need the time to think. I looked at his face and saw nothing but tranquility in his eyes. Yet still, I was suspicious. This sort of thing happened only between the covers of romances. In real life, I was

Keiko, the girl child who was fortunate even to have survived. The girl who had always been taught she was plain and worthless.

"You didn't see me because I didn't allow myself to be seen," Yo said simply. "But believe me, I was always there. Watching you. I was there when you climbed the mountain to capture the eagle chick. My heart was ready to die with you when I thought you were going to fall. I could do nothing but will you to live. At least Isamu took care of you then. If he had let you fall, I would have killed him to avenge your death."

He really had watched me, then. I searched my mind for a meaningful response. "I am unworthy of your interest," I finally managed to say.

I looked at him carefully. He was dressed in the same plain robes as he had worn in the Floating World, although close up I could see that they were made from the best fabrics and had been very well-cut. His features were extremely pleasing, but he was certainly not as handsome as Isamu. I doubted he was even the same class as me. He smiled at my thorough inspection, and I wondered at once how I had ever dismissed him as being less than handsome. His smile lit his face from within. He was attractive, almost magnetically so. I felt myself swaying toward him and schooled my body to keep its distance. What was I, some silly maidservant who believed in love at first sight? Such nonsense. It was nothing more than the magic of this strangest of nights. Yet still I listened as Yo's relentless voice went on.

"You are onna-bugeisha. You are the woman I dreamed of finding but despaired existed. If my sensei Riku had not told me that he intended to retire in great content, as he was sure he had finally found a pupil who was more skilled than he was, I would never have known you even existed. Now that I have found you, I will not let you go willingly. Believe me when I say that fate has bound us together." He kneeled gracefully before me and kowtowed so deeply that his head touched the tatami.

"Please, no." I was deeply embarrassed. This was the first time in my entire life anybody had praised me with such eloquence. I could not believe what he was saying. Instead, I concentrated on practical matters. "How long have you watched me? Why didn't I see you until tonight?"

"I've watched you since Riku spoke about you. He and I are old friends. He taught me how to fight long ago. I still visit him to make sure I haven't forgotten anything he taught me." I hid my disbelief, knowing that Yo was watching me intently.

"I've seen you sword-fight with your brother. I've watched you hover at the beck and call of your sister." I was confused; he sounded almost angry when he spoke of Emiko.

"I've seen you sit in the garden and heard the birds sing for you. I've seen how jealous your brother was when he realized that his dog had come to love you more than he did his old master." I shook my head, smiling. He was wrong about that, at least. A dog can have only one master, and Matsuo was Isamu's dog.

"It's true. Haven't you noticed that Isamu rarely takes Matsuo hunting anymore? I heard him tell your father that the hound had turned into a woman's lapdog and no longer had the courage in the hunt that he could rely on. I don't think Matsuo minds greatly. He's your dog now, and that's all that matters to him."

I considered his words. He had been so close to my

father and brother that he had heard them speak about me, yet he had remained unseen? That was impossible.

"How?" I asked. "How did you overhear them? Can you make yourself invisible? If you can, you must be a spirit, not a man at all."

Yo shrugged. "How do you see me?" he asked.

I thought carefully before I answered. "You seem human, and not some malicious spirit out to trick me. Apart from that, I don't know. You're not samurai. But you're not a merchant either. And certainly not a peasant." An idea came to me. "Are you an actor? They can appear as whoever they like."

"In a way." Yo was clearly amused. "I'm not an actor, although I love the kabuki. I will answer your questions, Keiko. All of them. But only if you can work out for yourself how I was able to be so close to your menfolk and not be seen."

Most people love riddles. Many of them are traditional, and every child knows the answers to them. Even though Yo was smiling gently when he asked me his question, I knew at once that the answer was important. If I was indeed onna-bugeisha, then I should be able to figure out the truth. I stood quietly and the answer came to me with a flash of certainty.

"You were invisible. You were disguised as a servant, weren't you?" Yo had no need to speak, his grin split his face like a slice of melon. "Neither Father or Isamu would ever notice a new servant. And they would speak freely in front of you because servants are beneath their notice."

"Well done, Keiko. That's exactly right. I might as well have been invisible as far as they were concerned. One of your house servants was suddenly taken with a virulent fever, and your steward was delighted to allow a clean, presentable man to take his place until he recovered."

"Did you have to bribe the servant very well?" I asked lightly.

"No. Very little. He was glad of the rest from his duties."

I smiled and then stopped myself. I had allowed this unknown man into my home. Was I prepared to allow him any further? What was wrong with me? Had I suddenly turned into Emiko, prepared to allow my heart to be stolen at the merest hint of flattery?

"So," I said briskly, "I have answered your riddle. Now will you tell me at last who you are? *What* you are? Why you are here? Tell me now. And if I don't like your answer, I'll shout for the guard." I reminded myself that for all her passion for Reo, Emiko had found the actual act of love-making disappointing. I had no intention of allowing myself to be disappointed like that.

"You know my name," he said quietly. "And I have already told you why I am here. I know your father has decided you should marry. He is already asking delicate questions amongst his friends to see if any of them is in need of a wife."

I shuddered. All of Father's friends were of his own generation. I truly was to be given to an old man, then. I raised my head in defiance.

"I will not marry someone as old as my own father," I said flatly.

"Of course you won't," Yo said simply. "It's impossible. You're going to marry me." I laughed out loud in disbelief. Who did Yo think he was to invite himself into my presence and tell me my future was decided? If it weren't so amusing, I would have called for the guard. But I did not, and he spoke intently, clearly misinterpreting my amusement.

"That is the important thing settled, then. As for the rest, it's easily told. As you guessed, I am no samurai. Nor am I a merchant, or a peasant. I suppose some would say I am a kind of actor. I am shinobi, Keiko. What the peasants call a ninja."

FIFTEEN

The pebble beneath
My shoe was once a mountain.
Were you with me then?

*M*y disappointment was so deep, it left me trembling. How very wise I had been to be cautious. I had been right all along. Yo was playing some sort of cruel joke on me. Or perhaps he and Isamu had planned tonight's diversion between them. That could have been how Yo came to know so much about my training with Riku. No doubt my iki brother was lurking in the shadows himself, listening with amusement as his little sister fell for this nonsense. And I had wanted to believe in Yo so badly, I had willingly let him make a fool of me. How they both must have been laughing at me all along. I was devastated, and worse still, I despised myself for falling for it. At that moment, I hated Isamu as much as I hated Yo, and I hated myself even more for believing him.

"Please go." I shuffled away from him and spoke coldly. At least I would have the small satisfaction of not letting either of them see how upset I was. "Now. I should never have let you in. Go now or I will shout for the watchman."

"You don't believe me." He actually sounded hurt, and my fury surged a notch.

"There is no such thing as shinobi, or ninja, or whatever you want to call yourself. They outlived their usefulness centuries ago. Everybody knows that," I said scornfully.

Yo seemed not at all worried by my words. "Really? In just the same way as onna-bugeisha no longer exist, I suppose? And yet here you are, onna-bugeisha yourself."

"That's different," I snapped. I was suddenly determined to find out all I could about this imposter, and in the morning I would confront Isamu about his "joke." At least then I would retain a shred of dignity. "Tell me, then. Explain to me how you come to stand before me claiming to be something that is no more than a legend."

"I am shinobi. I am ninja. Just as you are onna-bugeisha." His voice was the breath of wind in far distant reeds. I caught myself leaning closer to him to make sure I heard him correctly. "My family has kept the tradition alive all this time. We are unknown because it is to our advantage to be unknown. If we are legend, then we can go where we want, do what we want. Those who have use of our services know I am flesh and blood. Those who cannot afford me do not know I exist. It is how we have survived."

"If you are truly shinobi, then you are no more than a mercenary," I broke in abruptly. "You spy and fight and kill for the man who is willing to pay the most for your services. You are less than a beggar at the side of the street. Less even than the untouchables, the burakumin. At least they do not hide themselves as you do."

I was no longer angry. I would say what I meant to Yo and not hide behind a cloak of civility. My words were brutal, but nowhere near as harsh as the joke he had tried to play on me.

"Because I am not of your class I am a beggar?" Yo's voice was so calm I almost wanted to apologize. "I am not a daimyo. Nor am I samurai. But neither am I a burakumin or a beggar. My ancestors fought alongside your family in the Genpei War. We were there when the Minamoto clan took the victory. My ancestor was offered land and a title as a reward for his valor in the battle, but he refused the honor. He was shinobi and loved the freedom that came with knowing he had no master. I maintain that tradition. I am free, Keiko. Free in a way that you will never understand until you are willing to throw off the chains of your tradition."

I was bewildered. Although he had spoken quietly, his words were proud, and they had a ring of truth about them

"You don't believe me," he said flatly. "I promise, every word I have said to you is true. I am here because you are my destiny. When I saw you in the Floating World tonight, I knew I had been given my chance and that I had to take it. I was sure I would be able to persuade you to at least listen to me. If I was wrong, then I have no place here. Shout for your watchman. Better still, shout for your brother. I will allow the watchman to take me without a fight—he would only be doing his job. But I promise you, I will fight to my death with your brother. *That* would truly be a matter of honor."

He stood silently in front of me. My lips tried to form words, but no sound came from my mouth. I had gone from deep pleasure to the knowledge that I had been betrayed and back again in the space of a few moments. I was bewildered. Yo held his hands out to me, palms up, and I wanted to believe him. And I had called Emiko a fool!

"I thank you for your kind words," I said finally. "But you've wasted your time coming here. You must understand. I am onna-bugeisha, a samurai warrior woman. I must be true to the honor of my family. If my father chooses a husband for me, then I shall follow my father's will. I have no choice in the matter."

I spoke quietly. Could he understand that I would never be free? I was bound by too many centuries of tradition. Hadn't even Tomoe Gozen obeyed her husband's wishes at the very last moment even though it was against her own will? For once, the thought of the great warrior woman gave me neither comfort nor guidance.

"You are onna-bugeisha," Yo agreed. "You are as much a creature of legend as I am. You must see that we belong together. The gods will it to be so."

"I cannot go against my father's word," I repeated bitterly, "even if I wanted to. Can't you understand that? It's a matter of honor. Please, go now. There can be nothing between us."

The moment of madness had gone. Still, I would cherish the memory of it in my heart for many long years. I felt enormously guilty that I had misjudged both my would-be lover and my brother, although at the same time I was thankful that I had been wrong.

Yo stood. His movement was lithe and silent. I admired his body, but turned my head aside as if I was not interested in him.

I am onna-bugeisha, I repeated to myself silently. *My honor is to my family. To the samurai tradition we embody. That is far greater than my own desires.*

"Will you fight me, onna-bugeisha?" Yo asked. "Fight me hand to hand in the honorable samurai tradition?"

"Why?" What new tactic was Yo trying? If he was a man

of honor, couldn't he see that the time for him to leave had come and gone? That it was madness that he was here in the first place?

"Because that is the only way you will find out if I am your equal. If I am, what other man could you accept?" He made it sound so simple. A flicker of pleasure made me smile reluctantly.

"And if you win? What then?"

"If I win, then you are mine to command. If I lose to you, then I will be at your feet. Whatever you wish of me, I will do. If you still want me to go away, then you will never see me again."

"Truly?" I asked. "You would go if I told you to?"

"No." Yo smiled. "If you win, and you tell me you do not want to see me again, then you will not see me. Ever. I will be here. I will watch over you. But you will never see me."

"Am I never to be rid of you, then?" I asked lightly, although I observed his face carefully as I spoke.

"No, you are not," Yo said simply. "I've watched you for months. I've seen you grow from a shy, sweet girl into a true warrior. There is nobody like you. Now that I have seen you and spoken to you and told you what is in my heart, how could you expect me to leave you?"

"I will accept your challenge." I shocked myself with my own words. Had I truly gone mad? I supposed that I had, but it didn't matter. This was *right*. I had never been a great believer in the gods. What had they ever done for me? But suddenly, I knew that my fate was guiding me. The decision was out of my hands and in the palms of the immortals. "May I choose the style of battle?"

"Of course." Yo inclined his head politely, but not before I had seen the gleam of joy in his eyes.

"I choose jujutsu. Will you meet me at our dojo? Not

tomorrow night, the moon will still be full. In three nights' time, at this hour? The moon will be dark by then. We will not be seen."

"I will be here." Yo bowed deeply. I stood and bowed in return. Suddenly, almost hysterical laughter bubbled in my throat. Here I was, making arrangements to fight this man for my entire future, yet we were bowing politely to each other! I guessed Yo sensed my amusement. He put out his hand and ran his finger down my cheek. I bit my tongue to hide my pleasure at the touch.

"You are more beautiful than any woman I have ever known in my life, Keiko-chan. Not just the beauty that the eye can see, but you are beautiful inside."

He put the fingers that had touched my face to his lips and held them there for a long moment. Before I could speak, he had turned, fluid as a shadow, and opened the door. In the heartbeat it took me to cross the room, he had disappeared. I closed my eyes and listened, but there was nothing left of him. Truly, he might have been the spirit I had first taken him for.

I was no longer tired. I paced the room, going over everything we had said. A scratch at my screen made me jump. Hoping that Yo had perhaps forgotten to say something and had returned to me, I slid the shoji back quickly and sighed at my own foolishness. Not Yo, but Matsuo padded in silently. I ruffled the fur around his neck and smiled, absurdly pleased that it seemed Yo had been right after all. Matsuo had chosen me for his mistress.

"What is it, Matsuo?" He was padding around, sniffing suspiciously. I had smelled no trace of anything at all on Yo's body, not even the deliciously clean smell of skin fresh from the bath. I glowed at the memory. I watched as the akita

paused at my—or rather, Isamu's—discarded robe. He
pawed at it and whined deep in his throat.

"Does it stink of the Floating World?" I asked indulgently. "Well, if you don't like it, I shall hang it up. Tomorrow, I'll give it back to Isamu."

Matsuo watched intently as I picked up the robe and
shook it out. He growled softly, deep in his throat, as a
folded piece of paper fell out of the sleeve. I picked it up
quickly, just before Matsuo could get his teeth into it.

"Good boy," I murmured absently. "Quiet, now."

I turned the paper over in my hands, staring at it
thoughtfully. I almost threw it away as a bit of trash that got
stuck in my sleeve. Then I saw that the name "Jun" was
written on the back of the fold and almost dropped it in
shock. Matsuo growled again, peeling his muzzle back from
his teeth. I sniffed the parchment cautiously and thought I
understood his distaste. It smelled of scent. Not the usual
gentle fragrance of jako, the geranium musk seeds that
people often fold into their clothes to deter moths whilst
clothes are in storage. That was a subtle, pleasant scent.
This fragrance was intensely sweet and—to my nose at least
—not at all pleasing. How had it gotten into my sleeve? Was
it possible that Yo had placed it there? The thought made
me open it eagerly. I gasped as I read it quickly, and then I
read it again more slowly. Still, I could barely believe what I
was seeing.

It was signed with a flourish—Reo. Emiko's despoiler. I
spoke the words out loud as I read them, as if I expected
Matsuo to understand and comment.

Dearest Jun,

*Since I met you tonight, I cannot get you out of my mind. I
beg of you, meet with me! Come to the Floating World, to Hana's
Green Teahouse. I will be there on the fifth evening from now at*

the time of four bells. If you do not come then, I will wait for you on the tenth night. You will be wise not to disappoint me! I promise you, I will have such delights for you that you will forget all about Isamu. Such delights that you will forget your vow of silence to moan with pleasure.

Do not fail me!

I was furious. Not just at Reo's arrogance, but equally because his note threatened to overshadow the enchantment of this magical night. Then I saw the funny side of it and began to laugh. How was this possible? Yesterday, I had been nothing at all. The neglected, youngest girl child of the family. The girl who should be grateful to be married off to an old man. And now? Why, now it appeared I had a queue of would-be lovers desperate for my favor!

I was about to tear up Reo's note when a thought occurred to me and I pushed it deep into my futon, tugging the mattress firmly over it. I sat on the futon as if to squash the note. Reo had despoiled my sister and then discarded her like a scrap of food left on a plate. She had thought herself in love with him, and he had cared nothing for her. He had broken her heart without as much as a second thought. Since she foolishly still cared for him, I hated him on her behalf.

An idea came to me slowly, and once in place, it lodged stubbornly. What if it was in my power to avenge my sister? What if I could make Reo understand that not all women were as weak as he thought? Keiko could not do it. Keiko would never have the opportunity. But Reo was not interested in Keiko. Jun was the object of—if not his affection, certainly his desire. And Jun was a different proposition entirely. I laid on my futon, with Matsuo warm and bulky and comfortable at my side.

Yo was going to come to me on the third day from today.

We would fight. And I would win. I smiled at my certainty. It was not possible that I might lose. I would win, it had to be so. And when I did, would I choose to take Yo as my lover? I smiled to myself in the darkness. Even as my mind formed the word "perhaps," I felt anticipation coil in my belly.

And after that? I shivered at the possibilities of all that might be to come with Yo. I sighed as I knew I had to put all thoughts of him away, for the moment at least. No matter. There would be plenty of time in the future. I reminded myself firmly that I was bound by the code of bushido. Others had to come before me. Before I could enjoy my anticipation of Yo, there was the matter of my sister's honor to be avenged. Reo wanted to meet me in the Floating World on the fifth day from today. I would not disappoint him. I would be there. And my vengeance would be all the sweeter when I revealed to him that his nemesis was not Jun, but Keiko.

And after that? I didn't know. No matter how hard I tried. I could not begin to focus on what my future was going to be. How could I? I had never known anything but my life as it was now. I listened to my heart beating and willed it to slow. Finally satisfied with the rhythm of my body, I fell asleep with my arm around Matsuo, lost in wonder as to my new life.

Strangely, I did not dream of Yo. Not even Reo. Instead, my dreams were of the women hidden behind the lattice brothel. When I awoke, my hatred of Reo burned.

SIXTEEN

If you have never
Been knocked down, then how are you
To know how to stand?

"*T*hank you for the loan of your robe, brother." I handed Isamu his borrowed robe. He barely glanced at it, yawning and stretching as if he had forgotten I had ever worn it.

"And how did you like the Floating World, younger sister?" He smiled cheerfully at me and I felt guilty that I had ever thought him capable of playing such a mean trick on me.

"It was like nothing I could ever have imagined," I said truthfully.

"Well, you certainly made an impression. First, it was Hana, then Reo. You know, I thought at one time that Reo had taken a real interest in Emiko, to the extent that he might actually put in an offer for her. And I could see she was struck with him as well. But I guess not."

"Probably just as well," I said tartly. "If he likes young

boys, I hardly think he would have made a good husband for Emiko."

Isamu stared at me, his eyebrows arched in amazement. "Perhaps taking you to the Floating World was not a good idea after all. Emiko—and you, for that matter—will accept the husband father selects for you. And do it gladly."

"I am sorry for my impudence." I lowered my eyes so he couldn't see the defiance in my expression. "You are right, of course." I nearly had to bite my tongue to force the humble words out, but Isamu took my apology at face value.

"You didn't like Reo, did you?" I shrugged non-committedly. "I suppose he can be a little—what's the word I'm looking for?—a little flamboyant, shall we say? But he is wealthy, and he comes from a very prestigious family. If he had made an offer to take Emiko as his wife, I think Father might have been at least a little tempted to put poor Soji aside in his favor."

"Could Father have done that? Emiko's been betrothed to Soji since she was a child. I've never heard of such a thing happening." As soon as I said it, I felt foolish. Of course I would never have heard of it. Such things would have been handled with the greatest delicacy and never made public. At the same time, I was grateful Emiko had had no idea that she might have had a chance with her plans. If she had only mentioned Reo by name, everything might have been very different. "Surely it would have been terribly disrespectful to Soji."

"Father would never have considered it if it was anybody other than Reo. And Soji." Isamu shrugged. A sly smile quirked his lips at the corners. "You must remember that Reo really is tremendously rich. And his family is even higher-caste than ours. If he had decided to put his case to Father, who knows? I know it's virtually unheard of to break off a betrothal, but you have to remember that Soji—even though he's samurai, in name at least—is a bit of a milksop. I daresay if Father had spoken to him firmly and convinced him Reo was the best match for Emiko, he would probably have released her."

I took a deep breath and thanked the gods that Emiko had never mentioned Reo's name to Father when she had pleaded with him. The irony of it was making my head spin. Very reluctantly, I could see that compared to Reo, Soji would appear quite boring. Would Emiko truly prefer a rat who would break her heart every other day to a nice, sweet-natured husband who allowed her to order him about? I rather thought she would.

"What are you smirking at?" Isamu asked casually.

"Nothing at all. A touch of wind is all."

He dismissed me with a wave of his hand.

I pulled out Reo's note and re-read it as I drank my morning tea. The smug, arrogant tone of it still enraged me, but now something puzzled me as well. He had barely been out of our sight last night. How had he found time—not to mention a brush, ink, and parchment—to pen the note to me? I frowned over the elegant calligraphy. Reo had not written it himself! I remembered he had excused himself for a moment as we walked toward the lattice brothel, saying that he had to go for a piss. He had been gone so long that Isamu had become impatient, demanding to know how long it took to pass water. Not long at all was my guess. But long enough to dictate his message to a calligrapher, apparently. I sneered at the thought. He was supposed to be besotted with me, yet couldn't take the time and effort to compose his own love note? I longed to tell Emiko what a narrow escape she had had, but I held my tongue. Perhaps later—much later—when Reo had been sufficiently punished, I might tell her what I had done for her.

But not, I thought, until she was safely married to Soji. Knowing my sister, I would hardly be surprised if she didn't become intensely jealous at the idea that Reo had found me —or rather, Jun—attractive. She might even be so furious that his attraction would be kindled all over again. No, best to stay silent.

Besides, before I could contemplate showing Reo the error of his ways, I had my own destiny to confront.

To begin, I made discreet inquiries of the servants. It had always seemed to me that many of the staff felt sorry for me. They chatted with me in a way that they never did with Emiko. I soon found out that Father was absent. He was visiting our daimyo and was not expected back for at least three days. The maid seemed distracted, so I asked if she was unwell. She was startled and seemed flustered by my concern.

"Oh, no, Keiko-san. I am very well, thank you. It's just all these dreadful rumors about unrest amongst the peasants hereabouts. Why, we could all wake up with our throats cut one morning if some of them decided enough was enough!"

I hid a smile behind a serious face. Wake up with our throats cut, indeed! What was the silly girl going on about?

"What are you talking about, Emi? What unrest?"

"Don't you know, Keiko-san? The weather has been too hot this year, and there hasn't been enough rain. The rice harvest is very poor. And they say that it's going to be even worse next year, as the peasants will be forced to eat the bit of rice they have and there'll be nothing left to plant for next year."

This was by far the longest speech I had ever heard Emi make. I stared at her in surprise.

"I see. But surely that's not a problem here? Father can spare enough rice to stop our villagers from going hungry," I pointed out cheerfully. "Our rice granaries are full to overflowing."

Emi hesitated. I waited for her to speak, but she lowered her eyes and shuffled uncomfortably.

"Yes, Keiko-san. Of course. Was there anything else?"

"Thank you, no." I watched her go. Her whole posture radiated unease, and I was puzzled. I went back to see if Isamu knew anything about the likelihood of us all being murdered in our sleep, but his apartment was empty. I shrugged. It was all idle gossip. It had nothing to do with me. There were other things to keep me occupied. Far more important things.

I closed the door to my room and kneeled on the floor, thinking of nothing at all. For a while, I was still aware of the sounds of the household. Slowly, they faded from my consciousness as I slid into a state of contemplation. Riku had explained to me that my mind was the greatest weapon I possessed.

"Your mind must be focused," he said. "If your thoughts are distracted, how can you expect your body to function as it needs to?"

That made sense. I watched him as he sat cross-legged on the beaten earth of the dojo.

"Sit," he instructed. I slid to the ground in front of him. "What do you hear?"

"The birds singing. The wind."

"What do you see?"

"The sky. Clouds. You, master."

"Close your eyes." I obeyed. "Remember how you felt when I first deprived you of your senses? You were afraid."

I nodded. I had not been afraid—I had been terrified.

"But once you understood it was necessary, the fear left you. Now, you must find that darkness and silence within you again. Close your senses to everything outside you. Be still, within and without."

I stared into space, reaching for tranquility. The transition was so gradual, I barely realized I had left my earthly body behind me until Riku spoke again.

"Your body is asleep," he said softly. "All earthly desires and stimulations are gone. Now, you will fight in your mind. I am moving toward you."

Although I was staring at his body, which remained still as death, my mind told me that he had stood up and was facing me. I, also, was on my feet.

His hand shot out to grasp my robe. I slid away effortlessly and countered with my open hand in his face. There was contact, but I felt nothing. We moved quickly, but I never lost my breath. After an eternity, Riku slid to a halt and bowed deeply to me.

My body jumped as if the earth had moved beneath me. I blinked, surprised to find the sun was fully in my eyes. It had been early morning when we had begun, and the sun had barely been over the horizon. I felt the strangest sensation of something slipping away from me as my mind was forced back into the bondage of my body.

Riku was seated exactly as I had seen him last. "You do not need to divorce your mind from your body each time you fight." He smiled. "You are a good enough warrior to overcome most opponents. You will know yourself when it is necessary, Keiko-chan. And when that day arrives, prepare yourself. Fight your opponent first in your mind. Do it until you are certain that you can anticipate every move they can make. When you can achieve that, you cannot be defeated."

And now that day had come when a worthy opponent was before me. I knew that if Yo won, he would demand that I become his lover. I fully intended that it should happen, but on my terms, not his. I had been practically a slave for every hour of my life so far, dependent on the whims of my father. Whatever happened, I was determined I would never be a slave to any man again. I was onna-bugeisha. If the bargain was on Yo's terms, I was not fit to bear the title with honor. And without it, I would be nothing at all. I was not prepared to let that happen.

With my body and my mind relaxed, tranquility flooded my body. Then, and only then, did I picture Yo in my imagination. We fought in the dojo I knew so well. I saw our battle so many times in my head, each time slightly differently. Finally, I yawned and stretched and eased the crick in my neck. I realized with surprise that I was hungry. When I glanced at the window, I saw dusk was falling. I had sat for the entire day in meditation.

And it was not enough. I was still not confident that I had been the winner of my imaginary contest. And if I could not visualize my victory, then I knew it would not happen. I clapped my hands for food and tea. I ate half a bowl of rice and some pickled vegetables and then lay on my futon and slept. I did not dream of Yo, but of Riku, telling me with a sigh in his voice that I had forgotten something. I puzzled for hours the next day, trying to grasp what I had forgotten, but it would not come. Neither would my mind settle to meditation. I was too on edge, too deep in anticipation.

On the second day, I went to see Emiko. I found my sister brimming with glee.

"Guess what!" she said without preamble as soon as I entered her room. "Reo is back!"

I had often heard the phrase "my blood ran cold," but I had never understood what it meant. At that moment, I did. I was chilled from head to foot. I spoke without thinking about my words.

"Is he? Why are you so pleased? After what he did to you, I would have thought he was the last man on earth you wanted to see."

"Oh, that!" Emiko tossed her lovely head. "It was all a misunderstanding. I see that now. He obviously drew back from me because I was too keen. A sophisticated man like Reo needs to be the one who does the chasing. I've got it all worked out. This time, I'll be indifferent to him. *He* can crawl to *me.*"

"Reo's here? In this house?" The effrontery of the man! How dare he show his face here? No matter. He would be sorry he had ever laid eyes on Emiko, no matter what the silly woman thought she felt for him.

"Well, no. He's not here exactly." Emiko pouted. "He's gone on a hunting party at Akafumu's hunting lodge. Isamu's taken Father's eagle with him to impress Akafumu. I hope Isamu will bring Reo back with him when they've finished playing their games. Reo really is well connected, isn't he?"

Akafumu was our daimyo, our overlord. He was a great noble, close to the shogun himself. And it appeared that Reo knew him. I was delighted. The higher Reo's standing, the sweeter and harder would be his downfall. Once he was stripped of his veneer of iki, even my sister would see him for the shallow idiot he really was. Emiko obviously misunderstood my sudden good humor.

"Such a shame you didn't meet Reo last time he was here. You would have found him charming. And such a handsome man." She glanced at me slyly. "Of course, now that Father has decided to own you as his daughter, he may well introduce you next time he's here."

"I look forward to it," I said wryly. I glanced at her face casually and understood at once I had no need to take care. Her expression was dreamy and far away. It wanted to shake her. It was evident that she had convinced herself that Father could somehow be persuaded to release her from her betrothal to Soji. And when he did, she thought Reo would be waiting for her. For a wild moment, I wondered about the tangled outcome if Emiko did tell Father about her feelings for Reo, only to find her lover backing away in horror when Father confronted him.

Still, her news delighted me, but for no reason she would ever know about. Father was away. I doubted very much that Reo would come back to our estate. The hunting party would surely take at least three days. He would go straight from Akafumu's lodge to his assignation with me in the Floating World.

Which meant I was free to go on with my own plans with no chance of any of my menfolk seeing me. I truly began to believe that the gods were smiling upon me.

SEVENTEEN

Anything may be
Discarded from my life. All
But my memories

*M*y thoughts chased like scraps blown in the wind. I knew it was essential that I achieve tranquility, and that the ability to grasp it was in my mind. But each time I came close, it was gone before I could hold it. The more I told myself to concentrate, the worse it became. And I could no longer even meditate. Perfect peace eluded me.

Tonight, I was to meet Yo, but I wasn't ready! Panic flooded me. I was angry with myself. I had been so sure I would win. My mental state had to be perfect or I might as well not bother at all. I might be as skilled a warrior as Yo, in theory. But I knew he had the edge on me. He had fought when it mattered, when his life was at stake. My skills were excellent, but never had my life depended on using them.

Until now.

I could neither eat nor drink. Nor could I settle on

anything. Matsuo came and nudged my hand. I glanced at him and saw the appeal in his eyes.

"Do you want to go for a walk, Matsuo?" He wagged his tail and I smiled. Why not? It would at least pass the time until my dream of being onna-bugeisha lay in shards at my feet. Until the moment came when I went from being the slave of my family to being Yo's slave. I wondered sadly if anybody in my family would miss me for long, and then was furious with myself yet again for my self-pity. I had walked into this with my eyes open. I deserved no pity from anybody. Especially myself.

Matsuo led me out of the house garden. Every now and then he turned and looked at me, as if making sure I was following him. He finally stopped quite far from the house, at the side of the river that was diverted into smaller channels to water the peasants' paddy fields. At a price, of course. I noticed that the water was very low. In fact, I could not remember ever seeing it so far below the riverbank. Matsuo sat down. I sat beside him and pulled his ears gently.

The flow barely covered the riverbed. Small boulders that I had never seen before caused eddies in the water, forcing it to part with a sweet murmur of sound. I lay my head against Matsuo's coat and felt peace fill me. Lazily, I tried to recall what the river usually looked like. Eventually, I saw it in my mind when it was in full flood. Then, there was no gentle murmur, but a harsh roar as the current pushed fast and hard. White foam topped the water. Occasionally, a brave waterfowl allowed itself to be pushed and shoved by the current. So real was the vision that I stretched out my hand to scoop up some water and blinked in surprise when my fingers met nothing but air.

And at that moment, I remembered what I had forgotten.

I took a deep breath, wondering how I could have been so foolish. Now, it was easy. Of course I had not been confident that I could beat Yo. How could I beat him when I didn't believe it myself? Hadn't Riku explained that to me?

"If you cannot imagine something, Keiko-chan, then it cannot happen. If you can visualize it in your mind, then it will be so. But to do that, you must first believe in yourself. That is your power."

Perhaps it was because I had stopped petting his ears, but Matsuo gave a soft woof and nudged me. I smiled and nodded.

"Shush, Matsuo. I have work to do."

The peace of the river was in my body. I relaxed and once again I was at the dojo. But this time, there was no repetition of punches, no evasions or battle for supremacy. This time, only one scene filled my senses. Yo was on the ground, at my feet. He looked at me and raised both hands, palms out, in surrender.

I had won. My life was mine to do with as I pleased. I was onna-bugeisha, and no man would ever give me an order and expect to be obeyed ever again.

When I came back into my body and conscious thought was gifted back to me, I found tears streaming down my face. Matsuo licked them away for me.

If I could beat Yo in my mind, then I could beat him in the flesh. I no longer had any doubts.

hen it was close to time, I sat quietly on my futon. I listened for the heartbeat of the house, but there was nothing. From far away, I could hear Emiko's soft, even breathing as she slept. Apart from her, everything was silent. I counted down from a hundred and was rewarded by the clatter of the watchman passing my window. I noticed he had acquired a nasty cough. Yet more noise to betray his presence. I stood and stretched.

Emiko had given me a bottle of camellia oil for my birthday. I had used a little on my face, but had found it greasy and the bottle was still almost full. I stripped off my sleeping robe and poured a palmful of the oil into my hand. That went over my shoulders and belly. My legs, also, were smoothed with the oil. It was difficult to reach all of my back without help, but finally I managed it to my satisfaction. I left only my face naked, and that was in case the oil got into my eyes and distracted me. Finally, I tied up my hair. Not in a samurai knot, which might have given Yo the chance to get hold of it, but in the tightest, sleekest knob I could manage. I tugged at it until I made my eyes water in protest, but the pins holding it in place did not give way and my hair was naturally silky enough to make it very difficult to grasp the knot.

There was no moon. No matter, I had no need of light. I made my way to the dojo naked except for a pair of sandals to protect my feet. That was important. It was possible that my future would depend on my agility. I kicked the sandals off at the edge of the dojo and sat cross-legged in the deepest shadow.

I did not see Yo arriving. Nor did I hear him. I sensed movement, and then felt the tremor of air being displaced as he stood in the center of the circle, staring around him.

"Yo-san. I have been waiting for you."

His head moved a fraction in my direction. I felt his surprise, and I realized my stillness had been so complete he had not seen me immediately.

"Keiko-chan. Am I late? I apologize if I am."

"Not at all. I was early." How very polite we were! As if Yo had been invited to take tea.

I stood fluidly and I heard the almost inaudible sound of him taking a sharp breath. I had startled him. Good. I glanced down at my nude body and smiled, but carefully, so there was no light reflecting off my teeth to betray my pleasure.

"Will you take the contest clothed or naked?" I enquired seriously.

"I think that we need to be even." He sounded amused. "If I keep my robe on, then you will win in the first moments."

I was disappointed. He was right, of course. If only I were naked, I would have the advantage. I would have robes to grab and clutch while he would have only flesh. Then I remembered the oil I had rubbed into my skin and I relaxed. My skin was slippery while his would be dry.

Yo moved to the edge of the dojo and shrugged off his robe. It was quickly followed by his fundoshi. I noted that he wore his loincloth in much the same way as sumo wrestlers wore their far more bulky garments and I was quietly pleased. He had come prepared for a genuine fight, then.

His movements were so graceful they were almost feral. A memory came back to me sharply as I watched him.

When Isamu was much younger, he had been given a leopard cat as a present. He had been much taken with the wild creature and had given it a collar set with pearls and had ordered it fed only the best meat, carefully prepared in our kitchen. The wild cat was beautiful to begin with, but day by day, I saw its soul shrivel as it endured captivity. One day, it disappeared, leaving only its jeweled collar behind. Isamu always thought it had tired of captivity and had escaped. He soon forgot his pet, and I never told him that I had taken the cat's collar off and left the way open for him to escape before it was too late. I shivered at the memory. The cat had been beautiful—and wild. Underneath his veneer of civilization, was Yo also wild? I hoped so.

He stood facing me with his hands on his hips. I saw he was inspecting my naked body far more closely than I had looked at his. Excellent, the more I could distract him, the better. I saw that Yo's gaze was resting on my breasts.

I took my chance.

Before he could raise his eyes, I darted forward and seized his arm in a beginner's move. I was hardly surprised when he disengaged himself easily. A moment later, his arms were around my waist. My oiled flesh slid away almost effortlessly. I felt like a fish in the deep sea, confident and swimming in my own element.

Yo rubbed his hands together. "Now why didn't I think of that trick?" He was not at all breathless. His voice was light and easy. I smiled in response.

"Ah, Yo. As a helpless woman, I felt I needed all the advantages I could get," I said humbly.

"My apologies. I should never have considered fighting with you had I known you were no more than a feeble girl."

We both laughed, the banter a nibble before the main course was served.

We circled each other. Yo darted for me. I feinted to one side and almost managed to trip him. After that, he was far more careful. He gripped me around the waist again. He was far stronger than I was. I went limp, but he was not fooled and merely tightened his grip. As he was about to throw me, I wriggled and against his chest. He glanced down reflexively and I banged the crown of my head so hard beneath his chin that I felt the pain in my own skull.

Yo grunted and let me go. I spun on the balls of my feet and kicked out at the back of his knees. Or at least, I kicked at where his legs should have been, but he was no longer there. I turned quickly, guessing he would be behind me. He was not. He seemed to have vanished.

I stood absolutely still. I knew Yo could move like a ghost, in total silence. The night was so dark, there was not even a shadow to betray him. I had a moment of panic. Where was he? How could I fight what I could neither see nor hear? The answer came to me from deep in the instinctual part of my brain. I had no need for any physical senses.

I closed my eyes and deliberately refused to hear. I was deaf and blind. There was no breeze at all, so my sense of smell was effectively gone. I thought I had taken long seconds to close down my senses. It seemed to me that everything around me had slowed. I turned almost languidly, feeling in my gut that Yo was off to my left, perhaps a body's length away. He would come to me, I had no need to search him out. I felt him pause, puzzled by my apparent defenselessness. He shrugged, and I felt the movement. Then he was moving so fast that even if my eyes had been open he would have been no more than a blur of blacker darkness than the night that surrounded him.

I allowed him to come almost close enough to touch me before I stepped aside. The essence of jujutsu is to use one's opponent's strength against him so that the stronger he is, then the greater your advantage. Yo skimmed past me so closely I felt the hairs on his arm brush against me. He was moving so very fast he could not halt himself as quickly as he wanted and almost stumbled. In that tiny fraction of time, I was on him.

I pivoted and caught his wrist, bending his arm so he was forced to spin around. While he was off-balance, I played the ending to my move in my mind. Mentally, I saw his hands reaching for me. Quick as he was, I was quicker still. I swayed to the side, allowing him to skim past me. Once he was moving out of my orbit, I put the palms of my hands in his back and shoved, hooking my foot behind his knee and yanking hard at the same time.

All the time, I had my eyes closed. I watched the movements in my mind and only opened them when I heard Yo grunt. A split second later, I felt the thud of his body as it hit the hard-packed earth of the dojo. Even then, he might have been able to get up and continue with our contest. But I made sure he could not. I swooped down and slid my legs across his belly.

We were both panting. I leaned forward and splayed my fingers around his throat, less to cause him hurt than to emphasize that I was the victor.

"Enough?" I asked.

"Enough. I was foolish, Keiko. I should have believed Riku when he said that the pupil had come to be greater than the master. But if you had been a man, I would have beaten you!"

I laughed in delight. He was probably right. A man would never have thought to oil his body. Nor would Yo ever have been distracted by the sight of another man's nakedness. I didn't care. I had won. That was all that mattered.

"Will you allow me to rise, mistress?" Yo asked quietly.

I heard his words, and a little of my delight ebbed away. I had a sudden memory of our amah—our nursemaid—

reprimanding Emiko gently. My older sister had always been spoiled, always utterly sure that she was going to get her own way. Our amah had doted on her and had only ever chastised her in the mildest possible terms. Her favorite reproof had been, "Be careful what you long for. You may get it." Emiko had never taken any notice of her. She had simply tossed her head and sighed in exasperation, telling the poor amah she was talking nonsense. Even at such a young age, I had longed to look the same as everybody else, and no matter how I thought over the amah's wise words, I couldn't see that there was anything at all wrong with wanting to look normal. For once, I agreed with Emiko. In fact, it wasn't until I heard Yo speak to me in a voice that acknowledged he was mine to command that I understood that our amah had been right after all.

It had seemed the most important thing in my world that I should beat Yo. That only by doing so would I finally be free. Now, here he was—literally at my feet—asking my permission to rise.

And I hated it.

Perhaps it was because I had been a slave myself. Perhaps it was because I remembered how Isamu's leopard cat had languished in captivity. I didn't really know. All I knew was that I had no desire to have Yo as my slave. I wanted a man who was my equal.

I stood and held my hand out to him.

EIGHTEEN

> Ropes can fetter my
> Body, but nothing made by
> Man can bind my soul

*Y*o grasped my hand. It was so slippery with oil and sweat from our exertions that it almost slid from his grip. His fingers entwined in mine, and instead of allowing me to help him to his feet, he pulled me down to the earth at his side.

"Have you forgotten your beating already, Yo?" I teased. I was oddly breathless. I had not been short of breath at all during our contest.

"I have forgotten nothing, *mistress*," he said slyly. "I am at your command. That was our bargain, and I will keep to it."

My breath juddered in my throat. "Until today, it was I who was the slave." The words stuck and I cleared my throat with a cough. "Now, I am free. I would never make anybody else a slave. Like me, you're free. Go. Stay. It's up to you."

I thought again of Isamu's leopard cat. It had seemed to me that he had paused, balanced delicately, and given me a fleeting glance of gratitude before he took his chance and fled. Would Yo do the same? Would the lure of freedom be too much for him to refuse? I could hardly blame him if it were. Yet my stomach clenched painfully at the thought.

"You are truly an honorable samurai, Keiko. You have all the virtues of the bushido tradition," Yo said quietly.

I bowed my head, both to acknowledge the compliment and to hide my bitter disappointment. He had accepted my offer, then. He would go and—like the leopard cat—I would never see him again. It could hardly be otherwise. The loss of face would be far too great for him.

"You have given me the gift of choice. For that, I thank you. But you must know there is no choice at all for me. I cannot leave you. Not now, not ever, unless you tell me to go."

We were two shadows, whispering of things that would decide our fates for the rest of our lives—and who knew how many lives that were yet to come—in a night that was so dark we could not even see each other. I spoke without thought from the heart.

"You are free, Yo. Just as I am now free. If we are to be together, it has to be from choice and for no other reason."

"I love you." Yo's words were the barely felt breath of the wind on a still night. I closed my eyes so I could taste his voice. It was sweet in my mouth, and I knew he meant it. Nobody in my entire life had ever told me that they loved me before. I swallowed his words and kept them safe in my belly. "I ached to see you when Riku told me about you. Even then, I hoped you would be the woman I had been looking for ever since I was old enough to understand what love really was. I have taken many women, Keiko. Some of them have tried to keep me by their side, but I knew they were not right for me. Always, I walked away sooner rather than later so their hurt would be less when I had gone. As soon as I saw you, I felt you in my gut. Neither my mind or my body would forget you."

"But you waited. Why didn't you seek me out sooner?" I asked. I had to be sure. My life had seen so much pain, joy was foreign to me and I could barely bring myself to trust his words. I was not jealous that he had taken women before, but I did need to be certain that I was not going to be only one more among their number.

"I had to be sure that it was right," he said simply. I smiled, pleased that our thoughts were the same. "I knew that I wanted you. I knew that you called to me in a way that no other woman ever has. But when I found out you were samurai, I hesitated. I am shinobi. You told me yourself that I am less than nothing." I winced at my own words.

"So, I agonized, wondering if it would be better if I never revealed myself to you. I convinced myself that it was useless and that I would be less hurt if I never gave you the chance to reject me."

"Why did you change your mind?" I asked. My voice was steady and betrayed nothing of the emotions that were making my senses reel.

"When I saw you in the Floating World, I knew that you felt my presence. I am shinobi. If I do not want to be known, I am invisible and silent. But you knew I was there. That convinced me to speak. We are kindred spirits in a world that will never understand us. We are apart from everybody else. That was why I came to you. I was sure, finally. I couldn't wait any longer. Please, tell me you feel the same? That you can come to love me as much as I love you?"

I felt Yo staring at me intently, waiting for my reply. The

tender words seemed to have come easily to him, but I was bewildered; I had no response. The most affection I had ever received until that moment had come from our amah, who had assured me kindly that one day I would find somebody who would not compare me with my beautiful sister, but instead would value my loving heart. I longed to respond to him, to express my feelings, but I could not. I stared at his outline in the dark and wanted to cry with frustration. Finally, I reached out and touched his cheek, running my finger down to his mouth.

I gave a wordless cry as he parted his lips and took the very tip of my finger between his teeth. I put my other hand in front of my own lips, as if I could pluck the right words from where they lurked in my mouth. But I could not. Even though my body screamed "I love you!" I could not bring myself to say the words out loud. How could I? I had no idea what love really was. Was the tumult of emotions that boiled inside me love or desire or—and I shuddered at the thought—simply gratitude that Yo had declared himself to me? I shook my head helplessly.

I was astonished when Yo took my hand away from his lips and laced his fingers in mine. He spoke gently, as if he understood my hesitation. "Keiko, do you feel anything for me? I have known you far longer than you have known me. Do you want time to think? Shall I leave you alone to see how you truly feel?"

"No!" I cried out the single word in anguish. "No. Don't leave me. I don't want that. I..." I shook my head in deep frustration. Why was it so very difficult to say three simple words?

"I understand," he said softly. "I saw you with Isamu. I have seen you with your sister, as well. You walk with them, but you are not part of their world. You have a beauty and a spirit they can't comprehend, and because of that, you worry them. That's why they keep you apart from them. That will never happen with us, Keiko. You are more than just a woman of flesh and blood. You said I was a legend. Do you not understand that you are also part of that legend? The gods meant us for each other." He let go of my palm and kissed it softly. "I love you. More than that, I need you."

He paused. I knew he was waiting for me, but still, the words would not come. I was going to try and explain, to tell him that my emotions had been buried for too long to allow me to open myself to him.

"I love you," I blurted. I was astonished at myself. My lips had said the words for me. "I love you," I repeated with astonished passion.

I thought the earth was shaking beneath me, then I realized it was I who was trembling. I stayed still and mute with amazement as Yo reached out and traced the line of my breast with his thumb. His touch was delicate, but it aroused me so that I drew in a shocked breath. I put my hand over his fingers, not to take it away, but to enclose his hand around my breast. He squeezed, quite gently. The sensation was delightful.

Although I could not see his face, I sensed Yo was watching me intently. I had no need to tell him what I liked; he would know. The knowledge was intensely exciting. Reluctantly, I plucked his hand from my breast, but only so that I could lie down. The earth was very hard beneath my body, but I was as comfortable as if it was the softest futon.

Yo lay beside me and I tensed. I might be able to control my body in combat, but this was unknown. And every living thing fears what it does not know. I thought quickly of Emiko, disappointed in Reo's lovemaking. Would I be the same?

"Don't be afraid. Nothing we do together could be less than wonderful." Yo was smiling. I heard it in his words. I melted, opening my hands in invitation.

He leaned forward and kissed me. I almost gasped aloud with shock. Never—not even in Choki's shunga pillow book—had I seen men and women kiss. Yo paused for a heartbeat and then slid his tongue between my lips. His breath was in my mouth, his tongue pushing gently and firmly until he made contact with my own tongue. He flirted delicately with it, flicking back and forth like a snake tasting the air. I relaxed and began to savor the sensation. Daringly, I responded, caressing his lips with my tongue. My mouth felt very cold when he took his head away. I would have pulled him back, but he was following the line of my neck with his lips, and the sensation was increasingly delicious.

"All women can enchant their men if they choose to," Yo whispered. "Very few women understand that. And fewer still do it from love rather than the desire for power."

I raised my eyes to his face. There had been neither moon nor stars when we had begun our combat. Why, then, was the dojo now illuminated in the softest of glows? I sat back, astonished, and realized that the glow was from a multitude of hotaru that had made their home in the trees that sheltered the dojo. Although each firefly was tiny, together their pulsing light was astonishing. I knew that many people kept these tiny creatures in special cages, treating them as pets for the short time they lived. I had always hated the idea. Now, I wondered if these fireflies had chosen to illuminate our lovemaking in gratitude that I had never imprisoned them.

"So beautiful!" I whispered.

"Not as beautiful as you, Keiko-chan."

I threw my head back and laughed with delight. "You are the only person who has ever called me beautiful. And the only person who has ever said they loved me."

"Then everybody else who has ever known you has been either blind or so jealous of you that they wanted to hurt you," he said superbly.

Yo propped himself on his elbows and ran his tongue down the side of my face, pressing kisses into the space above my shoulder bones. His arms went around my neck and his lips found my mouth.

"What would please you?" he mumbled, his words muffled by my lips. "For tonight, I am yours to command. Tell me, what will give you very great pleasure?"

"I don't know," I moaned. "Anything. Everything. Show me what I want."

My words made little sense to me, but Yo seemed to understand instinctively. He rolled me off of him so that I lay on my back on the earth. As soon as his body broke contact, my skin felt so very cold. I reached out to pull him back, but he captured my hands and shook his head.

"If you don't know, then I will show you." He sounded so confident that my worries died a little. I watched his face in the unearthly glow from my friends the fireflies and held my breath. Last time we had met, I had thought him a spirit rather than a man. Bathed in the flickering, living light that was all around us, I wondered again. He touched my face with a single finger, his expression full of wonder, and I knew suddenly that he was looking at me in exactly the same way.

I spread my arms wide, inviting him to me. There was a fire in my belly that made me wonder if I was truly going to melt.

But Yo was not going to be hurried.

My mind whirled. My entire body was alive and vibrating with desire. I gasped, my mouth opening and closing without words. I arched against him, desperate to have him as close to me as I could force him. He lay against me, his lithe body quivering, taut as a strung bow on top of me.

"Keiko." Just my name, but it was spoken with love. I opened my mouth wide and howled with pleasure. He slid inside me suddenly and I was still, transfixed between longing and wonder that I had been able to take him into my body with such ease.

I felt something mounting deep inside my body and I pushed frantically against Yo as the need became irresistible. There was a sudden sensation of heat and wetness in my sex and I knew with blind instinct that Yo had burst his fruit inside me. While his tree still pulsed with life, my body exploded in my own yonaki. My toes curled so fiercely that they gripped the earth beneath my feet. My hands were on Yo's back, and I gouged my nails into his sweet flesh. My mouth fell open in a soundless scream. My pleasure peaked, the sensation ebbing slowly until I could contain it and savor the aftershocks that jerked my body. Yo stayed inside me all the time, his tree hard, until I fell back and let him go.

We lay side by side on our bed of earth. I could hear the fireflies pulsing. Smell the scent of pines on the flicker of breeze that fanned our bodies tenderly. Lazily, I turned my head and licked the sweat from Yo's shoulder. I thought it the finest taste I had ever known.

In Japanese, the word for orgasm—yonaki—means cries in the night. I had always thought the word slightly absurd. Now, I no longer thought so. My body was relaxed, and yet at the same time alert. Yo moved slightly, and my body missed him at once.

"Will it always be as wonderful as that?" I asked. I knew it was a naïve question, and yesterday I would have hesitated to ask it for fear of appearing foolish. Tonight, it was my right to know. The self-knowledge was joyous.

"No." Yo was smiling. I could feel it in the slight movement of his shoulder muscles. "It will get better. As we get to know each other physically, and we both learn exactly what is good for each other, enjoying each other's bodies will become heavenly."

Better than this? I thought. Something to look forward to!

We lay together until I noticed the light from the fireflies began to dim. I propped myself on one elbow and was astonished to find that dawn was lightening the sky.

"I know, you must go," Yo said. "I must be on my way as well. I have a certain business to see to in Sendai. I don't want to go, but I gave my word, so I must honor it. Will you come with me?"

"I can't." I closed my eyes and sighed. I sensed Yo staring at me. I wondered if he would speak, question my response, but he did not. He simply waited for me to explain to him. "Like you, I have some unfinished business. And like you, I can't just let it go. How long will you be in Sendai?"

"I don't know for sure. It depends on how things go." He paused, and I wanted to demand to know what he was doing in Sendai. Who was he working for? Was it dangerous for him? But Yo had treated me as his equal; he had not questioned my "unfinished business." I could do what he had for me and I remained silent, waiting for him to finish. "It could be a few days. It might be a good deal longer. I'm sorry I can't be more specific."

"As long as you come back for me, it doesn't matter. I'll be here for you," I said.

"I will come." Yo hesitated, and I understood he was searching for the right words. "Your unfinished business, is there danger in it for you? Can it wait until I come back and we can face it together?"

I was silent. During my training, Isamu had often spoken of the honor of the samurai. Of the importance of adhering to the code of bushido. But he had never explained to me *why* it was so important. He seemed to think I would understand that without being told. I did not, and eventually I had become bored with the repetitions and had closed my ears to it. Now, I understood. Bushido was the samurai tradition. It was more than just a code, it was a way of life. And Yo was bound to follow his own tradition, the way of the shinobi. He wanted to stay with me, but he could not. I looked at his face and saw the conflict in his eyes. He was being torn apart.

"There's no danger at all for me," I lied cheerfully. "Don't worry. It's just that...a promise should never be given lightly. It has to be fulfilled. And I gave my word."

The worry melted from his face and he smiled. He leaned forward and kissed my mouth. I was aroused by the simplest of contact with him and clenched my hands into fists to stop myself from grabbing for him.

"I shall come back as soon as I can. I'll wait until your noisy watchman has passed by and then I'll tap on your shoji. Will you let me in?"

I pretended to think about it, pursing my lips in a frown. "Oh, if I'm not so deeply asleep I don't hear you, I suppose I will."

Yo smiled at me. He gathered up his fundoshi and

knotted it quickly, pulling on his robe over the top. Every movement was so fluid, it was a joy to watch.

"Take great care, Keiko. I promise we'll watch the fireflies dance again as soon as I come back. And then, we'll face the world together."

He walked away from me with neither another word nor a backward glance. I sat for a while longer, wondering at the ways of fate. Yesterday, I had never known a man. Today, I knew what it was to be filled with the consummate pleasure of accepting my lover into my body. My lover! I took a deep, shuddering breath at the thought. I sighed and pulled my own clothes on. At the last moment, I remembered my hair was still tightly bound up, so I unpinned it quickly, bundling it back up loosely in case any of the servants saw me and wondered at the strangeness of my appearance.

I had no need to worry. I was back in my own room before anybody else—except Matsuo, who greeted me with an anxious whine—stirred. Reluctantly, I went to the bathhouse. There was no maid awake to rinse and soap me, so I did it myself. It was only when I slid into the steaming water that I realized that my mind might be totally relaxed, but my body was not. My muscles were knotted and tight, both from the combat and the night spent on the hard ground. I moaned aloud with pleasure as the hot water seeped into my joints. I sloshed my legs around lazily and yelped as the heat penetrated into my black moss, making my sex smart angrily.

"Oh, Yo, what have you done to me?" I said softly. But there was no reply, not even in my own mind.

I was climbing out of the bath when a thought stopped me with one foot lifted to the step. Yo had asked me to go with him, and I had agreed. But I had no idea where we were going. What had I committed the rest of my life to?

The idea was so liberating, I threw my head back and laughed out loud. The sound of my amusement echoed around the bathhouse, bouncing off the walls and seeming to cause the water to ripple. I only realized how loudly I was laughing when one of the maids poked her head timidly around the door and watched at me silently with astonished eyes.

NINETEEN

Your hand reached to me
But I did not take it. Do
I wish that I had?

Somebody was shaking my shoulder, quite hard. I awoke from my sleep joyfully, delighted that Yo had returned so quickly. I reached for the hand on my shoulder and grasped it with pleasure.

"Keiko, for the gods' sakes, wake up. I need to talk to you."

Not Yo at all. Emiko. I sighed my disappointment and then stretched and yawned. The sun was bright through my window. My bath had made me realize how exhausted I was and I had taken to my futon happily. And now Emiko was waking me after no more than perhaps a couple of hours of sleep.

"What is it? Is the house on fire? Is it raining fish?" I said jokingly. Then my eyes focused on Emiko's face and all desire to laugh faded. My lovely sister had been crying. Emiko cried often, usually when she was denied her own way. But she usually cried beautifully. She had this knack of allowing tears to trickle down her cheeks woefully while her eyes grew larger and more luminous. Even Father could never stay angry with her when she cried. But today, her eyes were rimmed with red and her mouth was screwed up as if she was in pain. "Emiko! What is it! What's happened?"

"I came to talk to you hours ago, but you weren't here." Emiko's lips trembled. "I couldn't believe even you had deserted me, sister. It was nearly the middle of the night and your futon hadn't been slept in. Where were you?"

I thought quickly and lied so easily I surprised myself. "I was wide awake for some reason, so I went into the garden and watched the fireflies." That part at least was true. "I must have nodded off on the bench. When I woke up, it was nearly dawn and I went to the bathhouse. That's why my futon wasn't disturbed. But never mind that, what's the matter? What is it?"

"Father." Emiko gulped on a sob.

I stared at her in fear. "Father? What about him? Has something happened to him?" My pulse raced. Father had taken ill, perhaps even died while I had been pleasuring myself with Yo? Common sense told me there was nothing I could have done, but my conscience screamed at me. "Emiko, what's happened to him?"

"Nothing!" Emiko almost shouted at me. "There's nothing wrong with him. I never said there was. It's me!"

I almost panted with relief. It was always "me" with Emiko. "Calm down," I said gently. "Explain things to me. You said it was Father. Now, you say it's you. Tell me."

Emiko pouted. Her tears had made her ugly. My heart went out to her as I understood that my lovely sister had nothing apart from her beauty, and that today her beauty was gone and she had been left with nothing at all. I opened my arms and she fell against me, her head against my shoulder. I stroked her hair and made soothing noises, as if I were the elder sister. It was her acceptance of my comfort that made me understand that something was very wrong. Usually Emiko drew back from my touch as if she might be contaminated by my ugliness.

"Tell me," I coaxed. "What's happened? Is Father back early? Have you had another argument with him?"

"No. He sent me a note. Just a note, Keiko. He didn't even bother to come home and tell me himself. I think that hurt almost as much as anything." Her voice choked to a standstill. Bewildered, I carried on stroking her hair, waiting for her to go on. "He says I'm going to marry Soji. He saw Soji's father yesterday, and they've both agreed on everything. The ceremony will take place as soon as is proper. It could be as early as next month. What am I going to do, Keiko?"

Is that what all this fuss is about? The words trembled on my lips. Then Emiko shook with more sobs and I chose my words carefully.

"That's sooner than you expected, for sure," I said cautiously. "But you've been betrothed to Soji since you were both children. I know you're not happy about taking him for a husband, but I thought you were resigned to it."

"I was. Or at least I thought so." Emiko had had enough of my comfort. She sat away from me and rubbed her hands over her face in a gesture charmingly like a child wiping away its woes. "But that was before Reo came back."

She was smiling through her tears. I spoke very cautiously.

"But Reo hasn't come back, has he? He's gone hunting with Isamu. You're clutching at broken reeds, Emiko."

"No, I'm not." She tossed her head, her mouth sulky.

"You're just jealous that a high-caste, sophisticated man like Reo would find me so madly attractive. Father's not the only one who sent me a note. Reo wrote to me as well. He's terribly upset that everything went wrong between us. He says he was horrified that he had allowed his overwhelming attraction for me overcome him to the extent that he had behaved dishonorably to me, and he has been out of his mind with worry since. He wants to meet with me privately. He says he'll come here to see me before Isamu and Father get back."

Emiko preened. I itched to slap her, to knock the gloating expression off her face. The sheer arrogance of the man! He intended to take me first, and then sneak back in for another go at my sister. I gave thanks that Emiko had never mentioned her hopes for him to Father. I spoke bluntly, hoping to force some sense into that lovely, empty head.

"And what do you think he wants to see you privately for? If he had any honor at all, he would be on his knees in front of Father, begging him to allow you to become his wife. No mention of that in his note, I suppose?"

Suddenly, I wondered if Emiko's note had been written by the very same calligrapher as mine. The idea made me almost tremble with fury.

"Forget him. He's not iki at all. He's a nasty, selfish, sneaking dasha kusai—a country bumpkin—with no more honor than a mongrel sniffing around a bitch in heat because he can't find a woman. If Isamu finds out, you won't be marrying Soji, you'll be in a monastery, and that's if you're lucky."

Emiko looked at me, her mouth dropping open. Sounds bubbled from between her lips, but no words. I was immediately sorry for my outburst. Emiko was Emiko. She had been spoiled the whole of her life. Was it really so surprising that she thought the world was hers to command?

"I'm sorry," I said quickly. "That was unforgivable of me. But you can't throw Soji aside for Reo. You just can't."

I almost told her then that I, too, was waiting for an assignation with Reo. Surely that, if nothing else, would bring her to her senses. I looked at her pouting, trembling mouth and sighed. What was the point? If I told her the truth, she would never believe me. Knowing Emiko, she would instantly decide I was making it up because I was jealous.

My thoughts spun madly. Father might have been willing to at least consider the union if the request had come from Reo. If Emiko dared to mention his name to Father, the first thing he would do would be to approach Reo—delicately of course—and ask him what his intentions were. And I had no doubt at all what Reo's response would be. A man of his status would never consider marriage to a girl who was not a virgin, not even if *he* had been the one to deflower her outside of marriage. But of course, Emiko would never see that.

I thought I had spoken reasonably. Emiko obviously didn't see it that way.

"You're just jealous. And stupid. You're as bad as Father," she spat. "You don't understand anything at all. Reo loves me. And I love him. If I can't marry him, then I'll go as his concubine, his number two wife. As long as I'm with him, that's all that matters."

"Emiko, no! You can't," I said urgently. "Think of the disgrace. Soji would either have to kill Reo or commit suicide himself. He couldn't live with the disgrace if you ran off to be Reo's concubine. Just think for a minute." I was now the one clutching at broken reeds, but I had to try.

"If you marry Soji, you can have the best of all worlds. You know he's besotted with you. Marry him next month and you can take Reo as your lover if that's what you truly want. I just know Soji would turn a blind eye to you having an affair if he thought it was making you happy. He's truly a good man."

Even as I tried to coax Emiko to see sense, I knew I was shouting into an empty cave. Would any woman really want to marry a man who would give his blessing to her taking a lover? And what would it be like to be caressed by your husband when your heart and soul were with another man? I shuddered at the thought. If the object of her love had been anybody but Reo, I might have even sympathized with her. But Reo was a nauseating, shallow, sneaking snake of a man. She deserved much better.

"You think so?" Emiko's voice was ugly. "You really think Soji's a nice man? I'm sure you're right in that he wouldn't mind me taking a lover at all. But not to make *me* happy."

"What are you talking about?" Emiko's expression was sly, and I was puzzled.

"Soji. You've always been half in love with him, haven't you?"

I shrugged. Before Yo had come into my life, I would have agreed with her. Now, Soji was nothing to me but the pleasant memory of small courtesies bestowed with a smile. Emiko frowned at me and I wondered if my thoughts showed clearly on my face. But she had never been one to notice anything that didn't concern her and she went on quickly.

"You always did think he was wonderful and that he could do no wrong. Well, it's *you* that's been wrong all along. He's not a nice man at all. In fact, he's not even a man."

"What?" I was bewildered.

"I saw him, Keiko." Emiko lowered her voice. "When he was here for Father's birthday celebrations last month. I saw him and Isamu. Together. In the bath."

I shrugged. "So? Everyone bathes together on occasion. We only have one bathhouse."

"You don't understand." Emiko wiped her lips with the back of her hand. It looked as if she was trying to rub away a foul taste. "I thought the bath was empty. I pushed the door open and I was going to call for a maid to get me ready when I saw them. They didn't see me, either of them. Oh no! They were far too busy with each other for that. Soji was facing the wall, with his hands on the side of the bath. Isamu was behind him. Our brother was mounting him, Keiko."

"No! You must have been mistaken, Emiko." I almost laughed at the absurdity of it.

"No, I wasn't." Emiko spoke flatly, with none of her usual drama. "I was so shocked, I just stood and watched for a moment. Isamu was splitting the melon with him. He pulled back so far, his tree almost came out, and Soji begged him not to stop. 'Harder, Isamu,' he said. 'Do it harder. I want to feel you inside me. Hurt me, please. Hurt me. Make me scream with pain.' Neither of them noticed me. They were too busy giving each other pleasure. I snuck out and stayed away until I was sure they had left the bath. Even if Reo hadn't come along, I promise you, I would never accept Soji as my husband after that."

She stared at me, her reddened eyes stony. I said nothing. I remembered Isamu calling Soji a milksop. There had been something strange in his voice when he had said it, something I had not understood at the time. Now, I wondered. Could it have been tenderness? I rather thought it had been.

Emiko was staring at me, waiting for me to respond. I felt an unexpected flood of pity for her. Poor Emiko. I was suddenly glad that I had not told her of Reo's interest in me —or rather, in the youth Jun.

"Well, I can understand why that must have been difficult for you," I said finally. "But it's not so unusual, is it? I mean, everybody knows about the way of wakashudo. Many samurai take a younger man as their protégé, and often they become lovers. But it doesn't stop them from marrying and having a family. I mean, you would hardly call Isamu effeminate, would you?"

"Not Isamu, no," Emiko said. "Although I have wondered why it's taking him so long to marry Himari. And you don't need to bother telling me that a lot of men like to enjoy themselves with men and women both. I understand that. But Soji's different. He's never so much as touched me, you know. All these years and he's never laid a finger on me. I thought it was respect. Now I know it is because he doesn't desire me. Not at all. If I wanted to arouse him, I would have to dress as a man and probably poke my sword up his behind."

I winced. If only Emiko knew how close she was to the truth, not just about Soji, but about Reo as well. At least— unlike Soji, apparently—Reo was also interested in women. But would my lovely, spoiled sister ever truly be willing to accept a husband who only gave her half his attention? The irony of it gave me no comfort at all.

"I don't know what to say. I'm sorry, Emiko," I replied awkwardly.

"I wouldn't mind so much about Soji if he were interested in women as well as men," she said sadly, almost as if I had spoken my thoughts aloud. "As you say, wakashudo is an ancient and honorable tradition. Isamu obviously thinks so anyway. But I'm sure from seeing them together that it isn't wakashudo at all with Soji. I think he's in love with Isamu. He probably has been for years. That's why he's so pleased about marrying me. It'll mean he can be closer to Isamu. Oh, it's such a mess. But you understand now, don't you? You see why I can't marry Soji? You were always the clever one, Keiko. You'll help me find a way out of it, won't you?"

Emiko pawed at my arm. Her hands were perhaps the only thing about her that weren't truly beautiful. They were rather large, and the veins on the back of them were very prominent. I stared at the hand that was clutching me and knew with a flash of pity that when she was old and her beauty had deserted her, Emiko would have nothing. Whereas I, the ugly, despised younger sister, would still have everything that mattered. Honor. A purpose in life. And—ironically—a man who considered me his equal, no matter what the ravages the years bestowed on me.

"I will help you, Emiko," I said quietly.

She was immediately happy, rubbing her eyes briskly and patting at her hair. "I knew you would think of something," she said cheerfully.

I already knew the answer. But it was not something I was about to share with Emiko. Suddenly, I was looking forward to my tryst with Reo even more.

TWENTY

> You ask, how deep is
> The sea? On the beach, only
> As deep as my toes

*I*samu had commented that the Floating World was a city of the night that never knew sleep. I saw clearly that he was right when I returned there. The day was hovering on the edge of dusk when I arrived at the waterless moat and handed my mare's bridle to the hovering groom. Although it was perhaps a little quieter than when I had first arrived, noise still spilled out through the main gate. The Floating World was alive and awake and looking forward to the evening as no doubt it did every day. And every night.

I was early. Reo had said he would meet me at the time of four bells. That was still some ways off. My excitement had been too great for me to eat during the day, and now I was thirsty and beginning to be hungry. I shouldered my way through the crowds and stepped inside the first teahouse I came to. It was nothing as elegant as Hana's

Green Teahouse, but the food smelled savory and I was glad to accept a plate of hot noodles laced with ginger and tuna and a steaming cup of tea. I ate with a good appetite, concentrating on my food, and I was astonished when a woman's voice interrupted me.

"Good appetite, my lord." I glanced at my side and found a yujo hovering, her fan flirtatiously before her face. She was quite young, and from what I could see of her eyes and smooth skin, I thought that she was probably pretty. "I don't think I've seen you here before. And surely I would have remembered such a handsome nobleman as you."

She sat down on the bench opposite me uninvited and folded her fan. I had been right. If she hadn't been wearing so much paint, she would have been very pretty.

"I'm afraid you're mistaken." I pitched my voice as low as I could manage. It tickled and I wanted to cough. "I have been here often, but I am a mere younger son of an unimportant samurai family, not a lord."

She assessed my—or rather Isamu's—robes cynically. As the sky was overcast, I had borrowed not only a kimono, but also one of Isamu's *kataginu*, a long sleeveless jacket worn over the top of the kimono. Like all of his clothes, they were sober in color but superbly elegant in cut and quality. Her hard eyes calculated the cost of my robes to the last coin. Obviously satisfied, she smiled broadly at me.

"Well, no matter. I can see you're on your own, good sir. My name is Effet." She put her head on one side, watching me to see if I appreciated the pun. "Effet" means virtue or chastity. Clearly, this was a yujo of some wit and not a little intelligence as her name was not only the opposite of her profession but intended to signal that she was clean and wholesome. Had I truly been a man, I thought I would have enjoyed spending the evening with her. "Would the honorable samurai perhaps welcome my company, if he is not already committed?"

"Alas, Effet. I'm bound to meet a friend at Hana's Teahouse."

Although her face remained impassive, her eyebrows rose in a clear signal of surprise. "Indeed, my lord. Well, I'm sure Hana's geisha will enchant your evening." She smiled archly. "Of course, in the unlikely event that Hana doesn't recommend further entertainment for you later, I can be found at the teahouse at the intersection of the Namida-Bashin. Perhaps I may hope to see you there later?"

"Perhaps," I said non-committedly. Effet rose gracefully, and, in spite of the fact that several men were looking at her with interest, she drifted out of the teahouse without so much as a glance at them. I finished my tea in great content. Surely if such an experienced inhabitant of the Floating World as Effet hadn't seen through my disguise, then neither would Reo. Or at least, not until I wanted him to know the truth.

The bells were sounding as I made my way to the teahouse. Hearing them, I stopped short and searched the street for Reo. For a moment, I was disappointed. I could not see him anywhere. Had he decided not to show? Had Isamu, deciding the joke had gone far enough, told him the truth? My spirits sank. I was about to turn away when my arm was grabbed.

"Jun! So punctual! You have no idea how I have looked forward to tonight. I have been out of town, hunting with Isamu these last few days, and I was tempted to ask him where I could find you so I could contact you and make sure you had not forgotten me."

I suddenly understood why Emiko found him so attractive. They were very alike. Just like her, Reo's thoughts were on himself to the exclusion of all else. It must have been rather like looking in a mirror at her own reflection. I stared at Reo silently. He was, I supposed, a handsome man in a flashy, flamboyant sort of way. Iki? No. Isamu was iki. Reo was too overblown, too in love with himself to be genuinely iki.

It was clear that Reo had mistaken my silent contemplation of him for delight that we were together. He smiled broadly and stroked me quite tenderly under my chin.

"Dear child, are you still holding to your vow of silence? Surely not. At least, do tell me how much you're pleased to see me."

"Of course I am delighted to be here with you, Reo." I spoke softly, trying to make my voice as husky as I could. "Shall we go straight to the teahouse?"

He grasped my arm as if he thought I might want to get away from him. I wasn't surprised. I wanted to put as much distance between us as I could. Reo glanced at me questioningly, and I smiled—I hoped flirtatiously. Did men handle these things differently from us women? I had no idea, and little time to find out. He grinned back and suddenly pulled me out of the road and flattened both of us against the wall of a shop. I set my teeth, thinking he had decided to taste my delights before we had even reached our destination.

I couldn't have been more wrong.

"Keep back." Reo put his arm across me protectively. I wondered if he would feel my breasts, but he was clearly so agitated he didn't even notice them. "If they touch us, we may be contaminated by them. Who knows what illnesses they carry on them. Judging by the way they stink, it could be anything."

Reo jutted his chin to the road in front of us. I had been so surprised by what I saw as his sudden attack that I had not noticed that what passed for silence in the Floating World had fallen on the street. Voices had suddenly become muted, and even the food vendors had ceased to cry their wares. Just like us, the crowds had pressed to the sides, leaving an empty channel in their midst. I stared in the direction he was indicating and saw two men walking our way. They walked casually, as if they barely noticed—and cared even less—about the sensation they were causing.

"Who are they?" I asked in astonishment.

My first thought had been that some great lord must be passing amongst us. A man so noble that the crowd had scattered before him. But these men were no lords. They were like no men I had ever seen before, and I stared at them with amazement.

Both were very tall. Far taller than Isamu, and he was a tall man. They were correctly dressed in robes made of good quality silk, but it was evident that they were not entirely comfortable in them. The way they walked was all wrong, and every few steps, one or the other of them plucked at their skirts as if they were getting in the way of their stride. I almost smiled as I saw their discomfort, but the smile faded to horror as they passed in front of a flaming torch and I saw their faces clearly.

In the torchlight, their hair looked so fair it was almost colorless. And both had hair on their faces! It made me itch just to look at it. And almost worse, their poor eyes were so misshapen, I wondered if they could actually see. Obviously they could, as they strode forward with apparent disregard for the way everybody else drew back from them. One of them glanced in our direction as they passed by, and he nudged his companion with his elbow. The other man looked at Reo and me and grinned widely before closing one eye deliberately. I was bewildered. Courtesy made me wait until they were unlikely to hear me before I began to question Reo about the exotic strangers. It didn't take long. The crowds closed behind them as they passed by. The entire incident took only a couple of heartbeats, but it left me gasping to know more.

Oddly, it reminded of the one time I had been allowed to accompany Father and Isamu when they went on a journey to inspect our estate. I couldn't remember why I had been allowed to go with them. Was it so Emiko would have somebody to chat with? Or had Isamu simply decided to be kind to me? No matter. Father and Isamu had traveled on horseback, with their retainers in front and behind them. Emiko and I followed behind the retainers in a palanquin. Our curtains were closed, of course, but we both peeked out from time to time. Emiko had quickly become bored with the unchanging scenery, but I had continued to look. This was my first glimpse of anything beyond our garden and the orchards that enclosed the house, and everything was of interest to me. The journey had long been forgotten, but the sight of the strangers awoke it vividly. In just the same way as the crowd had drawn back from them, their eyes cast down and their voices stilled, had the peasants drawn back from our procession whenever we went through a village. Wherever there was more room—on the roadside or when we passed fields where the peasants were working—the villagers hadn't just bowed, they had prostrated themselves full length on the ground. It had intrigued me, and I had pointed it out to Emiko.

"Father must be a very important man," I said timidly. "The peasants treat him as if he is a god."

Emiko looked at me as if I was mad. "Of course they do. He has the power of life and death over them. If he thought they weren't civil enough, he could have them executed."

This seemed extremely harsh to me, and I was stupid enough to say so.

"Oh, don't be so childish." My sister sighed at my ignorance. "That's the way it is. They're just peasants. They breed like animals, so one more or less isn't going to make a difference to anybody. Father is their lord. They owe him everything. And anyway, he's very merciful to them. All samurai are allowed to test the sharpness of their swords on any peasant they like if it pleases them to do it. Father and Isamu are both so enlightened that they say that's barbaric and would never do it. These people know when the gods have smiled on them. That's why they love and respect Father so much."

One of our bearers stumbled slightly at that moment, and Emiko was so busy shouting at him for his clumsiness that she forgot what we had been talking about.

The recollection came back to me now, vividly. I had thought at the time of our journey that there was no love at all in the villagers' behavior, simply fear. And that was why I remembered it now. Everybody the strangers had passed by had drawn back because they were terrified of the two men, just as they had done when our procession had gone through the countryside. I was intrigued.

"Who were they, Reo?" I demanded again. Reo drew himself erect nonchalantly, but I was not fooled at all. He had been as worried by the two men as everybody else in the Floating World.

"They're gaijin," he said tersely. "Disgusting foreign barbarians. You can tell just by looking at them that they're not normal men at all. Did you smell them?"

I shook my head. I hadn't been near enough to catch any odors from them, and I was sure that Reo hadn't been either. But that didn't stop him from wrinkling his nose in disgust.

"They stink of butter and meat. It seems to leak out of their skin. Not surprising, really. I've been told that they don't even use the bath every day. Ugh. Up until recently, the authorities made sure they were confined to the island of Dijima, where they could trade without spreading their vile, strange diseases amongst us decent people. Now, you can even see them in Edo itself, walking about as if they have just as much right to be here as the rest of us. The shogun must not know about it or he would do something about it."

I stared at him, fascinated. Reo obviously mistook my interest as he went on quickly.

"You don't want to have anything to do with them. Don't even get near them if you can help it. A lot of people don't think they're really human, but devils in disguise. Who knows what one could catch off them!" He glanced around and then lowered his head to whisper close to my ear. "I've heard tell that some of the yujo who were forced to go with them because they were desperate for the coins have said that they have tails. Yes! That's why they walk so oddly. And the yujo also say that the foreign devils seemed shocked when they saw their sex. They seemed surprised that they were normal. I think the gaijin women must keep their sex the wrong way around. Across instead of down. How hideous!"

He meant what he said. I nodded gravely, smothering laughter. The gaijin were certainly very odd-looking to our eyes, but I couldn't help but wonder if we seemed as strange to them. The incident had certainly added even more excitement to things, and now I was eager to get the first part of the evening over with. I had my plans in place. As soon as it was polite, I would pretend that I wanted to leave the teahouse to be alone with Reo. I hoped he would be delighted to think I was anxious to go to a house of assignation with him. It was true that I was looking forward to getting him on his own.

"Oh, forget about the gaijin, dear boy. I told Hana we would be here tonight. You see how sure I was of you? She said she would be delighted to see us again."

Reo had a fan in his hand and he used it to tap me lightly on my forehead. I bowed my head and smiled from beneath my eyelashes. Did he like his boys on the effeminate side? I thought he probably did. A moment later, I was sure. He put his hand on my backside and groped it thoroughly. He only stopped when the teahouse shoji slid open and the same maiko I had seen before welcomed us in.

"Good evening, noble sirs. Jun-san. Reo-san. Hana-san bids me welcome you to her humble house."

Reo muttered something I didn't catch. I guessed he was annoyed with the maiko's clumsy error. As the elder "man," she should have welcomed him first. I didn't want him angry yet and made great play of standing back and bowing Reo in before me.

"Welcome, my dear friends. Welcome. Would you like tea or sake?" Hana bowed to us. Her greeting was very warm, and I felt Reo bask in her pleasure.

"Hana-san, always a delight to be with you. You no doubt remember Jun? He was with Isamu-san last time you saw him."

Hana's expression never flickered, but I guessed she had understood the message behind Reo's words. I was no longer with her valued customer Isamu. Reo had stolen me off him, like the iki man about town he thought he was.

Hana stood aside and Reo brushed past her, sitting in

front of the tokonoma shrine alcove as if it was his right. I was appalled by his rudeness and waited silently until Hana smiled at me and indicated I should sit at Reo's right hand, the position for an honored male guest. Had I arrived as a female, my place would have been to his left. I drew a deep breath, all was going to plan.

Hana clapped her hands, and two geisha glided in. Before I could ask for tea, a cup of sake was pressed into my hand. I drank in tiny sips, smiling and nodding my appreciation of its excellence. The evening would, I thought cynically, cost Reo a lot of money. Such a shame it would not lead to the finale he was no doubt anticipating eagerly. He gulped his first cup in two swallows and held out the cup wordlessly to be refilled.

I had no need to make conversation. Reo saw to that. He laughed and joked with the geisha, who looked at him adoringly as if their lives had been enriched by his presence. He was, I suppose, good company if one had a taste for gossip from court circles and risqué comments.

"Really, Reo-san?" Hana raised her eyebrows in apparent amusement at a comment from Reo I had missed. "I had not heard that the shogun was inclined to such things."

Instinctively, I guessed she had entertained the shogun in her house, probably many times. Would she, I wondered, pass Reo's salacious tidbit about his personal habits back to him?

"Oh, yes." Reo had taken a lot of sake. He was bubbling with good humor, but not, I thought, actually drunk. It was some time since he had spoken to me, and I wondered if he had been distracted by the geisha who fawned over him. I soon found I was wrong.

Reo rubbed his hands together and leaned toward

Hana, smiling widely. "Dear Hana-chan, I think it is time we went on our way. Unless, of course, you could find a little something else to entertain us with?"

Hana smiled at him, her expression bland. "But of course, Reo-san. It will be my very great pleasure to recommend one of the best courtesan houses for you. If it pleases you, I will send one of the maiko out to alert them that you will be arriving shortly."

"Ah. I thank you, Hana, but that is not quite what I was thinking." Even the ebullient Reo seemed a little deflated. "Actually, I thought I might give young Jun here a special treat. I seem to remember last time we were here that you said he would be welcome in the Hidden House?"

The eagerness in Reo's voice was embarrassing. Hana inclined her head politely.

"Indeed, Reo-san. Jun is welcome to taste the delights of my flawed jewels in the Hidden House at any time."

I understood what she was saying immediately. It took a little longer for it to filter through to Reo. His grin faded slowly. He stared at Hana incredulously and licked his lips.

"Well, then." He paused, waiting for Hana to speak. She smiled, her head on one side, but remained silent. "In that case, shall we take our leave of you and move across to the other place?"

I squirmed with embarrassment. Surely, even Reo could understand what Hana was saying. I might be welcome in the Hidden House, but he was not.

"I think not, Reo-san," Hana said coolly. "If you're bored with the delights of my beautiful geisha, I will ask the maiko to see you out."

Her tone was courteous, but her words hit Reo like a slap in the face. I held my breath in amazement. Who was this woman who dared to treat a man from a noble family as if he were a peasant? I waited for Reo to get to his feet and knock her to the ground. He would beat her to a pulp for her insolence and nobody would offer him anything but approval for his actions. Shock made me gasp out loud as Reo cleared his throat loudly and actually smiled. A small, twitching sort of smile, to be sure, but a smile for all that.

"I could never be bored with your geisha, Hana," he said stiffly. "But I think you are right. Jun is a very young man, and like all youths, he loses interest very quickly. Perhaps it would be better if I took him out and showed him a few more of the delights the Floating World has to offer."

He stood and inclined his head. I took the hint and rose quickly. Hana rose with us, and—in spite of her earlier words—accompanied us to the door. As Reo bent to put on his shoes, she leaned forward and spoke in a soft voice.

"Do make sure you come back to my humble house, Jun-san."

By the time Reo had straightened, she had stood away from me and was bowing with every appearance of courtesy.

I was bewildered. Even more so when Reo was still silent when we were a street away from the Hidden House. Finally, my curiosity got the better of me and I spoke cautiously.

"Reo, I must beg your indulgence. As you said, I am nothing but a youth. I am not a man about town such as you are, and I have no knowledge of the world." I hesitated, wondering if I was laying on the flattery a little too much even for Reo. But I sensed him relax and knew I had not. By the gods, but the man was a fool! "But it seemed to me that Hana was discourteous to you. How dare she behave like that to such a great noble as you?"

Reo lifted his head, his expression sulky. "She is a stupid

woman," he said arrogantly. "You are right. She was most discourteous to me. Had it been anyone but Hana who had spoken to me like that, I would have struck her down on the spot. She and every one of her precious geisha."

"You were surely merciful, Reo," I fawned.

"I was, wasn't I?" Reo's good humor was nearly restored by my flattery. I chose my words very carefully.

"Is Hana perhaps an old friend?"

"No. I don't think I would call Hana a friend." Reo pursed his lips and tapped me quite hard on the shoulder with his fan. "I would advise you very strongly to keep away from Hana's teahouse, young Jun. Hana seems to have taken a fancy to you, and I must warn you, she is a very dangerous woman."

I was fascinated and waited for more. When Reo stayed silent, I persisted.

"Oh, surely not! She's only a woman, after all. Just because she has the good fortune to manage a very fine teahouse, I don't see how she could be any danger to me. Especially when she knows that I have such a powerful noble as you to protect me." I smiled at him with shy adoration and was surprised when he looked uncomfortable.

"Never take anything in the Floating World at face value, Jun," he muttered. "It's rumored that Hana has more power in the Floating World than you or I could ever begin to imagine. It's said that she actually owns both the teahouse and the Hidden House. Apparently, they were gifted to her by her lover, who was the most feared yakuza in the whole of Edo, just before he died. Now, his son has inherited his father's empire, and it's said he's very fond of Hana in his turn."

I was bewildered. "A yakuza? A mere gangster? What harm could he do to you? He wouldn't dare touch a noble. If he tried, the authorities would have his head off the next day."

"If it were anybody but the yakuza Akira, they would." Reo was obviously uncomfortable even speaking the yakuza's name. "It's whispered that he has all of Edo wound in his obi. He owns teahouses and shops and brothels. Great men owe him money. I've been told that he knows secrets that would cause such loss of face to important nobles that the greatest in the land turn a stone face to anything he chooses to do."

The words "even the shogun" hovered unsaid. I stifled laughter, hardly able to believe that even the arrogant Reo believed this nonsense. Yakuza, indeed! I was certain that either Father or Isamu would not have hesitated to ensure that Hana had gotten her just deserts had she dared to speak to either of them as she had to Reo. I hid a sneer. No matter. Very soon indeed, Reo would find that Hana's insult had been nothing at all compared to what I was about to do to him.

My sister was about to be avenged by my hand. I looked forward to it with very great anticipation.

TWENTY-ONE

My shadow is my
True companion. It is
Always there for me

"*E*nough of this chatter about Hana. I'm bored with her and her teahouse. I doubt you would have enjoyed the Hidden House anyway. I'm sure the tales about the place are exaggerated. No doubt she and her yakuza spread the gossip themselves to justify the shocking fees they charge customers. I daresay she was up to something similar tonight, trying to whet my appetite by teasing me."

Reo was talking himself into believing his own words. Was there no end to the arrogance of the man? I nodded thoughtfully as he took my arm.

"What real man has need of women anyway? I've always thought the code of wakashudo is the true way to follow for any samurai. I'm certain you've already found that Isamu thinks so!"

He leered at me. He was so close, I could smell the sake on his breath. I had a vivid memory of Emiko telling me about seeing Soji and Isamu together in the bath and moved away from him.

"I'm sure you're right, Reo," I agreed. I glanced around. We had come to a halt in a relatively quiet part of the Floating World. I thought there must have been a fire here recently, as there were a couple of plots with half-built houses on them and then a space where the earth was scorched and bare. Little enough here to entice the crowds. There was a narrow, unlit alley a few steps further on, perfect for my plans. I listened carefully but could catch no sound of life coming from down there, although the hum of life vibrated from the next street.

"Of course I'm right. Never mind Hana, I'm on fire for you." Reo grabbed my hand and placed it on his crotch. I had expected to find a rearing tree and was surprised to find it only half erect. No matter. Reo clearly had only one thing on his mind, and it suited my purpose perfectly. "Come along, Jun, There's nothing here for us. We need to get back into the Floating World proper. I know a very discreet house of assignation not far from here."

He made to move away, and I threw my arms around his neck in mock passion.

"Reo-chan," I murmured, "that will be wonderful for the rest of the night. But I don't want to wait that long. Look—this alley is nice and dark and deserted. Wouldn't you like to stop here for a while?"

He hesitated, peering down into the darkness. I thought he was about to refuse, so I rubbed against him seductively.

"Well, you might be right. It wouldn't be as comfortable as exploring each other on a futon, but it would be...different."

"Oh, it will!" I assured him. "And there's always the added spice that we might be discovered. So exciting!"

Reo was convinced, and he eagerly followed me into the alley.

I had no need for any light to see by. The small sounds we made bounced off the walls of the alley, so I used our echoes to find my way. The ground was fairly smooth beneath my feet, so I had no fear of tripping. Reo was less sure.

"Not so fast, Jun. I don't want to trip and injure myself." He sounded pettish, and I wished heartily that Emiko was here to see her lover's feebleness. Here I was, a "boy" he was supposed to be deeply in lust with who was finally offering himself to be taken, and what was this brave man's response? Fear that he might turn his ankle in the dark! Poor Emiko, deceived on all sides. But if my plan worked, at least one of her deceivers would be dealt with.

I reached the end of the alley and turned. Lacking my sense of the night, Reo took another stumbling step and stubbed his toe on the wall.

"Ouch! I really don't know about this, Jun. I daresay this sort of thing might be all right for your battle-hardened samurai lovers, but I'm used to a little more decorum in my affairs. This is most uncomfortable. And I just know that this wall is dirty. It's going to stain my robes. No, this just will not do. Come along. Lead me back to the street again. We will go to my comfortable house of assignation. Jun? Where are you?"

There was a rising note of panic in Reo's voice. I moved closer to him and tapped him on the shoulder. He screamed with surprise.

"I'm here, master," I teased from the other side of him.

"Jun, really. I don't know what sort of game you are playing, but I'm not interested. Come on, lead me out of this horrible alley, now."

I stayed silent, breathing very quietly. I could feel the panic rising in Reo like a physical presence. I touched his face, light as a moth's wings, and he screamed again, lurching away from me.

"Don't you want to play, master?" I whispered right next to him. "I have heard that you like to play games. Is that wrong? If it is, I am so sorry. I will leave you here to find your own way back out and go see if Hana really would like me to visit the Hidden House. But do be careful. I'm sure I saw rats when we came down here."

"No!" Reo's voice was as high pitched as a woman's with fear. He grabbed for me, and I evaded him easily. "I don't like rats. They bite. You can catch terrible things from a rat bite." Suddenly, he was wheedling. "I know what you're up to, my dear Jun. You're only a boy, after all. This is your idea of fun, isn't it? Well, I'm not amused. Not at all. Take me back into the Floating World and we'll say no more about it."

I stayed silent, listening to his heart pound. When it suited me, I giggled.

"But I thought you wanted me, Reo? Don't you find this tremendously exciting? Just the two of us here, well away from anybody who could see or hear us?"

"Go away. Leave me here on my own." Reo's tone was indignant, but I heard the bluster beneath his brave words. "I know we're not far from the main road. I can soon find my way back to the Floating World proper. I realize now that you have nothing at all I want. In fact," he added spitefully, "if you want to know the truth, I wasn't all that interested in you in the first place. It was amusing stealing you off Isamu, but I really only wanted you to get me into the Hidden House."

He was telling the truth, I could tell from his voice. I was

furiously indignant. How dare this weak despoiler of innocent virgins not find me attractive!

"Isamu is a thousand times the man you are," I whispered very closely to his ear. So close that when he jerked
his head in shock, he almost hit me. I bit down on my anger.
I had to be careful not to allow my personal feelings to
make me careless. When I spoke again, I was on his other
side. "*I* am a thousand times the man you are."

Ridiculously, I found myself wishing that he knew the
truth, if only to see the irony in my words.

"You and Isamu both are too in love with the code of
wakashudo," he sneered. Clearly, I had not frightened him
enough yet. He was regaining his confidence. "Neither of
you are real men. I daresay neither of you would even know
what a proper woman feels like. I'm not surprised Isamu
has put off marrying his betrothed for so long. I'm sure the
poor girl will get a terrible shock when her wedding night
actually arrives, if it ever does."

He cackled at his own wit. I steadied my body, counting
ten heartbeats before I moved. Reo had not only despoiled
my sister, now he had insulted my brother. And, oddly, me
as well. Enough. It was time he learned the lesson I had
ready for him.

I pinched his cheek, then darted away. His arms
thrashed about. A child could have heard him grunting, and
I evaded his flailing hands effortlessly.

"Jun! Jun!" he wailed loudly. "I've upset you by saying
those things about Isamu. I'm sorry. I spoke in anger. I didn't
mean it, not a single word. Look, lead me away from this
terrible place and I'll give you money. More money than
you've ever seen. I promise, you can go away and forget we
ever met. But please, don't tell Isamu what I said."

"He'll kill you with no mercy at all if I tell him." I stood very still in front of Reo. I could feel his terror. I had no pity for him at all. "When I tell him, shall I also tell him how you violated his sister?"

"What?" Reo's voice was a tremulous whisper. "I don't know what you're talking about."

Suddenly, it seemed he was far less interested in being led out of the alley. I felt him shrink back, as though he hoped the wall itself might part and offer him shelter.

"Emiko. You must remember her, surely? Isamu's beautiful sister. Daughter and sister to samurai. You went to her father's house and despoiled her beneath his roof."

"No, no. That's all nonsense." He laughed uncertainly. "Do you know Emiko? Is it she that told you all these lies? If you really do know the silly girl, you must know it's all nonsense. She's just a bored, rich, young girl, that's all. She makes things up. Do you really believe that a man from a noble family could ever do something so discourteous?"

Knowing my sister, I almost believed him. Then I recalled her red-rimmed eyes and the days she had spent longing for him to get in touch with her and I knew he was lying. And of course, there was the small matter of the note he had sent to her.

"I believe *you* would," I whispered. Reo was trying to slide away from me. He was holding his breath, as if that would stop me from hearing him! I moved swiftly to block his path. When I spoke again, he hissed with fear. "I saw the note you sent to her. Did you use the same calligrapher to write her note as the one you sent to me?"

He wailed in fear. "You can't know about that! Nobody can know! Who are you? Why are you doing this to me?"

"I am shinobi," I said softly. Where the idea came from for me to lie to Reo, I had no idea. But I was delighted by the effect my words had. He screamed like an animal in pain. I realized at once that he knew shinobi were no legend. Had he perhaps made use of their services himself? If he had, so much the better.

"No! By all the gods, no! Who is employing you? It can't be Emiko. She wouldn't know about such things. And if Isamu knew about it, he would have killed me himself. It doesn't matter. Tell me what you're being paid and I'll double it."

I allowed his scrabbling hands to grasp the front of my robes. Then, very gently, I patted his hand.

"You can't pay me enough. It's a matter of honor."

"Don't kill me, please!" Suddenly forgetting his fear of rats, Reo sank to his knees before me. He banged his head on the filthy ground in front of me, kowtowing as if I were the shogun himself. "Please, let me live. I'll never go near Emiko again. I'll write to her and tell her it was all a mistake. I promise."

He meant it, for the moment at least. It didn't matter to me, though. I had no intention of killing him. If I did, Emiko would spend the rest of her life grieving for her lost lover. My sister had a full—and I hoped long—life in front of her if I could save her from her own foolish romantic notions.

"Get up, Reo," I said. When he did not move, I gave him a brisk kick in the ribs. "Get up. That's better. Stand still."

I reached out and tugged at the obi that fastened his robe. Reo obviously misunderstood what I was after as he spoke eagerly.

"Please, take it. There's a gold koban and some silver in my purse, it's all yours."

A gold koban, enough to feed a man for a year. My disgust deepened. How could anybody be stupid enough to bring that much money somewhere like the Floating

World? It was asking for trouble. Well, Reo had found trouble, even if not in the way he had expected. His fingers scrabbled at the obi, trying to help me. "The netsuke is made from black coral and beautifully carved. You'll be able to sell that easily."

In his eagerness, Reo tore both the purse and netsuke from his obi, thrusting them both blindly at me. I had admired the netsuke earlier. The traditional fasteners that secured purses to the obi by silken strings were typically made of ivory. I had no doubt that this variation was quite valuable on its own. I took both the purse and the netsuke silently, tucking them into my obi.

"And the robe."

"What?" Reo seemed to have recovered a little of his bravado. I slapped the side of his head to remind him who had the upper hand here. He gasped in disbelief, and I thought cynically that it was probably the first time anybody had dared administer the mildest hurt to this spoiled noble. "You can't be serious!" he bleated.

"Oh, but I am. Take your robe off. And whatever you're wearing beneath it. I'll have your zori as well."

"I see." There was a questioning note in the words. I realized with disbelief that this arrogant wretch had begun to think I still wanted to play love games with him. And that —in spite of his words a few moments ago—he was more than willing to play. I was sure when he spoke again.

"Really, Jun. This is hardly the place, you know. Well, you've had your little joke. Do you know, I actually believed you when you said you were shinobi. Although how you found out about my little fling with Emiko, I have no idea."

I am onna-bugeisha, I said only to myself, concentrating on each syllable as if it was a lifeline. Which it was, but not for me. Without the rigorous mental training of a samurai warrior woman, I would have killed Reo where he stood without the least hesitation and felt the world a cleaner, better place without him.

He was reaching for his obi. I grasped his hand and slid my fingers up to his neck. I felt his relief. I allowed him a heartbeat of hope, and then pinched the pulse in his neck between my thumb and first finger.

Riku had taught me the trick.

"This has no part in the code of bushido, Keiko-chan," he warned. "It is not fair. It is not honorable. Even if they know of it, no samurai would dream of using it. But it may save your life one day." He had instructed me to stand still and had placed his fingers against my neck, exactly as I was doing now to Reo. "Now, carefully. A little pressure—just so! —and the world will begin to go away from you."

He was right. The earth rocked beneath my feet and suddenly I was incapable of moving a muscle. I could breathe. I could hear and see. But I could neither move nor speak. Riku released his grasp and I jumped with shock.

"What did you do?" I demanded.

He demonstrated with his own neck, showing me the exact point I needed.

"Try it," he invited. "There's no strength at all needed. It's just a matter of finding exactly the right point where the life's blood rushes to the heart and applying just the right pressure. A pinch as gentle as rubbing a particularly annoying itch is all that is needed to disable a man. But it must be right, and in exactly the right place. Too little, and all you will do is warn your opponent that you are up to something. Too much, and he will fall to the ground and never rise again."

He offered me his neck. I found the right place, but I was afraid of hurting him and my pinch was feeble. Riku threw me to the ground and waited patiently until I got to my feet again.

"Try once more. A little more pressure this time."

The next time, I was too fierce. I mewed with horror as he collapsed to the ground. I was sure I had killed my venerable sensei and kneeled beside him, my head on his chest, listening for a heartbeat. I was immensely relieved when he recovered enough to give me a clout around my ear.

"Better." He cleared his throat. "The pressure you need is between your two efforts. You must find the exact point yourself. I am an old man, and next time you may kill me without meaning to."

I remembered his instructions as I stroked Reo's neck. I could feel his pulse hot and strong beneath my fingers. I hesitated, remembering Riku's words. *This technique is not honorable. No samurai would ever use it.* Then Reo laughed, breathily, and all worries about honor and the code of bushido deserted me. This man had shown no honor to my sister—or me! He deserved no honor in return. I pinched his artery sharply through his well-fed neck and he slithered bonelessly to his knees. He stayed there, bent absurdly at the waist, his head almost touching the ground.

"Reo." I gave him a nudge with my foot to make sure he wasn't faking. His body rocked, but he neither fell nor straightened. Excellent.

His position made it a little awkward to take his robe and fundoshi off him. His undergarment was made of silk, not cotton. I might have expected it, but still it made me sneer. I picked up all his clothes and then gave his shoulder a hard push. Reo rocked back against the wall. If I had planned it, I could not have bettered his position. He ended up squatted on his heels, looking like a naked man who had been caught short and had had to take a shit, his arms held out for balance. It was so undignified, I giggled.

"Reo," I squatted down myself so that my lips were close to his ear. "I know you can hear me, so listen well. I am merciful. I could have killed you and gotten away with it. I have many names, and Jun is only one of them. Perhaps you believe me now when I tell you I am shinobi. This is the only warning I will give you. When you can move again, you will write to Emiko and apologize to her. You will be honest with her. You will tell her that she was only a whim on your behalf. That you had no intention of marrying her, not even of making her your number two wife. Oh, and you will write it yourself, not pay a calligrapher to do it for you. If you ever go near her again, I will know about it. If you ever visit Isamu again, I will know about it. And if I find out that you have disobeyed me, I will kill you without any hesitation at all."

There was a great deal more I wanted to say, but I held my tongue. I bundled up Reo's clothes and walked away from him without looking back. How he would manage to get out of the Floating World and back to his home naked and without a coin to help him, I had no idea. I sincerely hoped it would be degrading in the extreme for him.

It took only moments, and I was once again back in the restless crowds of the Floating World. I laid Reo's robe and fundoshi and zori in the lap of a beggar wearing nothing but a threadbare loincloth. He was so disfigured with leprosy that his hands were fingerless and his nose and lips had crumbled to nothing. I realized he was blind as well when he croaked his thanks without raising his eyes to my face. I was about to put Reo's coins in his begging bowl when I noticed a couple of drunks close by watching me with interest. Were they drunk enough to risk contact with the leper and steal the money from him? I rather thought they were and I moved on. At the next food seller I came to, I showered silver on to his tray.

"Do you fear the gods, my friend?"

He raised astonished eyes to my face. "I am Shinto, sir," he managed to say at last. "All living things that are put on this earth are sacred to me." He gestured at his tray, which contained noodles and vegetables, but no meat. "I try to live my life with respect for all."

I peered into his face and believed him.

"You see that leper over there?" He nodded. "Feed him for as long as that silver lasts and you will please the gods greatly."

I glanced back as I walked away and was delighted to see the noodle seller moving toward the leper.

I could feel Reo's netsuke and purse as a lump in my obi. I did not want the koban. How could I ever enjoy spending money that had been tainted by him? The netsuke tempted me. It was very unusual and very beautiful. I reminded myself that it had been close to his body, and its beauty lessened. I paused, considering what I should do before I finally quit the Floating World. A voice spoke softly nearby.

"Do you have need of my services? I can cure all bodily aches and pains."

An anma, one of the blind masseuses, had stopped close to me. I had been deep in my thoughts, but still, I was surprised I had not heard her approach.

"Thank you," I said courteously. "But I have no need of your services."

Instead of finding her way with a stick or being led by a child as anma usually were, this one was guided by a dog, a mongrel of many breeds that wagged her tail at me and thrust her nose into my hand. The anma shrugged and was about to move away when a thought came to me.

"Anma, do you know a street where there was a fire recently? Quite close to here?"

"I do. I was here the night it burned. If I recollect correctly, two houses are already being rebuilt and work is to start on a third very soon. It was said that the man who lived in one of the houses went to sleep with his pipe in his hand, and when it dropped, he set fire to not only his own house, but those on either side. Why are you interested? They're in a back alley, and even when the houses are rebuilt, they will be cheap, working-men's homes."

She seemed to be looking at me. Even though her eyes were white with the disease that had robbed her of her sight, I schooled my face to show no expression. Clearly, this woman relied on senses other than her vision; my voice had told her that I was no peasant. To find my own abilities reflected back at me was disturbing. I thought of Reo, crouching naked and incapable of movement or voice in his alley and felt a twinge of guilt.

It is not honorable. It is not bushido. But it may save your life one day. I had used Riku's technique carelessly, not to save my own life, but purely for revenge.

"I was curious, that's all." I felt in my obi and took out Reo's purse. I threw the purse away—the dog immediately ran to it and sniffed it, but finding it held no interest it came back to the anma's side at once—but held the koban in my fingers. "I have no need of you, anma. But there is something that you could do for me."

She said nothing, just put her head on one side.

"At the end of the alley, close to where the fire burned, you will find a man. I have no need for your massage, but I think he will welcome it." I put the coin in her palm, and her eyebrows shot up in surprise. "I would appreciate it if you would wait for a while before you go to find him. Say, until the revelries are at their very height and the streets are crowded?"

In spite of my remorse, I swallowed laughter. If I had left Reo to come to his senses naturally, it might have taken hours. Although the Floating World never slept, I would prefer it if he staggered out of the alley when the crowds were at their thickest, rather than in the morning when there were relatively few people about to witness his shame. I examined my conscience and decided he deserved no more.

"With great pleasure." The koban disappeared into the sleeve of her robe. "That is a great deal of money for a simple massage, my lady." I caught my breath. Truly, this blind woman saw far more than those who had use of their eyes. "I can only hope that my customer merited whatever has caused him to need my services so urgently."

"Oh, he has," I assured her. A thought struck me, and I added, "Does your dog take good care of you, anma?"

"Indeed, she does, my lady." Her hand found the dog's head unerringly. "You're fortunate. She obviously likes you. Some of my customers seem to think they are buying more than a massage to ease their aches and pains. They have not been so lucky."

I smiled as I turned and was swallowed up by the crowds in the blink of an eye. The anma and I understood each other perfectly. I was still smiling as I walked to the great gate. There was a great deal I still had to learn about the code of bushido, but I was pleased. I had avenged my sister, and—I thought—turned her life away from the dark and to the light. Soji was a great disappointment to me, certainly. The man I had worshipped from afar for so very

long had turned out to be deeply flawed, but I was still sure
he would make Emiko an excellent husband. After all, she
would go into the match with her eyes open, which was far
more than could be said for most marriages. She must learn
to take the bad with the good. It was just a shame she had
been spoiled for so long.

"Jun." I was so absorbed in my pleasurable thoughts
that I thought I imagined the soft voice calling my name. I
hesitated for a pace and was about to move on when the
voice came again. "Jun, over here."

I turned and my smile widened. Effet was standing well
back in a deeply recessed doorway. She leaned forward and
beckoned me to her.

"Effet." I lounged in the doorway, doing my best to copy
Isamu's iki slouch. "Surely you haven't waited for me all
evening? I'm deeply flattered, but I'm afraid I must be on my
way."

"Oh, surely another few minutes wouldn't hurt?" She
pouted. Even though I knew perfectly well her sorrow was
all pretense, I was flattered. She was looking at me in
apparent approval, smiling as if she liked what she saw. Her
gaze lingered on my obi, and her eyes widened with
genuine interest. Reo's netsuke. It still dangled from my obi.
I was filled with wicked amusement. It was the only part of
him I had not given away. Now, it could go to a good home.

"Do you like my netsuke, Effet?" I asked. "Well, truth to
tell, it wasn't mine earlier in the evening. It was given to me
by a...friend. I don't really care for it. Would you like it as a
souvenir of our brief meeting?"

Her eyes were wide and greedy. I handed the netsuke to
her and felt cleaner for its loss. She licked her lips and the
coral disappeared into her wide sleeve.

"You are most generous, Jun. Are you quite sure there is

nothing I can give you in exchange?" I shook my head, and she leaned closer to me, putting her lips close to my ear. I waited indulgently for her whispered enticements. She said nothing, but pinched my ear lobe and stroked my face. Her fingers were very soft. This close, I could smell her scent. Something light and flowery, but at the same time vibrant and feminine. It was delightful, and I inhaled the perfume with a lingering intake of breath. I had to smile. Had I truly been a man, I would have found Effet irresistible.

I relaxed for a moment, content to linger in her presence. Why not? I had achieved all I had come to the Floating World to do. The excitement was finally beginning to ebb from my body, and I realized I was exhausted.

"I have a long ride in front of me, Effet," I said gently. "I must leave you."

She made no effort to stop me as I turned. I had not left the shadow of the doorway when I collided with something as solid and unyielding as the mountain I had climbed with Isamu. I was plucked off my feet effortlessly. Whatever had hold of me tightened its grip, and I felt as if my ribs were being crushed into my lungs. I heard Effet's voice from somewhere behind me, although I could not make out her words. I didn't waste my time trying to answer her. My mind spun, trying to make sense of what was happening to me. My feet were dangling in space. My face was pressed into what felt like flesh, but flesh that was harder than anything that I had ever touched. Something was wrapped around my entire body, holding me firmly. I tried to wriggle. If it were possible to escape from this trap, then I would do so. Once free, I could think about fighting back. But not until then.

My legs were free, so I could kick. I slammed my feet hard against my captor. When that had no apparent effect, I swung my lower body as far back as I could. It was only perhaps a hand span, but I reckoned it would be enough. If this was truly a man that had hold of me—and judging by his reek of hot flesh he was—then there was a quick and, for me at least, easy way out of this situation. I slammed my knee crisply into where I reckoned his kintama should be. I expected his hold to be relaxed at once. When nothing happened, I tried again, a little higher. And then lower.

I thought I had finally reached my target when the hold on me was relaxed very slightly. Not enough to allow me to get away, but enough for me to raise my head to see what manner of creature had captured me. A face as wide and full as the moon was looking down at me. Given that the owner of the face still seemed intent in squeezing the life out of me, it wore a curiously gentle expression. The vast moon head bent down to me and full lips smothered my mouth. I felt the air being sucked out of my very lungs. My protests were lost in his mouth. I tried to breathe through my nose, but my whole face was squashed against his cheeks. I was being smothered by flesh. I went limp, hoping he would think I was already unconscious. When that didn't work, I tried to kick his kintama again. My last thought before my body finally accepted that I was about to die was one of great sadness that Yo would come back for me and I would be gone.

TWENTY-TWO

If my spirits are
Sad, then the brightest summer
Day is overcast

*T*he terrible pressure had lessened slightly, but my chest still hurt. With the pain came the knowledge that I was alive. What use would a spirit have for pain? Instinctively, I wanted to move, to stretch each limb to see if anything was broken. But my training had been thorough. I lay still and kept my eyes closed, sensing my surroundings.

I was lying on a comfortable futon. It smelled of nothing except crisp, clean linen, but the texture of the bedding was foreign to my skin. I parted my lips fractionally, smelling and tasting the air much as a snake does when it flicks its tongue. A faint odor of incense. Further away, the smell of cooking. A bird was singing outside. The wind was blowing lightly. And above all that, the sound of someone breathing close by me. A woman.

"You might as well open your eyes. I know you're awake."

I did as the voice instructed. There was no point pretending if she could read my reactions as keenly as that. Besides, I was curious. The voice itself was familiar, but there was an edge to it that made it seem strange. I opened my eyes and sat up, relishing the chance to stretch. At the same time, my brain took stock of my situation instantly. I was still fully clothed apart from my zori, which were missing. I had never seen the room I was in before. It was quite large, but gloomy. The feel of the air against my skin assured me it was daytime, and warm, but the sun was excluded from the room by very thick silk screens.

I turned my head and blinked. Hana. She was staring at me intently. I hid my bewilderment and smiled at her.

"Hana-san," I said courteously. "I am in your debt. I have no idea what happened to me, but I was viciously assaulted. How did I get here? How long have I been here?"

She inclined her head. I thought her lips quivered with amusement, and I tensed.

"You are indeed in my debt, *Jun-san*." She rolled the syllables around her mouth as if she was tasting them. "A nice enough name, but I don't think it suits you."

I glanced casually around the room, giving myself time to think. There was no one else close by, I was sure of that. The room had the usual shoji around it on three sides; the other wall appeared to be made of solid stone, without windows. No matter, it would be an easy thing to break through the silk and lattice screen walls if I had to. I could get out of here whenever I wanted. As I was indoors and Hana was with me, I assumed I was in the Green Teahouse and almost smiled. A few geisha would hardly be able to prevent me from leaving.

"I thank you, Hana." I patted my obi. Not surprisingly, my purse had gone. "I've obviously been robbed, I'm afraid.

If you will wait until I can get home, I'll be delighted to pay whatever you think is appropriate for rescuing me. Of course, no amount of money can repay you for saving my life. I'm forever in your debt."

I bowed my head deeply, using the polite movement to give me time to think. Something was very wrong here, but I had no idea what.

"Such exquisite politeness!" Hana tittered. She was jeering at me, I could tell from her voice. The small hairs on the back of my neck prickled erect in warning. I began to get to my feet, and her voice lashed. "Sit down. You're not going anywhere."

"And you think you can stop me?" I said coolly.

"Of course I can."

I shook my head in real amusement. She had no idea of what I was capable of. I almost felt sorry for her.

"Sit down, Keiko." I froze for a second, my heart galloping with shock, and then I laughed. My voice sounded shrill, and I was annoyed with myself.

"Keiko? Who is Keiko? My name is Jun, you know that. Not that it matters. I'll be on my way now."

"No, you will sit down," she snapped. "You are not going anywhere at all. I know who you are, Keiko. I know you're Isamu's younger sister. And I know about that oaf Reo and what he did to your sister, Emiko."

She watched as I sat down slowly. I breathed deeply, relaxing my body. This was shockingly unexpected, but I decided quickly that it didn't really matter. Both Reo and Isamu had told me that nothing happened in the Floating World without Hana knowing about it. I had doubted them at the time, but obviously, I was wrong.

I relaxed. At least I knew what to expect now. I would have to buy her silence, probably sell some of my trinkets to do it. At the same time, I was intensely curious. How had she found me out? Had I made some sort of slip? Did I want to know how I had gotten here? Or *why* I was here?

"How did you find out who I am?" I demanded. "And what happened to me? Did you arrange to have me kidnapped? Why?"

Instead of answering my volley of questions, Hana simply stared at me. I stared back unblinkingly. Hana broke the silence first.

"All you samurai are just the same. Men and women alike," she sneered. I raised my eyebrows in surprise. "Always thinking you're better than anybody else. That you have rights nobody else can lay claim to. At least most daimyo manage to be polite, but not you samurai! Not so much as a please or a thank you."

"I'm sorry if I have been less than courteous, Hana," I apologized. "All this has come as a great shock to me and I'm baffled. Please, if you would be so kind, explain to me how you guessed who I am. And how I come to be here."

I bowed my head and allowed my shoulders to slump as if I was fatigued. I guessed intuitively that Hana would be able to read my body's language just as well as she could understand my speech. This was a very clever woman. It would not do to underestimate her...again.

"I will tell you." She spoke grudgingly, but I caught the undercurrent of malicious pleasure in her voice. "First things first. You want to know how I knew who you were. I was puzzled right from the start. Something felt wrong to me about the pair of you. It was Isamu who gave the game away. It was partly the way he looked at you now and then, as though he was trying not to laugh. And the way he spoke to you made me think you were either very old friends or relatives. Not lovers. He never touched you at all. Had you truly been lovers, he would never have been able to resist touching your face or patting your arm. And he paid far too much attention to my geisha. At first, I thought he was trying to make you jealous. Then I saw it was nothing of the kind. He was simply enjoying their company."

I nodded reluctantly. "I see. But I still don't understand how you found out I was Isamu's sister."

"I was obvious when I thought about it," Hana said calmly. "You don't look a great deal like your brother, so that was no help. But once I had decided you were not lovers, I watched you both carefully. I realized that you knew each other very well indeed. You were comfortable together, the sort of comfort that comes between very old friends. You had no need to speak; Isamu spoke for you. All that puzzled me greatly. If you really were old friends, then why was Isamu trying to pass you off as his lover? I pondered it after you had gone. I wanted to know what game Isamu was playing.

"As I said, you do not look like your brother. But you both have a certain way of putting your head on one side when you are listening to something that interests you. You're doing it now." I held my head perfectly still, considering. She was right. "There were other signs as well. I do not have any brothers, but one of my geisha has four brothers, and she commented when you left that Isamu looked at you in exactly the same fond way as her eldest brother looked at her when she had done something he approved of. She found it quite touching. Once I thought it all over, I realized that you had to be his sister. But you couldn't be Emiko. I have heard she's very beautiful, and equally stupid. And you are neither."

I reconsidered my situation quickly. Hana was truly a clever woman, and one who would make a dangerous enemy. I mentally recalculated the amount that would be needed to buy her silence and let me go.

"I see. Did you wonder why Isamu had brought me to visit you?"

"I suppose it had simply amused him at the time. But I was still interested," Hana went on. "When you both left me, I sent word out to find out where you had gone. I soon found out that you had both met Reo. The calligrapher he used to write his note to you was only too pleased to tell me what he was up to. I was puzzled at first, but that was quickly solved with a little thought. I already knew Reo had seduced your sister." I nodded reluctantly. There was no harm in confirming what she already knew. "He had boasted about it to his cronies here in the Floating World. The idiot seemed to think it would give him some sort of respect in their eyes."

"He thinks of himself as being deeply iki," I interrupted. "And he's vain enough to think that deflowering an inno-cent girl will enhance his reputation. Especially when the girl in question comes from a high-caste samurai family."

I thought of Reo, naked and unable to move in the filthy alley, and regretted asking the anma to minister to his hurts. I should have left him there in hopes that the rats would find him and recognize he was one of them.

"The man's an idiot," Hana said calmly. "He deserved all you did to him, and a lot more besides." I was startled. Was there anything Hana didn't know? "If it had been me, I would have killed him when I had the chance. But you couldn't do that, could you? It wouldn't have fit in with the code of bushido. In your eyes, it would have made you even worse than him."

"I've taken away his pride. Stripped him of his vanity. To Reo, that will be worse than being dead. And I hope I've convinced him to keep away from Emiko." I paused, gathering my thoughts. Hana watched me calmly. "But I still don't understand why I'm here. Why did you have me abducted off the street? I'm surprised that a woman as subtle as you needed to be so dramatic."

I wanted to annoy her, to get under her skin. Had I succeeded? I had no idea. She turned a stone face to me.

"I felt it was necessary," she said calmly. "I didn't want you to leave the Floating World, and I didn't want to draw attention to you. The easiest thing was to use Abi to collect you. It was your own fault, you know. If you hadn't been so courteous as to allow Effet to claim your full attention, you would have seen Abi before it was too late and could have evaded him. He's surprisingly quiet for his size and can move very quickly—although, not as nimbly as you—but disguising his presence is as difficult as hiding a whale on dry land."

Abi? Who or what was Abi? I was almost willing to believe that Hana had a pet demon under her control. Then I remembered the stink of the flesh that had wrapped itself around me and I knew that Abi was no devil. I guessed Hana would never tell until I asked, and I needed to know.

"Abi was the giant who took me from the street?"

"He is. Once he had hold of you, you could never have made him let go. If you had managed to stick a dagger in his ribs, it might have slowed him down a little, but I doubt it. If you knew the Floating World a little better, you would have heard of Abi. He is a sumo wrestler. No, I do him an injustice. He is not just a sumo wrestler, he is yokozuna. The very best, and because of that, he has the very best patrons. My own dear Akira is amongst them."

Akira. I remembered Reo saying he was a gangster, the most feared in Edo, and the son of Hana's lover. Was that how she found out so much, through people's fear of the yakuza?

"But I kicked him in the kintama," I said wonderingly. "Hard. No matter how big he was, that should have stopped any man."

"You think so? But you must remember, dear Keiko, that sumo wrestlers are different from all other men. They are taught to massage their kintama and to work on their internal muscles until eventually they have the art of drawing their kintama back inside their bodies. They do it before every match. They have to. If they left them in their natural place, as soon as their opponent grabbed their fundoshi to lift them up, they would be screaming in agony and the game would be over at once. Once they are relaxing in the bath afterward, they let them down again. Abi tells me the pain is exquisite."

We were both silent for a moment, thinking of it.

"I see. Well, that is something else I have learned today, Hana-san. Now that I know how and why you saw through me, I will be more careful in the future. I thank you for the lesson, even though it was a hard one. Now, tell me how much you want for teaching me and I will be on my way." I glanced down at my bare feet. "Or at least I will when you give me back my zori."

"Go? You think you have enough money to persuade me to let you go? I'm afraid you don't know me at all."

TWENTY-THREE

When the sun hides her
Face from us at night, does she
Sleep just as we do?

*H*ana stirred, pretending she needed to find comfort.

"Ah, my poor legs!" she moaned. "Why do the gods allow our bodies to age when the mind is still alert?"

I stared at her stonily. She was playing with me. She was not old, nor was there anything wrong with her legs. I was not interested in her games. I wanted to go home, now! I doubted Isamu would be back yet, but there was always a chance, and I needed to be there to confess my story to him before he found out I had vanished and became angry. And even more importantly, what if Yo returned and found me gone?

"Tell me what you want. However much it is, I'll get the money," I said bluntly. Hana regarded me thoughtfully. I was shocked into silence when she spoke.

"There has been a great deal of gossip in the Floating World recently. It's said that a creature of legend has arisen again. That once again there is one who is onna-bugeisha amongst us." I fought to keep my face neutral. "A samurai warrior woman who will right the wrongs of the world. I had dismissed the rumors as nonsense until Abi told me how you fought against him. He told me that few men could have put up a better fight than you did. But perhaps I'm wrong. I always thought that perception was a great part of the onna-bugeisha's weaponry." Hana shrugged. "You don't seem to understand me at all. I told you. I don't want your money. Nothing you can offer me will be enough. I have *you*. Daughter and sister of samurai. Even better if you truly are onna-bugeisha. All that is worth more to me than any amount of money."

I shook my head in disbelief. I stopped myself from glancing at the flimsy screens around me, but Hana's sense of perception was sharp and she answered my unspoken thoughts.

"You could break out of this room as soon as I left you. You would not find it quite as easy to get out of the house and back into the Floating World. I have two enforcers who would be delighted to try and match their skills against you. There is always the chance that you could beat them. And then—barefoot or not—you could easily find your way back to the gate and away from here."

"I suppose so," I agreed cautiously. Hanna was smiling, and I did not like that at all.

"Naturally. You are samurai, escape from capture would always be your first thought. But you are not going to leave here, Keiko. Not until I am ready to let you go. And when that day comes, I doubt you will find welcome in your father's house."

"And what is going to keep me here, Hana? You? Your enforcers? Or are you going to post Abi at my door? Even he must sleep some time, and when he does, I will get past him. You can't really believe you can keep me here."

Even then, I thought she was simply trying to frighten me. To make me accept whatever sum she named. I was still slightly amused at her insolence. How Yo would laugh with me when I shared the joke with him.

"You must remember, Keiko. I am not samurai. Still less am I onna-bugeisha. I have no code of honor. I don't care who I hurt in this life as long as it is for my benefit. I suppose I might pay for it in another life, but this body will know nothing at all about that, so I don't let it worry me. I already have money. More money than you would believe possible. A little more is always welcome, to be sure, but that's not what I want from you. You can give me power. That's what I want, and that's what you are going to give me."

"I don't understand what you're talking about."

"Don't you, samurai's daughter? Then listen to me. My men found Reo where you left him. The anma you sent to him had restored life to his body, but I'm afraid he wasn't at all grateful to her. If it hadn't been for her dog, he might have hurt her. Reo was most grateful to my boys. He tried to tell them that you had lured him into a trap where he met a band of armed robbers at the bottom of the alley who beat him up and stole everything he had."

"Why?" I was so angry, I forgot my own position. "Why did you help him? You said yourself that you would have killed him if you'd been me."

"You still don't see, do you? For all your supposed instincts, you can't see the obvious. I had Reo taken to my teahouse. I allowed him to bathe and gave him new clothes.

I even gave him sufficient sake to make him brave and full of bluster again. And then I explained to him that I knew exactly what had happened to him. That he had been taken and left for dead by a single green boy. I also told him that I knew what he had done to your sister. And what did this great, big, iki man do? He threw up on my tatami and fell to his knees, begging me to never tell anybody, especially Isamu. Reo comes from an important family. His father is an advisor to the shogun. Reo is the spoiled brat of the family, but from now on, he is mine. His father will find a great change in his eldest son. Suddenly, he will be very interested in affairs of state. He will display an intelligent appreciation of what is happening at the highest level. His father will be delighted. As will I, when he passes the information on to me. From this day on, Reo is my pet. Knowledge is power, and I have a great deal of knowledge."

"And you think I'll do something similar for you? I'm afraid you're going to be disappointed, Hana. It amuses Isamu to allow me to be onna-bugeisha. My father barely knows I exist. To both of them, I'm no more than an inconsequential girl child."

"It's not what you are, Keiko, it's *who* you are, and what you can do for me."

"And what's that? Am I going to join your thugs and become a guard?" I grunted with laughter. "Do you think it's going to amuse your patrons to find a woman guarding the geisha? Is that it? And you really think I'm not going to get away as soon as I get the chance?"

"Do joke, Keiko. It will be a long time before you laugh again." Hana was smiling, but I could see no humor in her eyes. "You are going to become the greatest treasure of my house. As you are samurai, you no doubt already have all the talents I normally look for in a girl. I'm sure that you will be able to dance and sing and play the samisen, as well if not better than any of my geisha. Alas, you do not look to me to be the type who will willingly look so adoringly at a patron that you make them feel like a god, but under the circumstances, I will overlook that fault."

I was so sure of myself, I shrugged and smiled broadly, shaking my head.

"No, I thought not. No matter. Take a good look at this room, Keiko. It will be your home until I decide to release you."

"Really? And what am I going to do that will please you so much, Hana? Whatever you have planned for me, I'm not going to cooperate, you can be sure of that."

"You will be the greatest jewel in my collection." I laughed, pointing my finger between my breasts. Me? "Yes, Keiko. I have it all planned. All my patrons are wealthy, influential men. Many of them have so much power and money, they have tasted every earthly delight and are constantly hungry for something different. Something new. That is why they come here, to the Hidden House."

That stopped the laughter in my throat. I was in the Hidden House? The place Reo had been so desperate to enter? Suddenly, I was less amused by Hana's nonsense.

"And you're going to try and keep me here?"

"I am not going to try and keep you here, Keiko. You will stay because you want to, I assure you of that. You will stay because you are onna-bugeisha. Because you have a foolish belief in the code of bushido. You will stay because if you do not do exactly as I tell you from this moment on, I will allow the whisper of how your foolish sister has betrayed the honor of your great house with Reo to reach your daimyo.

Don't think he wouldn't believe me. He would. Lord Akafumu has been a patron of my teahouse for many years, and I know him well. He is a man of great pride. I understand he is already furious with your father for allowing Emiko to delay her marriage to Soji. Any further scandal, and it will be the last straw for him. He could not deprive your father of his wealth, but he could strip him of everything else that matters to him. Suddenly, he will find he has no position court. None of those men he calls friends would so much as talk to him. Your father would lose so much face, society would be closed to him forever. And of course, it would also reflect on Isamu. He would no longer be iki. He would be nothing at all. His betrothed's family would decide they had waited too long for the marriage and find her another husband. Nor would he be able to get another bride from a good family. Who knows, the family line might well die out completely. And it would all be your fault, Keiko. Could you live with such disgrace on your conscience?"

She was wrong. She had to be. But I glanced at her icy face and knew I was fooling myself. She could do it. She *would* do it.

"And what can I do that is so important to you?" My voice sounded rusty. I had already given in, and Hana knew it.

"You will remain here. In this room. I will supply everything you need to live. I will give you clothes and feed you. There is a small bathhouse through there." She nodded at one of the shoji. "If you like to read, I will supply you with all the latest books. If you want a pet, I will even arrange for you to have a cat, or possibly a small dog. Am I not the most generous of women?"

"And what do you expect from me in return?" I asked.

"You will be mine. You will do exactly as I tell you. I suppose, just like your stupid sister, you've allowed some man to take you already?"

Her words were so unexpected, I flinched. Hana obviously took that for agreement. She sighed.

"I thought as much. Who was it?"

She was grinning, and I thought quickly. She had not mentioned Yo. If she knew of him, she would have let me know. He was my only chance to get out of here. And far more importantly, my only chance of saving the family honor. I spoke reluctantly, allowing my body to express my revulsion.

"A visitor to our house. A friend of my brother's. I didn't like him at all, but he forced himself on me. I couldn't tell anybody. Even if Isamu believed I was innocent, he would have been forced to believe his guest, not me."

I spoke bitterly, and for the first time, I was grateful for the memory of the dreadful Choki. Hana appeared to believe me.

"You see? So much for the code of bushido. It is fatally flawed, child, trust me. But you're not going to trust me, are you? You're samurai, and it would be far beneath your dignity to entrust yourself to a woman such as me. A pity you're never going to be able to get your revenge on the man who violated you. But it doesn't matter to me." Suddenly, she was brisk again. "I can soon get a surgeon to put a stitch or two in the right place. The man who wins you and becomes your danna will never know the deception."

I licked my lips and found them dry. "You expect me to service your patrons? To be a common whore?"

"Certainly not," Hanna snapped at me. "There is

nothing common about the girls in the Hidden House. My flawed gems are sought after by the very best of society. All of the girls are as superbly talented as the very best geisha in the whole of Edo. My geisha in the Hidden House delight a man's every sense in every way possible. An evening with one of them costs a small fortune. They are not whores. They are as far from it as the sun is removed from the earth."

She was genuinely angry about the way I had referred to the Hidden House. I tucked the knowledge away, in case it might be useful to me someday.

"I don't know how to delight a man in bed. What use am I to you?" I said.

"I told you. The patrons who come to this place are bored with ordinary life. They are seeking something different. Something that will arouse their jaded senses. And what better than you, an apparently untouched girl who is obviously from one of the best families? Although, we will never truly share the secret of your identity with them, I will ensure that enough hints are dropped so that they understand they are buying not just any girl, but a true samurai. In any event, they will see from your bearing that you are from a good family. And I think that we will add a little spice by inventing an interesting past for you."

She was smiling happily. I shrugged, pretending not to be worried.

"So? What difference will any of that make? All your patrons are here to pay for their pleasures. Why should they care what class their whore comes from?"

"Ah, only a samurai could think like that." Hana covered her mouth with her hand, hiding laughter like a geisha. "You really have no idea how much your class is hated by those beneath you, do you? Many of my patrons are high ranking men. Some of them were born to high estate. Others are men who have clawed their way up through society by their own efforts. But for all that, they are not noble. Not one of your precious samurai would give them the scrapings from their rice bowl. When the lucky patron who finally wins you takes you to his bed, he will see himself spitting in the face of all those who have sneered at him and called him a riverbed beggar behind his back. That will be your unique enticement, the notion that they are despoiling a samurai with no fear of reprisal. Wonderful!"

"And what will you gain from that, Hana? Why take the risk of keeping me here? You must know Isamu will take the Floating World apart piece by piece to find me, if only for the honor of the thing."

My mind was cold. My thoughts were already beginning to work on my escape, which I hoped would be sooner rather than later. I would not allow this terrible woman to use me to destroy my family. Nor would I allow her to force me to prostitute myself. In the meantime, I wanted to know everything I could. I felt that anything—the smallest word—might be able to help me. Although I had spoken bravely, in my heart, I guessed that Isamu would think I had gotten bored with my life as a neglected younger sister and had simply run away. He would be disappointed in me and too angry to spend much time looking for me. Yo would find me eventually, I was confident. Whether it would be in time was a different matter. In any event, I would not allow myself to depend on him. If it were somehow possible, I would escape from this place by my own efforts.

Hana grinned openly at me. "You will be worth a great deal of money, of course. But you'll be worth far more than anything money can buy me. Even when you have been bought and paid for, I have no intention of letting you leave the Hidden House. You will remain here, in this room. No doubt at first your danna will want to keep you to himself. But after a while, he will want to show you off. I'm certain that he'll allow his most favored friends to enjoy you, both to show off his secret treasure and to impress them with his generosity. I promise you will learn, very quickly, what pleases each one.

"Some will want you to bow to their will. Others will love it when you bite and kick. They will feel they have mastered you when they finally put their tree in whichever of your orifices appeals to them. You will learn to be all things to each of them. I have no doubt at all they will be entranced with you.

"And you will listen to the words they whisper to you, Keiko. Because they think you're hidden away from the world, they'll gloat over you. They'll take pleasure in sharing with you the secrets of their souls, things they would never tell their concubines, and still less their wives. And you will tell me. You will tell me their fantasies. What they like to do to you. Whether they like to inflict pain or receive it. And even better, when they whisper to you of their ambitions, of their hopes for advancement, of the risks they are willing to take to get it, you will also tell me that. And each word you say to me will increase the power I have over them. And the real joy of it is that they will never know. Until the day comes when I choose to use that power, and then it will be far too late."

"I hear you," I said. Hana was clearly mad. But that was no help. My thoughts darted, but no matter which direction they turned in, I could find no escape—for the moment, at least. I bowed my head as if in defeat. "If it saves my family, then I will do it. As you have pointed out to me so clearly, I have no option if I wish to live with my conscience." She smiled with real pleasure in her expression. "But first, tell me one thing."

Hana tilted her head to one side, her expression considering. "That depends on the question. Ask, and I will see."

"Who hurt you so badly that you feel the need to take revenge on my class?

TWENTY-FOUR

I speak to you and
You do not hear. Does that mean
My words are silent?

*A*lthough my room was large, I suddenly wished that it was much larger and that Hana was a great deal further away from me. I sat very still, instructing my body not to flinch away from her. Even on the day I had climbed the mountain with Isamu, I had not felt as much fear as this. Then, I might have died, but this was worse still. Hana had the power to make my life a living hell for as long as she wished.

Her expression did not waver, but I felt her body tense. I breathed slowly and easily, pretending an ease I did not feel at all.

"Perhaps you truly are perceptive, onna-bugeisha. Nobody else has ever looked for a reason behind my whims."

Hana stared at me, and I met her gaze firmly. It was very much like being confronted by a vicious dog, and just as when facing a dangerous animal, I knew it was essential to show no fear. She nodded finally.

"So, I shall tell you. There's no harm in it. You'll never be able to make anything of it. My father was a middle-ranking civil servant, an ambitious one. He knew he could never rise above his class, nor did he want to. But he was clever enough to see where the real power, and money, lay. His superiors in the civil service were the men who held the court and titled classes in their hands. Samurai and daimyo alike crawled to them with full purses when they wanted a favor. Without such men, nothing would get done.

"That was what father dreamed of. He wanted to become a top-class civil servant. A modest enough ambition, you might think, and he was well on his way. His superiors were coming to rely on him. It was whispered amongst his peers that he was the coming man. Already, his word was being sought widely.

"I was his only child, and he saw beyond the fact that I was only a girl and recognized that I had inherited his sharp mind. He talked to me about his ambitions, and I was as excited as he was. Our future was clear and the gods were smiling on us."

She stopped. I waited. My patience broke first this time.

"So, what happened?"

"A samurai happened." Hana bared her teeth in a smile. It was like watching a wild animal peeling its lips back. "This man—Mon Anjin—saw me out shopping one day. He took a fancy to me and made an offer to my father. He wanted to take me as his concubine. Not even his number two wife! I would have been number three wife.

"Father refused him outright. That only served to whet Anjin's appetite. He came back with a better offer. It would be perfectly legal, he assured father. There would be a ceremony of 'marriage.' As the daughter of a minor civil servant, I should be flattered, he insisted. As should my father.

"The insinuation was there, of course, that he could help Father in his career. It would be an excellent match for me, and Father would get the promotion he craved. Father asked my opinion, and I refused. I would have turned the samurai down anyway as a matter of pride, but by that time, I had met Akira. You have heard of him?"

Akira, the yakuza Reo had mentioned. I nodded, wondering.

"Speak, child. Your thoughts are written on your face anyway," Hana said sourly.

"You rejected a samurai for a yakuza," I said. "Even if you had begun as his number three wife, if he liked you enough, he might have put aside his number two wife for you. And if his first wife died, you could have stepped into her place." Even as I said the words, I guessed that Hana would never have let anybody stand in her way. I doubted that Mon Anjin's wife would have survived for long after his "marriage" to Hana. "That didn't entice you?"

"It did not. I had met Akira, and that was that. He bewitched me from the start. He was different from anybody I had ever known. He spoke to me as if I was his equal, not a mere woman. He knew everybody that mattered. He was rich, and in his own way extremely powerful. And so very charming and handsome. My skin itched with lust every time I met with him. He was older than I was, but that didn't matter at all. He told me that he had a wife, and that he was fond of her. He would not put her aside, not even for me. I respected him for that, and in my turn, I told him I would never become his concubine. We would be equals. I was so happy, I smiled all of each day."

"And your father approved of him?" I scoffed.

"Father didn't know about him. I took great care that our relationship was secret. Nobody knew. Even Father—much as he loved me—would never have considered Akira a suitable match for me. In fact, he did his best to persuade me to accept the samurai. When I dug my toes in and refused the wretched man, even Father became angry with me. He locked me in the house until, as he put it, 'I came to my senses.' I was devastated. I couldn't believe that Father had turned on me.

"It didn't take long for Akira to get tired of waiting for me. One day, when Father was away on business, he simply walked into the house with some of his fiercest henchmen and took me out of my prison. We made love that night for the first time, and I was his from then on. We stayed as equals, both in bed and in our business dealings."

"A pretty tale with a happy ending," I commented. "But I still don't understand why you hate samurai so much."

"Because the samurai who had wanted me took my rejection of him in favor of a mere yakuza as a personal insult. He broke my father to get his revenge. First, Father was demoted, and then he was discharged from his position on some trumped-up accusation. Mon Anjin made sure nobody else would employ him. Father turned to opium for consolation. He ended his life as a beggar on the street, spending the few coins he earned on opium pipes. He died of hunger and cold the winter after I left him."

"Why didn't you help him? You said your lover was rich. Couldn't you have bought a house for him? Kept him in luxury for the rest of his life?"

Hana stared at me. I was very glad she wanted something from me. To judge by her expression, if I had been useless to her, my life would have been very short. Suddenly, I understood how truly ruthless this woman was.

"If I had known what had happened, he would have lacked for nothing. I would have forgiven him everything." I thought there were tears in her eyes, but it could just as easily have been fury. "But Mon Anjin was cunning and cold in seeking his revenge. I wrote to my father often but never received a reply. I was heartbroken. I thought he had put me aside and no longer cared about me, but wasn't so.

"I found out after Father died that the samurai had bribed his servants to intercept all my letters. Of course, once Father fell on hard times, that was no longer necessary. The house was sold and the servants dismissed. Nobody knew where I was. Even if they had known, they would have been too frightened to contact me.

"I had no idea what was happening, nor did I understand how much Mon Anjin hated me for the loss of face I had caused him. I found that out when Father died. The temple where we used to worship buried him out of charity. And do you know what the damned samurai did?" It was a rhetorical question, but I shook my head anyway. "After Father was buried in a pauper's grave, he made sure that word reached Akira what had happened. I only knew when it was far too late. Mon Anjin couldn't get to me, I was far too well protected. So, he killed my father instead. I suppose that is the so-called code of the samurai."

"I'm sorry." I meant it. Although I had never met Mon Anjin, I shared Hana's fury at his wickedness. "But not all samurai are like that. Many of them are good men who try to live their lives in accordance with the code of bushido."

"You really think so?" Hana sneered at me. "I have heard that it is only recently that your own father could be bothered to acknowledge that you exist. And now that he has owned to you, he is doing his best to arrange a marriage for you to an elderly widower. A man who has already outlived two wives. That is the code of bushido, is it?"

I was at a loss for a reply and asked a question instead. "We are all in the hands of the gods, and sometimes it's difficult to understand their humor. What happened to Mon Anjin? Did you take your revenge on him? Or did he prosper in spite of everything?"

"As you say, we are truly the puppets of the gods." Hana nodded serenely. "Oddly enough, I had no need to avenge my father. It happened that Mon Anjin's daimyo had a dispute with a neighbor. He called upon Mon Anjin to raise troops to help him, but by some mischance, the message was never received, and as a result, the skirmish went against the daimyo. He was successful in the end, but he never forgave Mon Anjin for what he saw as cowardice.

"Mon Anjin protested his innocence, naturally, but the daimyo was mortally offended. He stripped the samurai of his lands and cut off all contact with him, so he was reduced to being a ronin, a samurai without a lord. For some men, that would have been a challenge, but Mon Anjin had become soft and idle, and he was lost and bewildered. He forgot his pride to the extent that he threw himself at his daimyo's feet and begged for mercy."

Hana broke off, smiling gently and happily, more as if she were telling a child a story than reciting a dreadful history.

"What happened? Did his lord forgive him?" I asked.

"Alas, no. He was so enraged by Mon Anjin's weakness, he ordered him to commit seppuku to atone for his errors. Even then, Mon Anjin was too much of a coward to take the honorable path. I heard that the daimyo had to order some of his men to hold him down so another samurai could inflict the ritual cuts on him. He died in great agony like the coward he was. The daimyo bestowed everything that had been Mon Anjin's on the samurai who had inflicted the seppuku cut, and Mon Anjin's wife, his concubines, and his daughters were sold off as slaves. You see? Sometimes the gods are very just."

"It would seem so," I agreed. "But I can't help but wonder if they didn't have just a little help? It seems strange that such an important message from a daimyo to his samurai should go astray?"

"Even the gods need a little help sometimes." She shrugged and looked at me pityingly. "You're a blind and foolish slave to the code of bushido, Keiko, whereas I am free to follow my own code, to live how I choose. In some ways, we are very much alike, you and I. The main difference between us is that you will always be a slave while I am free. That's a shame. I rather like you, child. If you were less stubborn, and less a prisoner of your class, we might deal very well. As it is, you are now my prisoner. I almost feel sorry for you."

"Don't waste your pity on me, Hana. I don't want it, and I don't need it. And we're not at all alike. I have honor. You live only to suck the life out of the men who wander into your whorehouses. You have only bitterness, no matter how you like to dress it up."

I had offended her. Her expression didn't change, but I felt her fury vibrating in the air between us.

"I will break you, child," she said, quite calmly. "Not too soon, I hope. I want to see you learn how to cry." She stared around the room and began to smile. "It is rather dull in here. Almost like an overcast evening, don't you think?"

I stared straight at her, waiting. I was expecting more threats, but her next words puzzled me.

"You are different from anything I have ever offered. The rest of the girls here in the Hidden House are available during the afternoon and the night. To emphasize how special you are, you will be on display to very carefully selected patrons only at night. Generally, my patrons like enough light to see what they are buying. But in your case, I think a special kind of illumination is called for. I will light your prison, but not with lamps. From now on, your name is neither Keiko nor Jun. You are Hotaru—Firefly. And that is how your room will be lit, by fireflies, caged just as you are."

She stood and walked away without a word. The shoji slid back as she approached it and a tall, handsome young man glanced at me as he closed it behind her.

I stared into space, seeing nothing. I remembered the fireflies that had lit the night when Yo and I had made love. Was Hana able to read minds, I wondered? I could credit her with almost anything. Or were the gods mocking me? It didn't matter. I waited until I was sure I was not overlooked, and then I took a deep breath and closed my eyes.

The fireflies had been my friends when Yo had become my lover. I had felt then that they had exulted with us as we found joy in each other. Now, they would light my darkness. Every time Hana brought their cages into my room, I would remember nothing but Yo and the happiness we had shared.

I thanked Hana silently.

TWENTY-FIVE

How strange! My words will
Echo from a mountain top
As well as a cave

I thought often of the golden eagle Isamu and I had stolen for Father. Just as often, I apologized to his spirit for the terrible thing I had done to him. At the time, I thought only of delighting Father. Now, I understood how the free spirit of the bird must have suffered in his captivity. Just like him, I craved the freedom I had lost.

Hana was true to her word. My room became my entire world. The shoji were too thick for me to see out. The sounds of the streets were muted and far away. One or the other of two handsome young men slid the door open a fraction frequently and looked at me, grinning, but neither of them spoke. I knew when Abi was outside my door, as the shadow of his bulk could not be hidden even by the dense silk of the screen. Strangely, the fact that I was constantly under guard gave me hope. If Hana thought I wouldn't escape—that it wasn't possible for me to escape—

why bother with a guard? Every pulse of my friends the fire-flies reassured me. During the day, I missed them and looked forward to their company at night.

I found it very difficult to sleep. That first night was very terrible. My futon was comfortable, but I could find no relaxation on it. I lied awake, my thoughts circling in my mind until I gave myself a headache. Father would not notice my absence. Often, months went by before I so much as glimpsed him. Emiko would surely miss me—she would have nobody to complain to. But given her own delicate position, would she dare ask what had happened to me? I doubted it. Would Isamu really think I had run away? The longer I thought about it, the more I hoped it would be so. My brother was a shrewd man. He would recollect how much I had loved the Floating World. He would assume I was here. But also, might he think that somebody in the Floating World had seen through my disguise? And that that same somebody had taken me against my will? If that were so, then he would gather our guards and they would take the Floating World apart until they found me. The thought filled me with dread. If Isamu did find me, a pris-oner here in the Hidden House, he would kill me without a second thought. The honor of the family would have been compromised; he would have no option. The irony of it was not wasted on me. My mouth puckered into a sour smile at the thought. Whatever happened, I had only myself to blame.

The knowledge was not in the least comforting.

Hana visited me on the first day of my captivity. She sat and stared at me for a long time. Eventually, she began to speak as if she was taking up the threads of an interrupted conversation.

"Don't bother thinking about trying to bribe Abi," she

said abruptly. "He's besotted with one of my geisha. He's tried to buy her out time after time, but I've always refused him. Since you arrived, I've dangled hope in front of him. Told him if he makes sure he keeps you safe and secure, I might consider letting him have Machi at some time in the future. The silly girl is mad about him as well, so she's begging him to make sure he pleases me."

I did not answer, and after a few moments, Hana left me. When I was alone, my thoughts whirled uselessly. There had to be a way out of this impossible situation, but I could not find it.

One of Hana's young men slid my shoji open as dusk fell. He carried two small bamboo cages in his hands and hung them carefully on hooks on opposite sides of the room. He went away as silently as he had arrived. I stayed very still, sitting cross-legged on the tatami, and watched the fireflies begin to pulse as pure darkness fell. I heard the voices soon after.

The first time, a man spoke very quietly, and Hana answered him. I stretched, glancing around casually. I soon saw a slightly darker patch on the screen to my left. I guessed that there was a peep-hole there and that somebody was watching me from the darkened room beyond it. Soft though his voice was, I could hear the man's words clearly.

"A treasure indeed, Hana. And you say she's samurai?"

"Just so, my lord." Hana's voice was unctuous. "And I must tell you, she comes from one of the very best families. My lips are sealed as to her true name. But be assured, if you heard it, you would know her family. She is unique, I think. Nobody else has seen her yet. I knew you would be interested, so I saved her for you."

That was the beginning. Another man came later that

night and the play was reenacted. The same the next night and the next, until I began to become quite confident that none of Hana's patrons were as interested as she had expected. Obviously, none of them were willing to meet the price she was asking for me. My confidence was misplaced and the gods frowned at my presumption. One evening, there was no peep-hole. Instead, my shoji slid back and Hana ushered in a well-dressed man.

"This is the one I spoke of, my lord. Her name is Hotaru. Do you find her pleasing?"

The man squatted down in front of me. I stared straight in his face, refusing to bow my head. I rejoiced in my own rudeness and hoped he was offended.

"Her?" It was a cool night, but the man was sweating through his silken robes. I could smell it, and I wrinkled my nose in distaste. The man stroked my breasts through my robe. His hand was trembling. He glanced at Hana; she nodded approvingly. "She is very slim. Almost boyish. One has to be certain, of course. You're asking a very high price for the pleasure of taking this precious flower."

I felt Hana mentally urging me to lash out at him, to bite and kick. She wanted me to show spirit, as it would probably amuse her patron. Instead, I sat completely still, refusing to be baited.

"Well, my lord?" she prodded, her head tilted to one side almost flirtatiously.

"You may put my name down on the list of bidders, Hana. I find this creature of the night very interesting."

Even though I knew from his words that he would be followed by more, the knowledge did nothing to abate my disgust. Each night, my fireflies came to keep me company, and following in their wake were the men. At least one each night, sometimes two or three. I had thought the first man bad enough, but he was as nothing to those who followed.

All of them wanted to touch me. They patted my face, touched my breasts. Some wanted much more. I was ordered to stand, to take off my clothes, to stand naked before them. Some of them squeezed my breasts. Others pawed at my rear. One actually opened my mouth and ran his fingers around my teeth. I felt like an animal at market.

And always, I stood or sat or squatted—whatever my inspectors demanded—passively. Very soon, I found it easy to allow my mind to fly away. Although I felt their caresses, it meant nothing at all to me. I was stone. Hana knew and hated it. I rejoiced in her anger.

"A lovely thing," one man commented. "But it seems a little lacking in spirit?"

It? I forced my limbs to remain relaxed. *One day*, I promised silently, *I will no longer be imprisoned. And when that day comes, you will discover how passive I truly am. You and all the rest who treated me as if I was a horse to be purchased at some country market.*

"Well, truth to tell, I have to slip our lovely Hotaru a little something in her food to keep her quiet. Otherwise, she would be as a howling wolf. My first concern is always for my patrons, my lord. Of course, when she is finally purchased, she will be as wild and free as the wind. It will be up to the man who is fortunate enough to possess her to tame her spirit in any way he sees fit."

"Really?" He was impressed, I could see. "And she is whole, you say?"

The inevitable question! I had become irritated by it. Why, in the name of all the gods, did it matter so much? Had I been about to become their wife or concubine, I could understand it. But there was no honor in what they wanted from me. Would I care if they had taken a hundred women before me? Of course not. Even with Yo, who had aroused my heart and body in ways I had never even begun to imagine, I had not thought to question if I was his first lover. He was so skilled in the arts of love while, it didn't matter to me. So long as I was the last, of course. What fools these men were. I regarded them with contempt.

"But naturally. I told you, she is no common yujo. She comes from one of the very best families. She has been guarded well. Until now. And she will remain that way until the day arrives that she is taken by her danna. But she is no novice when it comes to arousing the body, my lord. She has talents that any man would find exciting beyond belief, I promise you."

Hana paused, timing her silence perfectly, waiting for the patron to give in to his curiosity. Most of them at least pretended not to be interested for a while, but this one gave in almost at once.

"Really? How can that be, if she is still a virgin? You say there's some mystery about her?"

"Oh, yes." Hana lowered her voice so that the patron had to lean forward to listen to her. I remained perfectly still, distancing them from my thoughts until their words no longer mattered to me. "She is from a very good family. But not one that you would be aware of, my lord. She originates from one of the outer islands."

"Really? I have heard interesting tales about those places. They say the inhabitants are still almost savages, and little more than animals in their ways."

His voice was eager. I turned my head to gaze at him in contempt. Out of all the fools who had inspected me, surely he was the most gullible. I almost laughed as he smiled at me.

"Look! She likes me! As I said, these primitives are just like dogs. Once they hear the voice of their master, they're happy to obey. Hana, do tell me. How did she get here to the Floating World?"

"Her father had arranged a suitable marriage for her, but this wild thing would have none of it. She had already taken a lover. A woman. The two ran away together and found their way to Edo. Once here, the other woman came to her senses and quickly realized that there were things a man could do for her that another woman could never match."

My would-be patron was almost drooling with excitement. I had heard Hana's nonsense so often, I knew exactly what she was going to say next. I allowed my thoughts to drift away again.

"This one was the masculine side of the relationship. She was arrested when she tried to steal some food. Of course, when she was taken into custody, her true self was discovered. Fortunately for her, the captain of the guards was a patron of my teahouse. He understood at once that she was a treasure I might find interesting and offered her to me. She cost me a very great deal of money, but I knew at once that she was something unique. Something that would delight only the most discerning of my patrons."

"Of course. You may certainly put me down on the list of bidders for her. Are there many names already on the list?" He was too keen. Hana saw it at once and smiled.

"The list of those who long to pluck this wildflower contains the most important names in Edo and beyond. I have ensured that only the most discriminating are even aware of her existence."

The man preened, and I saw my price rising in Hana's smile.

None of it bothered me in the least. I was sure that none of the men who prodded and poked me would ever possess me. I did not yet know how it would happen, but somehow, I would escape from my firefly prison. And far more importantly, I would ensure that the honor of my family was not stained by my foolish actions.

I was equally certain that Yo was close. I felt it in my spirit. I could think of only one way he could get close to me. I began to look carefully at each of the men Hana brought before me, hoping each time that I would recognize Yo.

I did not. Still, I hoped.

TWENTY-SIX

Do not fret your life
Away. All has its season.
You cannot change it

"You've got Hana quite worried." The elder of the two young men who guarded me kneeled down. "She natters at us nonstop to make sure we keep a close eye on you. Myself, I think she exaggerates both your intelligence and your spirit."

I didn't answer him. It was daytime. He had surely only come into my room to amuse himself by taunting me. I would not give him the pleasure of thinking he was getting to me.

Unlike the patrons who came in the night, this young man appeared to have infinite patience. He glanced down my body with interest, but made no move to touch me. I met his eyes and saw something reflected in them that put me instantly on my guard.

"I'm Hana's prisoner." I glanced around my room sourly

and made sure I sounded dejected. "I'm guarded day and night. If Hana thinks I can escape, I'm flattered."

He seemed delighted that I spoke to him as if we were equals.

"So you should be. I find it quite amusing that you've got Hana flustered." His grin widened, showing excellent teeth. "But I also thought that it was only right that you should understand that escape isn't an option. You can try, and I do hope that you do something desperate. Hana's promised us that if you try and escape and we stop you, we can teach you a lesson you're not going to forget. We'd make sure that there were no marks, of course. The patrons would never stand for damaged goods. But we could hurt you in ways that would make you scream for us to stop and never leave so much as a bruise. We'd enjoy that greatly."

I cowered very slightly, my glance sliding away from his hot eyes. He liked that. I guessed he had come to taunt me, to try and make me afraid of him. He was a fool, then, just as much as the patrons. He stood and stretched, tossing his final words casually at me.

"In any event, it's not going to be long now. Hana's named her starting price for you. She's only accepting bids above that, and there's only a handful of men who can afford to carry on. I daresay the surgeon will be with you quite shortly."

The room seemed to have become cold all at once, and I would have liked to pull my kakebuton around me for warmth. I guessed that my guard would have liked for me to show weakness, so I did not. I stared into the air in front of me, refusing to acknowledge his presence. He became bored quickly and left me.

I knew my guard had been right when no more men

were brought to inspect me that night. Only my fireflies kept me company. When I thought I was alone, I scraped a tiny hole in the corner of one of the screens with my finger-nail. The silk was very thick, and it took me many hours to do it. By the time I had made a hole large enough for my fireflies to pass through, the nail on my right index finger had been worn down to the nail bed. My finger pad was bright red and throbbing with pain. I opened one cage door, and then the other, shaking the bamboo gently against the opening. It seemed to me that my companions didn't really wish to leave me, but eventually one, and then the other firefly accepted their chance of freedom. I smiled as I watched their light vanish. I rejoiced that I had been able to give them their freedom even as I wished that my own prison could be left so easily.

The cages were removed the next morning, as always. I wondered if either of my guards noticed that my fireflies had gone. Before I found out, I had another visitor.

I watched Abi suspiciously as he squatted in front of me. He was truly a giant. Even hunkered down as he was, the top of my head barely reached his chest. I guessed he weighed at least three times as much as me, possibly more. Yet he had none of the menace that the other guards carried with them, and his movements were curiously graceful. Unlike the other two men, he had never entered my room, never even glanced in at me. Why now? More threats, perhaps? I was wary.

I couldn't have been more wrong.

"Hana has told all of us how we must be very careful to keep a good watch on you, Hotaru." His voice was star-tlingly pleasant. Not the baritone I had expected, but a deep tenor. Did he have a beautiful singing voice, I wondered? If he did, did he ever have reason to sing? I doubted it and felt sympathy for this mountain of a man.

"So your companions have said," I replied neutrally.

He nodded seriously. It was like watching a wave break on the beach. "Yes. You need to be careful of them. Big and Bigger are not good enemies to have."

I coughed to hide a giggle. The guards were really called Big and Bigger? They were tall, certainly, but next to Abi, they were insignificant.

"I had not heard their names before; they amused me," I explained. "Why do they have such silly names? They sound like characters out of a kabuki play."

"If you were one of Hana's geisha, you would know how they came by their names. They are Hana's enforcers. If any of the patrons get out of order, they sort them out. If any of the geisha cross Hana in any way, she sets them onto them. It never happens twice. I have seen them in the bath, Hotaru. I am a big man, for sure, but their trees of flesh make mine look like a wilted twig. I have heard it said that no woman could take either of them into her body without screaming with pain. I believe that."

I recalled the way the elder of the two had looked at me and I shuddered.

"Thank you for telling me, Abi-san," I said politely. "I will take great care not to annoy either of them."

By now, I was intensely curious. It was kind of Abi to come and warn me about the guards, but surely that was not enough to tempt him into my prison cell. He was nervous, glancing around constantly.

"Hana is not here," he said finally. "She has gone to negotiate an event that many of the geisha from the Green Teahouse are to attend. Her boys have gone to the kabuki, leaving me to guard you." I raised my eyebrows in amazement. I would never have thought of my guards as "boys," although I thought that next to Abi any man would appear diminished. He paused, and I nodded encouragingly. His nervousness was contagious. I had to resist the temptation to fidget.

"I see. So why have you come to talk with me, Abi? I think Hana would not be pleased to find you here."

"She would not." He nodded gravely and then took a deep breath that parted the front of his robe. "A person has spoken to me."

He fell silent again. I watched his anxious face and chose my words with care.

"And what has this person said to you, Abi?"

"He told me that Hana will never release Machi to me. He says that I'm too valuable for her ever to lose her power over me. Do you think that's so?"

"Yes," I said simply. "Who has spoken to you, Abi?"

"I don't know his name. He came to me a few days ago and told me he was your friend. That he wanted to release you, to take you away from here. When I told him that I couldn't talk to him, that I wanted to know nothing about any plans he had, he told me about Machi. Explained to me that we would never be together. I didn't want to believe him, but if even a stranger like you can see it, I think it must be so."

Yo! It had to be Yo. He had found me. My spirits soared.

"Thank you for telling me this, Abi. You have made me very happy. Will you see this man again?"

"Oh, yes. He told me I was to speak to you and he would come to me again tonight to hear your answer. What shall I tell him you said?"

"Tell him..." How could I possibly explain to this

stranger? I gave in and simply said what was in my heart. "Please, Abi. Tell him..." I spoke in a rush. "Tell him I love him. But tell him as well that Hana has the power to destroy my family if she wants to. That I can't see any way I can escape without her taking revenge on me. Tell him that. He'll understand."

"He said you would say that. He said that I was to tell you that Hana is lying to you." He paused, his massive brow wrinkling in thought. "He said that Emiko married Soji last week. Soji knows everything and has forgiven her. Does that make sense to you, Hotaru?"

I licked my lips and nodded. Words were fighting to get past my lips, but only a foolish bleating sound came from my mouth.

"He said that if I helped you escape, he would take Machi from the Green Teahouse and make sure we both got away from Edo. He said that sumo wrestlers were much in demand in Kyoto and that he would have a patron waiting there for me. Is he telling the truth, Hotaru? Can he do it?"

"His name is Yo," I whispered. "He is shinobi. He will keep his word to you, Abi. I promise you."

The great man's face cleared like a child whose thoughts flit with every heartbeat.

"Then I will help you, Hotaru. But not just yet. I will see your shinobi tonight and tell him I have spoken to you. When I hear his plan and am sure Hana will never suspect I was involved, then I will help you leave this place. It has to be done quickly. I heard Hana say that the final bids for you will be opened soon. She's arranged a ceremony where the three men who are still bidding will be present. I've never seen her so delighted. She's gloating about them knowing they're competing against each other for you."

"We have a little time, then." I sighed with relief.

Abi shook his great head and frowned. "No, you don't understand. You don't have much time at all. The surgeon is going to attend to you tomorrow. Hana wants to be sure that your surgery is healed before you go to your danna."

TWENTY-SEVEN

There is sorrow in
Parting. But far greater joy
In reunion

I had expected the surgeon to be an old man. He was not. Barely middle-aged, I thought, but crouched about the shoulders, no doubt from spending so much time bent over his patients. He put two furoshiki—the traditional large, silk squares used to bundle anything and everything—on the tatami and unwrapped the knot of one of them with a practiced flick. I stared at the array of needles and odd-looking implements it contained in horrified fascination. Behind the surgeon, Big and Bigger exchanged a glance, and I saw the flicker of excitement in their expressions.

"I think that's all in order," the surgeon said crisply. His voice was rather low-pitched and extremely reassuring. If I had been facing any routine surgery, I would have found it comforting. "Now, gentlemen. I need only one more thing.

A large pot of freshly boiled water, if you please. The biggest pot you have."

"What? What do you want that for? Hana said we were to keep an eye on you. She never mentioned bringing you water." Bigger frowned, his beautifully plucked brows arching suspiciously. The surgeon raised his head and stared at Bigger until he dropped his gaze resentfully.

"I can't help that, young man. Hana has told me that it is vital that this operation is carried out successfully. I have no wish to disappoint her."

Big grinned, nudging Bigger gleefully in the ribs. But Bigger was not to be distracted.

"What do you want water for? She's clean enough, isn't she?" he said.

The surgeon sighed. He stabbed his finger in the air fiercely, as if he was addressing a room full of students rather than the two feared enforcers.

"Young man, I have been a successful surgeon for many years. And I have been successful because I take great care to adhere to the teachings of Buddha. The Lord Buddha teaches us that all life is sacred, from the largest to the very smallest. You are surely aware that of the five precepts of the Buddha's teaching. By far the most important is the first precept—one must commit to never killing a living being." I could see my guards' eyes beginning to glaze with boredom. But the surgeon had not finished with them yet. "As a surgeon, it is perhaps even more important to me than others. I do not know why it is so, but over the years I have seen many patients die, not from the pain of their operation, but because the wound became infected and poisoned their whole body. Many surgeons say that the open wound has enticed an evil spirit to feast on it and their breath has contaminated the patient. I do not know the truth of it. But I do know that before I operate, if I take care to wash the patient in water as hot as they can stand and steep my instruments and thread in boiling water before I use it, then I do not cause Buddha grief by inadvertently killing my patient. Or at least, not often."

Bigger rolled his eyes and sighed theatrically.

The surgeon shrugged. "Very well. I will operate without my cauldron of hot water. But be sure, I will explain to Hanna that you refused my wishes. If the girl dies, I will not have her death on my conscience."

The boys glanced at each other. Eventually, Bigger shuffled his feet and grimaced.

"You'll have to wait," he said sulkily. "If you really want the biggest pot the kitchen can provide, it's going to take a while to heat it up. It'll take both of us to carry it. You don't want to be taken in by her innocent face. If we leave you alone with her, she's likely to break your neck."

"Really?" The surgeon pursed his lips. "Well, given that I'm about to cause her a great deal of pain, I can't say I would blame the poor girl. But I have a solution for that." He took a small vial from the furoshiki and shook it vigorously. The contents stirred slowly, as if they resented being disturbed. "Would one of you big, strong gentlemen hold her down for me? In my experience, it's always the smallest dogs that want to bite. This will have her asleep before you can both leave the room."

Big moved toward me quickly. I managed to land a good, hard kick on his shin before his arms were around me. He kneeled on my legs, leaning away from me so I couldn't reach him to bite.

"Quickly, man," he instructed the surgeon. "She's a wild cat, and no mistake."

The surgeon held my nose and poured the pearlescent

liquid down my throat. I held it there for as long as I could, but when he put his palm firmly over my mouth, I was forced to swallow so I could take a breath. It tasted delicious, like melon. A heartbeat later, I slumped to the tatami gracelessly.

"By the gods, but that was quick! How long will it last?" Big demanded.

"Long enough for you to obtain my boiling water for me. If the girl is fortunate, it may keep her asleep until after I have stitched her up. On your way, gentlemen. The sooner I get my boiling water, the sooner I can restore this one's maidenhood to her. I can't believe she'll wake up before you two get back. But even if she does, if she's trouble, I can always shout for help from the honorable sumo wrestler you've left in the corridor. I doubt any woman ever born would cause him a problem." The men shuffled out. The slap of their zori died away before the surgeon spoke again. "Unless, of course, her name happens to be Machi. Come on, Keiko. We must move fast."

I tried to get up so quickly, my feet tangled in my robe and I sprawled on the floor again. Abi pattered in on silent feet and stood me on my feet with as much care as if I was precious to him. I stared at the surgeon and wondered why his figure seemed to be misty. The potion he had given to me, perhaps?

"It was nothing more than melon juice." He wiped the tears from my eyes very gently with the back of his first finger. "Do you really think I would risk hurting you?" We stole a moment to stare at each other, and then Yo was brisk again. "Come on. We must be quick. Here, Abi. Drink this." He handed a large flask to Abi. The sumo wrestler took it and downed the contents at a gulp. "Keiko, put these on."

He was untying the second furoshiki as he spoke,

handing a threadbare robe and a pair of peasants' straw waraji sandals to me along with a deep straw hat. I tossed off my silk kimono and wrapped the cotton robe and greasy obi around me quickly, tugging the straw hat down over my face. By the time I had changed my clothes, Yo had exchanged his sober surgeon's robe for a merchant's well-cut kimono and a silk obi. He straightened and I understood at once that it was less the clothes that had changed him as his bearing and expression. He was smiling and looked at least fifteen years younger than the serious man who had prepared to operate on me.

"Just one more thing." He reached back into the furoshiki and pulled out a strip of dirty cotton. "Bind your eyes with this when we get outside and then take my staff. Once we leave here, you are an anma."

"Abi!" I cried as the big man slumped to the floor, his eyes glazed and unseeing. "Is he all right?"

"He will be." Yo took my arm and tugged me to the screen door. "I've given him an immensely powerful sleeping draught. He won't wake up until tomorrow morning. When he does wake up, he'll tell Hana that the honorable surgeon told him he looked a little yellow around the eyes and kindly gave him some medicine to drink. A moment later, and he knew nothing. He'll wait for a while until Hana forgets to be suspicious. On a certain day, Machi will go out shopping. Her maid will be grabbed by a couple of thugs and Machi will disappear into thin air. Abi, of course, will be beside himself with grief. He will search the whole of the Floating World for her, but he'll find no trace. Eventually, he'll be so heartbroken that he'll tell Hana he's going to leave the Floating World. That's the last anybody in Edo will hear of either of them, but in due course, Kyoto will discover it has acquired a very talented sumo wrestler who has moved there with his wife."

Yo spoke very softly, pulling me down the corridor as he spoke. He had chosen his time well, early afternoon, when even the servants were allowed to take a rest before the surge of customers later in the day. We stopped dead as a bedroom door opened. A geisha stared out at us, her eyes huge with amazement. She glanced down the corridor at my open screen door. Yo took a step toward her, but the girl shook her head and put all her fingers to her mouth and then threw her hands open. She had no need to speak; her gesture said as clearly as words that she would stay silent. As she turned and moved away from us, I realized that one of her legs must be much shorter than the other as she lurched fiercely to one side, almost losing her balance. The arm that caught at the doorframe for balance was badly withered as well. One of Hana's flawed gems, no doubt.

"What happened to the real surgeon?" I whispered.

"Nothing." Yo smiled reassuringly. "He was happy for me to take his place. It discharged a substantial debt he owed me. When Hana asks him how a strange man came to take his place, he will be astonished. He will insist that he sent her a message explaining he had been taken with a particularly virulent fever and could not attend her. Being a skilled surgeon, he will have no problem in appearing to have all the necessary symptoms."

I nodded and spoke urgently. "How do we get out of here?"

"We walk out." Yo hustled me forward, his hand on my elbow. "Down here. This door leads into the garden."

We slid through silently. In a few steps, we had crossed the raked gravel and he was pushing at another door so faded by the weather a casual glance would never have noticed it. The alley outside was quiet and almost secluded for the Floating World.

"We need to separate," Yo said quickly. "Hana will be looking for a man and woman together, so we have a better chance this way. There's a ryokan two buildings down from the brothel Isamu showed you. Go there, take a room. I'll join you as soon as I can. And listen, this is important. If you're found, *don't fight.* Not unless it's that or risk death." He pushed a slender purse into my obi and wrapped my fingers around his staff. I fastened the bandage around my eyes and turned and walked away. I had to. At that moment, I was more woman than onna-bugeisha. If I had lingered, I would have hung on to him, refusing to let him go. But he was right, we had a far better chance separated. But the pain of finding my lover only to lose him at once was very great.

The bandage gave me no problem at all. In fact, I closed my eyes beneath it, the better to allow my other senses to see for me. I had been so long in near-silent captivity that the roar of voices and traffic hurt my ears. I found myself walking carefully, my shoulders hunched, as if I expected a blow at any moment.

"You've got money, anma?" The innkeeper was only interested in whether I was going to be able to pay. I fished in my purse, handing him two coins. I had no idea if it would be enough, but I realized instantly that I had been generous when he snatched them off me. "Business must have been good. That'll do for a room to yourself and some supper. Follow me. Mind the stairs," he added grudgingly. I followed him, taking care to tap with my staff.

I had no need to take off my bandage to know my room was filthy. It stank of sweat, old food, and the remains of sex. No doubt my host rented out his rooms to any yujo who had a customer who wanted to rut in privacy for an hour or two.

In spite of that, I sank onto the futon with relief. Something ran over my hand and I snatched it away with disgust. I sat very still, listening to the sounds of the street, the clatter of pans from the kitchen below, the enticements of the whores captive in the lattice brothel. My visit there with Isamu felt slightly unreal, rather like a very vivid dream. I tensed as I heard footsteps in the corridor.

"Here you are, then. Supper. I've put it on the table for you." I heard his breath quicken. His voice was suddenly sly. "I don't suppose you've got that much money, anma. And the days are turning cold now. I daresay you might want somewhere to stay for a while. I've got this dreadful back-ache. If you could do something about it for me, I daresay I might see fit to let you stay here for a while in return for your services."

"The master is most kind," I said respectfully.

"We'll see, then. I've heard tales about you anma. I've been told that you make up for being blind by concen-trating on all your other senses. If that's right, I'm sure we can come to some sort of agreement."

He walked over to me and thrust his hips out, waggling his tree a hand's breadth away from my face. I kept my head down, wondering about the sort of man who could expose himself to a blind woman.

"Yes, master," I said. Apparently satisfied, he tucked his tree away with a grunt of satisfaction.

"Get your supper, then."

I left my bandage in place and groped my way carefully to the table, holding on to the edge as I sat cross-legged on the prickly tatami. I guessed the innkeeper was the sort of man who would enjoy watching the yujo entertain their clients, and I was taking no risks. I had been ferociously hungry, but now I found my appetite was dead. Just as well.

I poked at the food on my plate. A whole fish, mackerel by the smell of it, and far from fresh. I ate a mouthful and then put my chopsticks down. Even had I been starving, it would have taken willpower to swallow the rank flesh.

I tensed. There were new noises in the street. Loud voices—loud even for the Floating World. Voices raised in complaint and pain.

Instinctively, I reached for my staff. I was about to take off my hat and bandage when, as clearly as if he were beside me, I heard Yo's voice. *Don't fight. Not unless it's that or face death.* I froze with uncertainty and then moved quickly. I was glad I had left most of my stinking mackerel untouched. I ripped off the oily skin and smeared it on my hands and face, and as an afterthought on my feet and legs. I gagged at my own smell and closed my nostrils to the odor. My lazy landlord had left the guts in the fish. I scooped them up in my fingers and smeared them over my black moss. With a mental apology to my own body, I shoved more inside my sex. By the time my shoji slid open with a bang, I was back on my futon, my head lowered and my shoulders hunched in fear.

"This her, is it?" Not Hana's boys. I was grateful for that; I doubted my disguise would fool them for a second. "Arrived a while ago, you say?"

"That's right. I don't know what's going on here, but I can't see what you lot want with a blind anma."

"If we want your opinion, we'll ask for it. Hana sent us to look for a man and a girl. We know they haven't left the Floating World. The guard wouldn't dare lie to Hana, so they're both still here somewhere."

I heard the innkeeper's sharp intake of breath at Hana's name. Suddenly, his tone was oily and deferential.

"Well, she's the only guest I've got at the moment. I can't

imagine she's the one you're after, but I'll leave you both too it."

"That's right," the other man said. "Get out of our way and leave her to us."

The shoji closed. No hesitation this time, the innkeeper hastily gone.

"You." The man who had spoken first poked me with his foot. "Anma, are you? What's your name?"

"Nara, master," I whispered. The name had popped into my head. I wondered if I had made a mistake when he laughed.

"Blossom from paradise, eh? What do you think about that, Jiro? Suits her, I don't think!" Both men cackled.

"Better be on our way," Jiro said

"Oh, I don't know." The other man was licking his lips. I heard the whisper of his dry tongue. "Even Hana can't begrudge us a bit of fun, surely. And it seems a shame to waste a bit of manko when it's going free."

I could feel the lust coming off both men. I turned my head from one to the other, instructing my body to be small. Humble. Afraid.

"What do you say, anma? You wouldn't mind servicing two big, strapping chaps like us, I daresay? You'd probably enjoy it, eh?" He reached down and tugged my robe apart.

"She's a bit flat-chested." Jiro sounded disappointed.

"Don't be so fussy. As the saying goes, 'a padded jacket is an acceptable gift, even in summer.' You're having her below the waist, not above it."

As he spoke, he reached down and yanked at my robes. The obi caught, and he cursed. I crouched into myself, like a child who expects to be beaten. Finally, the obi gave way and he and Jiro grabbed my shoulders, forcing me back on the tatami. I would wait until the first man tried to enter me. Then he would regret it. Both of them would.

"By all the gods!" Jiro reeled back, retching. "If you want to put your tree in that, you're welcome. But I'm not having any of it. She must have some sort of disease. She reeks. And look—her manko's full of green slime!"

Both men jerked back from me. I wanted to laugh, but instead clutched at Jiro's robe.

"Oh, no, master. There's nothing wrong with me, I promise you. Please, don't leave me now. It's been days since I had a man, and I could really do with a good seeing to. I'll be that grateful. I won't even charge either of you."

I rose to my knees and shuffled across the tatami, hanging on to Jiro's robe. He screamed like a woman in childbirth and yanked his robe from my grasp.

"Come on, let's get out of here. I wouldn't touch you if you paid me, never mind about for free."

I heard their footsteps moving away far quicker than they had arrived and smiled to myself. Yo had been right, I understood that now. If I had fought the two men—and I had no doubt at all that I could have beaten them easily— the innkeeper would have known instantly that I was the one Hana was searching for. Although he could not have kept me, his cries would have alerted the whole street and I would have been discovered.

Ah, Yo. I am in your debt. Come here and I will settle that debt!

TWENTY-EIGHT

When you sail upon
The sea, I long to be a
Wave beneath your keel.

*T*he bathwater was so hot, it was almost unbearable. As is so often the case in life, that subtle difference was the dividing line between pleasure and pain.

"I thought you were never going to come and take me out of the Hidden House."

"Liar." Yo smiled. "You knew I would be there. You just couldn't contain your impatience."

He shimmied his hips and water splashed on my neck. I sighed with pleasure. Still, I had one doubt.

"Hana won't find us here?"

"No. This house belongs to Jokan-Ji Temple. It's the temple where all the whores who gave their lives to the Floating World are buried. It's not somewhere the men who visit the pleasure quarter want to know about. Quite often, the women die of neglect or disease, and their bodies are just dumped behind the temple for the monks to find and give a simple burial to."

I nodded soberly, feeling a knot of guilt in my belly. Just like the men who used them, I had never given a thought to all the women who spent their lives laboring for their pleasure.

Yo smiled at my serious face and went on quietly, "The kannushi of the temple used to be a comrade of mine. We have helped each other many times in the past, until the gods called him and he renounced the life of a shinobi and ended up in Jokan-Ji Temple. He was the one who gifted this house to the temple. More importantly, he may well be the only man in the Floating World who isn't afraid of Hana or her yakuza. They keep a respectable distance from him; he has a great deal of power and influence, even now. He knows everybody worth knowing, and they have much respect for him."

I relaxed. If Yo believed we were safe here, then it was so. It was a very good feeling.

After Hana's men had left me, I had sat silently, waiting. After a while, I heard cautious steps outside my room, then the innkeeper's voice whispered through the screen.

"Anma, are you all right? The men left very quickly. Have they hurt you?"

"Oh." I tried the effect of a moan. It quite pleased me, so I did it again. "Oh, master. I don't understand it. They were both going to take me, but when they took my robe away, they both lost interest. They seemed to think there was something wrong with my manko. Do you think you should come and have a look at it yourself?"

He backed away so quickly, I heard him trip over the tatami. "Not just now. I'm swamped. I have somebody who wants your room tomorrow. Make sure you're gone by first light, anma."

"But how am I to know when it's light, master?" I wailed. "You must come and wake me. Help me to dress."

"Just go!" he shouted as he fled down the corridor.

I waited so very long, I thought I imagined it when I felt Yo's presence. He took my fish-stinking hand and helped me up.

"Stay close to me, anma." He spoke in a normal voice, and I wondered if the landlord was hovering nearby. "I have need of your services to help cure a terrible stiffness in my neck and back. You were recommended to me by a friend as the best masseuse in the whole of the Floating World. It's taken all day to track you down. I was beginning to think you must have been caught up in the trouble outside. I have no idea what's going on, do you?"

The landlord *was* listening, then. I answered dutifully.

"No, master. I heard the noise and two men came and questioned me, but I don't know what it was all about."

"No matter. Come along and we'll see what you can do for me."

I pursed my lips with amusement at his wickedness and followed my lover meekly. Now, Yo watched me, smelling my arm with obvious amusement.

"Are you never going to be satisfied, woman?" he asked. "Isn't it enough that I rescued you in the first place and then turned myself into a maid to make sure you were clean before you got into the bath?"

I lowered my arm into the water quickly. Yo had rinsed and soaped me repeatedly from head to foot. I knew that I no longer stank, but a gleam of mischief made me hold out my hand to him.

"Are you sure I don't smell like gone-off mackerel?"

He took my hand and sniffed it elaborately before taking one of my fingers in his mouth and sucking the pad. The sensation was divine.

"You smell and taste delicious. Shall I eat you up to make sure?"

"Yes, please," I said simply. I breathed so deeply it was a groan. "Yo, stop."

His expression was bewildered as he raised his face to look at me.

I paused, considering my words. "I can't forget that I owe you my life. That's not something I can just put aside. If it hadn't been for you taking me from the Hidden House, I would have killed the man who finally met Hana's price and then myself."

"Of course you would have," Yo said simply. "It would have been the only honorable thing to do. But that didn't happen. The gods decided that it wasn't time for you to die. You owe me nothing."

I shook my head. My escape had nothing to do with the gods and everything to do with Yo. I struggled with my pride, but the words had to be said.

"I am in your debt, Yo. I owe my life to you. It's an obligation I can never repay."

"Really?"

I stared at him incredulously. He was smiling at me as if I had said something that amused him. Could he not see that I was laying myself at his feet in total humiliation? I ground my teeth together so hard they hurt, determined the bitter words in my mouth would never leave my tongue. I began to relax as he went on.

"Then we're equal, aren't we? You let me rise from the dojo when you beat me. You could have killed me, but you didn't. You could have said nothing and watched me slink away like a hurt dog, my pride gone forever, but you didn't. You said then that we were to be equals. But saying something doesn't make it so. Now, I have returned your mercy. We are truly equal, onna-bugeisha."

He leaned the short distance between us and kissed me quite hard, full on my lips. I waited for a second, searching for the flaw in his argument, but I could find none. I opened my mouth and let my tongue explore his teeth and tongue. Only for a heartbeat, all the breath was knocked out of me as Yo put his arms around me and tightened them with crushing force.

The hot water surged around us. I thought it was angry that we had excluded it from between our bodies. Yet we had not; we were both slippery and hot with it. My hand knocked against his groin and I felt a hard ribbon of flesh. I was sure that had not been on his body when we had made love on the dojo and pulled away from Yo's embrace to look.

"Yes, it's new." He ran my fingers over the scar. It was as long as my hand and ran from his black moss up into his belly. "I was a fool. My opponent begged me for mercy. He promised that if I spared him, he would live a righteous life. He was on his knees before me, babbling that he would change. For some unknown reason, I believed him. I turned away, and next second, he had a dagger between my legs, slashing at me. If I hadn't been so quick, he would have opened my kintama with his knife and no doubt enjoyed watching me bleed to death."

"You killed him," I said flatly. Of course he had. A dog that bites once may be shown mercy. Twice is once too much.

"I did. I cut his throat. A merciful death compared to what he planned for me. Trust me, he deserved it. He had killed many men. If he'd had a conscience, he would never have slept at night. But it didn't bother him in the least."

"And you, Yo?" I asked curiously. "Do you sleep well?"

"Yes," he said simply. "I consider myself an honorable man. I take only commissions that seem to me to be right. I would never take another's life unless my own life was threatened. And I pray for the soul of each and every man I have helped into the next world." I would have let it drop there, but Yo was not finished. "You remember how I told you not to fight unless you had to?"

"I remember. And I didn't."

"You should always remember that. If you had dispatched the men who came for you, the landlord of the inn would have run into the street screaming for help. Others would have come, too many for you to fight. As it was, you used your brains and survived."

So I had! The thought pleased me greatly. "I am onna-bugeisha."

"You are," Yo agreed gravely. "And you are also my lover. Have you forgotten that, onna-bugeisha? Do I have to make you remember?"

I laughed in delight, all seriousness gone. All thought of us being equals fled into the rising steam as I lay back against the wall of the bath and held my arms open in invitation.

"Please do." Fleetingly, I thought how very strange it was that the touch of his hand was so arousing when it had given me nothing but disgust to think of what Hotaru's would-be patrons had planned for me.

"Good?"

I had no need to answer. My body thrust forward on its own, and Yo smiled. I pushed back fiercely, at the same time allowing my first finger to trace the line of his scar. It must have been tender still as he moaned, although it could have been with pleasure. We were already at the stage where pain and pleasure become intermingled so that one brings as much delight as the other.

Finally, my mind lost control of my body. As the waves of my yonaki rolled through me, I felt Yo tense and heard him moan. His seed burst inside me, hotter even than the water that beat around us, and I gasped, feeling the intensity of my orgasm like a living thing within me.

I had no concept of how much time passed; time had ceased to have any meaning for me. The intense pleasure of my yonaki had given way to a glow that seemed to inhabit my whole body. I had no wish to move, for fear I might disturb it.

"Mistress." Yo spoke softly.

I smiled and lay my head on his shoulder. "Master." We were truly equal, and it delighted me.

We were silent again, everything that needed to be said between us done. Finally, my thoughts became my own again and I stretched and sighed.

"I must go home. See Isamu and explain things to him. I hope he'll understand. I would have liked to have said goodbye to Emiko, but I can't. How long has she been gone?" I felt intensely guilty that this was the first time I had thought of my sister since I had been captured in the Floating World. I comforted myself with the thought that she would not have spared a thought for me.

"She must have married Soji very soon after Hana took you."

My thoughts were bitter. All I had suffered had been needless. If I had known, I could have laughed in Hana's face and found a way to break free. Yo seemed to read my face.

"You didn't know. Hana made sure of that. But nothing ever happens without reason. You are stronger, more certain of yourself now than you were before she took you. You've survived the worst that fate could throw at you. Nothing can ever hurt you again like she tried to do."

I thought, *You're wrong, Yo. You could hurt me.* But different words came from my lips.

"No, I couldn't have known. But it doesn't matter. I'll leave at first light. If I dress as a noblewoman and ride a decent horse, I can't imagine that even Hana would dare try and stop me, even if she recognized me. Will you wait here for me?"

I expected Yo to argue, to insist that he had to go with me, to keep me safe, but his words took me by surprise.

"I understand that you feel you have to go alone. But be careful. I've heard that there has been a great deal of unrest amongst the peasants this summer. The weather's been too hot, and there hasn't been enough rain. Many villages are starving where the crops have failed entirely."

"I heard about that before I came back to the Floating World. Why should it bother me? The worse that can happen is that I get pestered for alms. No peasant ever born would dare attack a samurai woman, even if she was on her own."

Yo shook his head and took my hand, squeezing my fingers as if to emphasize what he was saying.

"You've changed, Keiko-chan. You're no longer the innocent girl that I first met. And the world is changing around you. There are men who tell the peasants that they are as good as anybody else. They listen and look at the rich men and wonder why they have food on their tables. Why their babies are not dying because their mothers have milk to give them."

He sounded so concerned, I almost gave in and asked him to come with me. A passing memory of me telling my maid that we had no need to be worried, that Father would make sure our villagers had enough rice, came back to me. Had he shown them charity, I wondered. Or had he simply shrugged and turned away when they had no money to meet his price? My back prickled with unease. I pushed the sensation away and smiled.

"I'll be watchful," I promised. And at the same moment, I promised myself that before I left Isamu, I would ask him if our own villagers were hungry. And if they were, I would make him promise to speak to Father, to persuade him to open our rice stores for the peasants. He would do that, I was sure. They depended on us. The code of bushido was clear—we must take care of our own.

Still, I felt a flash of anger for those men who were lying to the peasants. There was no need. We had all lived lives in the past, we all had lives to live in the future. Who knew? In my next incarnation, it might be me who had an empty belly, and one of our villagers who threw me scraps from his table. That was the way it was. One's fate was decided even before birth. To fight against it was futile.

I dressed in the kimono and obi Yo provided for me. Being Jun had been amusing, but it felt so very good to be in my own skin again. Yo escorted me to the gate and helped me mount a horse that I had never seen before. I wondered what has happened to my nice, docile mare and then glanced at Yo's face and decided not to ask. Perhaps I might find her at home, waiting for me. I hoped so, even as I knew I was wishing in vain.

"I'll be back as soon as I can." I smiled down at Yo, wickedly amused that my extra height on horseback gave me the advantage.

"I'll wait until the mid-day meal tomorrow. If you're not back by then, I'll come for you."

"Stop worrying." I flicked my reins, anxious to be off. "I'm going home. Isamu will be furious with me. Apart from that, what's going to happen to me?"

I was still smiling, secretly delighted with Yo's concern for me, as I urged my horse to a trot and passed over the dry moat of the Floating World.

TWENTY-NINE

The single petal
That falls from the rose to your
Hand lays like life's blood

*S*omething should have prepared me. Some instinctual sense of unease should have made me silent and wary as I approached my home. As it was, I sang most of the way, only stopping when my throat became dry. I stopped once to allow my horse to take water from the stream—a tributary of a much wider river—that marked the boundary of our land. It was lower than I had expected. My mount had to nose water from the bare trickle that ran grudgingly between pebbles. When he raised his head, his muzzle was sandy rather than wet. I nodded to myself. No matter how angry Isamu was with me, I would speak to him about our villagers. If Father hadn't yet opened his rice stores to them, I would tell Isamu that he must. I would *tell* Isamu what Father should to do? I giggled to myself. Truly, Yo had been right when he said I had changed.

I tried to jog my mount into a trot as my home came into

view. He hesitated, shaking his head and standing his ground. I gave him a kick and shook the reins fiercely. I felt his reluctance and began to worry.

Something was not right. A high wall shielded the house and garden. I could just make out the roof of the house peeking over it. There was one high gate set in the wall—easily wide enough for two horses to pass through, side by side. This gate was always closed. Today, it was not only open, but each gate was flung wide. They were not latched back neatly to the wall, but hanging at odd angles as if they had been thrown apart and simply left. My fingers gripped my reins tighter. I paused outside the gate and called out. When nobody replied, I called again.

Wrong. All wrong. A man should have been stationed at the gate. He was there day and night. There should have been servants in the garden, raking the gravel and plucking weeds from it, picking up any fallen blossoms and leaves. My thoughts skittered warily as I listened to the silence.

I slid off my horse and tied the reins to the great door knocker on the gate, then walked into the garden as silent as a shadow. My glance darted from side to side. I had no idea what had happened here, but I was alert for any sound or movement. Yo had insisted I take a dagger with me, which I had tucked into my sleeve. I slid it down, ready to flick it into my hand if I needed it.

"Hello?" I waited for somebody to answer. Nothing. The main house shoji was open, and I walked forward cautiously. I knew the house was as empty as the garden as soon as I walked in. There was no scent of cooking, even though it was near the time for the mid-day meal. No servant scurried to greet me. I walked into Isamu's apartment unchallenged and stared around bewildered. He had been here. A book was discarded on the floor. His futon was made, but the kakebuton lay ruffled, as though it had been caught by a hasty foot. I called his name and listened to the echoes.

I was shaking—less with fear than worry—as I moved to Father's apartment. Long habit made me pause outside the door and call my name out humbly. It was only when I was met with silence that I pushed the door aside and looked in. The outer room was empty, as was Father's bedroom. Knowing it was pointless, I glanced into his bath-house and caught my breath. The bath was continuously filled by a trickle from a hot spring that ran nearby. It should have been full and steaming. I stared in disbelief as I saw the water level was far below what it usually was and that there was no steam rising from the surface. This could not be! The hot spring outlet must have been closed. Unable to believe my own senses, I kneeled and dabbled my fingers in the water. Cold enough to make me shiver.

Suddenly, my body was filled with urgency. I ran from the bathhouse, shouting wordlessly. Only echoes came back to me until I went outside to the stables. There were no horses in there, but I was greeted by a volley of barks. Matsuo! It had to be.

He had been closed into the feed room and the door latched behind him. I jerked the door open and he almost fell out, whining and winding around my legs. I went down on my knees and let him lick my face. I patted him all over his body, looking for wounds, but there was nothing. Had Isamu left him here to keep him safe? And if he had, safe from what? Yet another uncertainty on this strangest of mornings.

"Matsuo! Good boy." I patted his shoulder and he panted at me, finally lying down and laying his head on his paws. "What happened? Where is everybody? What are you doing locked in there? Ah, if only the gods could make you speak!"

Matsuo wagged his tail at me and then jumped up. He glanced at me and moved to the stable door, clearly waiting for me to follow him. I rose quickly, cursing my own stupidity. Matsuo had no need of words. All I had to do was follow him.

He moved so quickly, I had difficulty keeping up with him and had to call to him to wait. Each time, I sensed he was becoming more impatient. He whined, deep in his throat, and moved off even before I had reached his side. I followed him out of the garden and through the peach orchard. Absently, I noticed that the peaches—which had been still green and small when I left for the Floating World —had been harvested. Not one remained. One more small oddity to add to the tally. The trees were carefully pruned and situated to ensure that not all of the fruit ripened together. Usually, the peaches were picked from each tree in turn to ensure a supply of fruit for as long as possible.

Any thought of peaches fled as we passed through the wicker gate that led out of the orchard. A man lay face down on the ground, a gardener, judging by his clothes. His body had the stillness of death. Suddenly, I found it difficult to breathe. Matsuo sniffed briefly at the corpse, then whined and trotted onward. I followed, understanding finally that I had no choice.

There were other bodies. Two more gardeners. A groom —I recognized him as he had fallen face upward. A little further on, the clumsy night-watchman. Three guards strung out in a row, their empty hands clenched as if their swords were still there. Next to them, more bodies. These I did not recognize, but to judge from their poor dress, these were—or had been—villagers. I looked away, distressed and bewildered in equal measure. Had some marauding pack of bandits attacked my home, made bold by need? Could there have been so many of them that Father or Isamu had called upon the villagers to help? Ah, poor souls. If that were so, they had died for us, just as they had served us in life. Matsuo slowed and turned back me, as if asking my permission to carry on. I swallowed bile and nodded.

I am onna-bugeisha, I told myself, stressing each word. Tears stung my eyes and I understood with a bitterness that surprised me what the words actually meant. I had never seen death before. Never smelled the stink of blood and shit that lingered on bodies from which life had been ejected suddenly and violently. For all my training, for all the arts of war I had learned, I had had no real idea what battle meant. It had amused me to pretend to be a warrior woman of the samurai. Now, I no longer found it so entertaining.

Now I understood what being onna-bugeisha truly meant. And it made me tremble. *I did not want this.* I wanted no part of this destruction of all that was dear to me. I wanted to be a girl again. Yet my mind refused to listen to me.

"I am onna-bugeisha." I realized I was saying the words out loud and shook my head fiercely. A fat black fly flew away from me at the gesture and landed on a gardener's body. I looked away, watching the ground at my feet.

"I am onna-bugeisha." I blinked the tears away and called to Matsuo, telling him to come to me. I could do nothing here. We would go back to the house. I would get on my horse and ride as quickly as I could back to the Floating World. To Yo, who had seen death many times and would know what to do.

Even Matsuo knew that I was lying to myself, and he would not come to me. Instead, he walked forward, almost delicately. He passed from my view down to the dip that led to the river, and I heard him howl.

"Matsuo, come here." Less a command than a plea. He whined again. I wanted to walk away from him. Leave him here with the dead and get back on my horse and go back and let Yo deal with this horror.

But I had come so far, I would not allow myself to take the coward's way out. I began to walk forward, not quite steadily. I slid down the riverbank, the earth crumbling beneath me. There was no water in the riverbed...but there was blood. Not enough to flow like current, but great pools of it. I noticed with a clinical coldness that seemed to come from somewhere outside myself that it was beginning to congeal. The night had been quite cool for the season. I calculated that the fight had taken place yesterday, probably late in the evening. A great cloud of the hideous black blowflies rose as I approached. I walked through them as carelessly as if they were the sweetest rain.

While I had been pleasuring myself in the bath with Yo, my family and our servants had been slaughtered like so many animals. I didn't count, but it seemed to me that there were dozens of bodies strewn carelessly on the dry riverbed. More of our servants. Still more guards. Villagers. More villagers than anything else. Some of them had scythes clutched in their hands. Others held nata, the all-purpose tools used for cutting and hacking. A few had picks. Some were empty-handed, their fists clenched into the only weapon they had possessed in life. All were facing inward, as if even in death they were worshipping the two armored bodies that lay where they had finally fallen at the opposite side of the riverbank.

Father. Isamu. I had seen their elaborate suits of samurai armor too many times to hope I was wrong. They lay side by side, and I could read the battle in the way they had fallen. They had fought to the last, giving way stride by stride. Finally, they had fought back to back. Their swords —both the long katana and the shorter wakizashi sidearms —were still clutched in their hands. I sank to my knees and pushed Isamu's elaborate visor away from his face. It seemed important that I should understand how they had died. On both men, the armor was battered and dented in places, but still whole.

The stink of blood and bowels evacuated at the moment of death was all around me. I breathed lightly through my mouth, retching as one of the disgusting blowflies tried to crawl between my lips. I turned Isamu's head gently to face me, as if he could still feel pain, and I saw at once how he had been overcome. His menpo—the iron face mask— covered only the upper part of his face, leaving his mouth and nostrils uncovered so he could breathe more easily. There was a ragged hole in his face, just beneath the lower edge of the menpo. I stood wearily and moved to Father's body. Just as was the case with Isamu, his menpo had been pierced. In his case, there were round indents in other parts of the mask where iron balls had struck and bounced off.

The arquebuses that Isamu had sneered at had killed both my father and my brother. I moved back to Isamu, absently treading on a villager's hand. I apologized silently to his spirit.

I had been wrong. It was obvious to me now. No marauding bandit gang had destroyed my family. Driven by a desperation I could not comprehend, the peasants from the nearest village had gotten ahold of one or more arque- buses. Far from dying trying to defend my family, it was our own villagers who had *killed* my family.

I sat quietly, Matsuo at my side. My father and my

brother had died as they would have wished, side by side in battle. Pride at the manner of their death rose in a hot flood in my breast. My gaze moved to the bodies of the fallen villagers and I cried out loud. They were so very thin. Even their elbows were sharp. One had fallen on his back, his robe flung aside. I could count each rib that had been exposed. Ah, Father! If only you had been able to put aside your greed and open your rice stores for people who were under your protection! Not quite family, no. But they were part of us. Still, they should have been governed by the code of bushido.

Sorrow for the villagers who had been driven by such hunger and despair I could not even begin to imagine piled on the searing pain of my menfolk's death. Anguish finally overcame me. I wept in pity for the hopeless villagers with almost as much grief as I felt for my own father and brother.

A shadow swept overhead, circling lower and lower. A spasm of revulsion made me snarl. Monk vultures, gathering to pick at the dead. I gripped my dagger. They would not find these bodies easy prey. Still less me.

I was wrong. A huge bird winged down. It landed beside Father, and through my bleary eyes, I watched as it threw its head back and cawed with what sounded like pain. I held my hand out and Soru, the golden eagle I had stolen from its nest, hopped across to me. Suddenly, I was drained of all feeling. Exhaustion slipped through my body. I was no longer hungry or thirsty. The gods were merciful to me, and even the fires of grief burned to low embers.

There was a water-smoothed stone near me. I slid down and placed my head on it. Matsuo moved at once and lay down full length against me. I heard the rumble of his sorrow from deep in his belly and managed to stroke his

head, although the effort left me weary. An unexpected soft-
ness brushed my face, blanking out the light. The riverbed
was hard. The stone beneath my head harder still.

My men had died an honorable death. Emiko was safe
with Soji's family. She bore his name now, rather than ours.
I was the last samurai of our line. I was onna-bugeisha, and
the burden of the family's honor was upon me. I lay silently
alongside my brother and my father, no living spirit except
for father's eagle and Matsuo with me.

There was no one to see my tears, and I was grateful for
that.

MANTIS

WARRIOR WOMAN OF THE SAMURAI BOOK TWO

https://books2read.com/u/3LYLW1

Keiko's men are dead, slaughtered by peasants in a desperate attempt to obtain food for their starving families. She is the last of her line; without her, the noble and ancient house of Hakuseki will die.

In order to try and save her family name, this noble samurai warrior woman is forced to humble herself at the feet of the local *daimyo*. When he ridicules her and takes the family estate for himself, the samurai code of bushido says there is only one thing left for Keiko.

Vengeance.

Keiko plots to take revenge for the actions of her greedy noble lord and revenge against the men who wanted to buy her and keep her as their slave.

Just like the praying mantis, Keiko lures her enemies into a sense of safety before taking her revenge...

ABOUT THE AUTHOR

 India Millar started her career in heavy industry at British Gas and ended it in the rarefied atmosphere of the British Library. She now lives on Spain's glorious Costa Blanca North in an entirely male dominated household comprised of her husband, a dog, and a cat. In addition to historical romances, India also writes popular guides to living in Spain under a different name.

Website: www.indiamillar.co.uk

ABOUT THE PUBLISHER

VISIT OUR WEBSITE
TO SEE ALL OF OUR HIGH QUALITY BOOKS:

http://www.redempresspublishing.com

Quality trade paperbacks, downloads, audio books, and books in foreign languages in genres such as historical, romance, mystery, and fantasy.